Where the Heart Is

L.S. Pullen

Where the Heart Is

Published by: L S Pullen
Edited by: Cassie Sharp
Cover Design by: Angie @ pro_ebookcovers
Formatted by: Brenda Wright, Formatting Done Wright

Dedication

Mum, my best friend.

“How blessed are some people, whose lives have no fears,
no dreads, to whom sleep is a blessing that comes nightly,
and brings nothing but sweet dreams.”
Bram Stoker, Dracula.

Table of Contents

Prologue

Summer – 1994 - Age 7

I swipe at my face when he calls my name—the last thing I need is for him to see me like this. He'd tell me to stop being such a baby.

"Flick, are you up there?"

I sniff back my runny nose. *It's probably redder than Rudolph's.* I'm not going to answer him. Nope. Where else would I be?

I wrap my arms around my middle, listening to the creaking of the wood as he climbs the ladder, followed by the tell-tale squeak of his stupid trainers making contact on the overused floorboards as he joins me on the balcony.

I know this is a memory, I'm dreaming—of course I am—but it's so vivid, and if I could be anywhere right now, it would be right here with him.

The tree house was the last present he'd received from his parents. I remember the look on his face, how his eyes shone like fairy lights, and his smile—bigger than his scrawny face. But it was what he said that I'd never forget.

"Thank you, but it's missing the most important part."

His dad crouched down in front of him. "Oh, and what's that, son?"

Looking over his shoulder in my direction, he smirked before answering. "Flick's swing, of course."

It gave me a funny feeling in my tummy—like when you're going down a steep hill on your bike too fast.

His dad let out a soft chuckle, winking to Nate. "Of course, you're right. We knew something was missing, but we couldn't put our finger on it, could we, sweetheart?" Standing to his full height—a giant in a child's eyes—he pulled Nate's mum into his arms and kissed her right on the lips. *Gross!*

She held her hand out at Nate. "Baby boy, you have such a big heart."

His cheeks turned red—like how your tongue goes after you've had one of those Gob Stoppers. She squeezed his hand before he slipped his fingers free, making a beeline for the ladder. As usual, I was hot on his heels.

Beside me, his legs mirror mine, dangling over the edge. "So, this is where you've been hiding?" He nudges me in the side.

"I wasn't," I say, crossing my arms and sniffing, my nose still yucky from crying.

His eyebrows make a wiggly V, causing his forehead to crinkle. "If you say so, but my Nan said she hasn't seen you since I left for the party."

"So what?" I don't even care that I'm acting like a baby.

"Come on, you could've come if it was my party. I brought you some birthday cake." He holds out a square wrapped in party napkins. I raise my hand, but then drop it quickly. He pushes it toward my lap. "It's your favourite. Chocolate. Don't be an idiot."

Whatever. He knows I can't say no. I take it, trying not to look too eager. I love chocolate cake…a lot. "Thanks." I want to spend as much time with him as I can possibly get. He's my best friend. I don't care if he's a boy or even if Sophie says they're smelly. To me, he smells like grass and bubble gum.

"Don't be upset," He says.

"I'm not," I lie. It's pointless. He can see right through me.

"So, tell me. Why is your face all blotchy from crying?"

I take a deep breath. "I have to go home soon and won't get to see you again for ages."

He looks down, picking at some fluff on his jogging bottoms. "You know it doesn't change anything, right?"

I nod. It doesn't bother him—me being a girl—and he's never once left me out. There was only that one time when his friends came over. He was showing off and threw the coke can at my face. It split the top of my lip open; I still have the scar.

A look of mischief crosses his face, his dimple poking out with it. I smile. He pulls out his Swiss Army Knife—the one Lawry told him was only for camping—and flips the blade open. He begins carving into the floorboard beside him.

I grab at his arm. "Stop. What are you doing?" I hate the idea of him getting into trouble.

"You'll see. Besides, it's *my* tree house."

I'm terrified he'll get caught, but he finishes after what feels like forever and blows away the loose shavings. Chuffed as punch.

"See? Done," he says, snapping the blade closed.

My tummy becomes warm as I lean over to see what he's done. He's carved a heart shape. It's silly, but I love it. Unable to resist any longer, I unwrap the cake, picking a piece off the corner. He chuckles, nicks a chunk, and wraps his arm around me. I attempt to pull away; he doesn't budge. And then it hits me—a thought—and I can't help the giggle that springs forward.

He steals another piece and pops it into his mouth. “What’s so funny?” he asks with his mouth full.

“When we grow up, I’m going to marry you.” Warmth spreads across my face.

He pulls his head back and chokes on his cake. “What? For real?”

I nod; he raises his eyebrows. With an exaggerated shudder, he puts two fingers in his mouth and makes a fake gagging sound. I elbow him in the ribs.

“Yes, stupid, for real. But I want chocolate cake, not the horrible fruitcake my Mum’s friend had at her wedding. It was *dis-gust-ing*. And I want to get married here.”

He tilts his head to the side, sucking his bottom lip between his teeth like he always does when he’s thinking.

“Well, if I marry you, I wouldn’t have to kiss you or do any of that other yucky stuff. But why here? Why not some church?”

I look at the view and inhale deeply. “Churches smell funny. And besides, this is my favourite place with you.”

His smile is both familiar and comforting.

It’s home.

I blink. Everything around me is fading into a mirage. It begins to disappear, and I’m free falling into a dark abyss. My stomach feels queasy, like it’s going to jump out of my mouth. My whole body lurches when I come to a stop. I open my eyes but don’t wake.

I’m back in a room I’d never seen before that morning—a room that will forever be tattooed into my memory. The musky stench. The sheets beneath my partially naked body are rough against my bare skin. The *tick–tick–ticking* of a clock.

My breath quickens, my pulse racing. Frozen in place, unable to make a sound, I squeeze my eyes closed tight. *Wake up*. Come on, wake the fuck up, already.

Chapter One

Present - Summer – 2007

I can't remember the last time I thought back to that moment in the tree house, let alone dreamt it. But my dreams end like they always do—a waking nightmare—barely able to catch my breath. With sheets twisted around my body like vines of thick poison ivy. Slick with a cold sweat, and my nightshirt damp. My heart thunders a thick staccato rhythm as I suck in shaky breaths.

Unable to rid the all too familiar sense of dread, each night I relive that same moment over and over again. Each night, I'm caught in the nightmare of waking in that same ghastly room.

But I'm not there.

I wipe away the crusty remnants of sleep from my sore eyes and untangle myself from my bedding. I stifle my yawn, hunched over, still weary from sleep, and toss my damp sheets in the linen bin. *Great, more washing to do.*

Cold shivers roll over my body and down the back of my neck, as though someone has walked over my grave. I try to rub away the eerie sensation. *Pull yourself together.* My body is protesting. Tense and stiff, I force myself to the bathroom.

I'd hoped coming to France with Nana would give me some semblance of normal—a reprieve from my demons. Evidently not. Two weeks we've been here, and thus far, every morning I've woken at the crack of dawn in pretty much the same state. Something feels…off. I can't shake it. I tug at the hair band around my wrist.

Somewhere in the recesses of my mind, the anxiety begins to curl its way around my gut. I squeeze my eyes shut, expecting the worst, although I've come a long way since…everything changed. I left my house and got on a plane. That's progress, right? I tug on my hairband, twisting it, and then pull it back as far as it will go before I release it, the sting welcome.

By the time I join Nana in the kitchen, I'm lightheaded from my erratic breathing. *In through your nose, out through your mouth.* I repeat it to myself over and over, until my heart settles and I can find air.

Placing a soft kiss on Nana's cheek, I make my way over to the breakfast bar. I need tea. I fixate on the task at hand. When I shake the kettle, the swoosh alerts me it's only half full. I pour the water away and refill to the brim, then light the stove before settling it on the centre hob. Where's my cup? Oh, right where it always is, front and centre. Searching the cutlery drawer, I rifle around until my fingers connect with the teaspoon I want. Removing the lid from the tea caddy, I dig my hand in to pull out the third tea bag from top, flicking it once, twice, three times, before dropping it into my cup.

The smell of freshly brewed coffee is strong in the air. Nana still makes it every morning—Papi's coffee—though he's been gone for years now…and we both drink tea. I've never had the heart to mention it. Nana's a creature of comfort, and she misses him.

"You didn't sleep again?"

I study the ceiling, trying to ease the tension in my neck.

Nana taps her wedding rings against the cup she's holding, and the bone china chimes. "Things will get better in time. Granted, time doesn't heal all wounds, but it does add a layer over the scars they leave. And you learn to carry on, despite the fact—"

Her phone interrupts her speech, and she pauses to answer. Only one person calls her apart from me. I get a deep, sinking feeling right in the pit of my stomach. Clenching my hands onto the worktop, I will the lightheaded feeling to pass.

It's Evie.

Her voice rings through the receiver. Nana keeps the volume on high, holding it away from her ear. *Radiation,* she once told me. I wanted to laugh, but I didn't fancy a clip around the earhole—something you're never too old for from Nana.

From what I overhear, Evie's distraught.

Lawry passed away in the early hours this morning. It's not long before Nana's sobs join in with hers and their combined grief vibrates through me.

Bile threatens to rise, my stomach unsettled. Swallowing hard, I turn to her, watching the tears cascade down her face. Tea discarded, I move over to her side, taking her hand in mine in an attempt to offer her comfort.

The news, although it was inevitable, is still hard to process. My already fractured heart shatters a little bit more.

I want to cry, but the tears don't come. Not that I'm surprised—they've been dry for a long time, now. I shake my head, pushing away wayward thoughts.

It only takes one emotional conversation after Evie hung up, and I'd consoled Nana, that had me promising I'll come back to England with her. As if I was going to let her travel back alone, especially without Papi at her side.

I scroll through my recent call list, dialling Simon's number. He answers on the first ring

"Hey beautiful, how are you holding up?"

I pull up the hem of my dress and begin picking at the scab on the inside of my thigh.

"I'm not sure it's really sunk in yet." I hiss through my teeth as the scab comes away, and seconds later blood seeps through the thin cut.

"Well, he was practically a Granddad to you."

I let out a puff of air. "I should've gone to see him, though. Do you think he knew how much he meant to me?" I fall back on my bed, covering my eyes with my forearm.

"Of course, he did, Sweetness."

"I hope so. I booked our flights home. I still can't believe this is happening."

I hear him clear his throat. *Here it comes.*

"You'll have to see Nate again. With the exception of the occasional Facebook post or postcard here or there, you two haven't spoken. Are you ready for this?"

Simon doesn't beat around the bush—one of the things I love about him. I've never told Nate what happened. My family agreed it was my story to tell, but I wasn't ready then. And I'm sure as hell not ready now.

"Nope. But what choice do I have? Besides, we were best friends once, and regardless, he's still like family. I need to be there for Nana and Evie. And…if Nate needs me, I'll be there for him, too."

I let out a shaky breath, resisting the urge to laugh at the thought of me being strong for anyone when I can barely take care of myself.

"Listen, I'm not trying to make you more anxious… I can't stand the thought of you hurting and me not being with you. But it *is* about time you put the past behind you."

Unable to keep still, I stand and begin pacing in circles, making myself dizzy in the process. My stomach is churning, and there's a thickness in my throat when I speak. "I don't know what I'd do without you sometimes. I'll let you know when I'm back, okay?"

"Okay, I miss you. Have a safe flight. Remember, you managed to get there, so coming home will be a piece of piss."

"I've never understood that phrase."

"What? Piece of piss?"

"Yeah." I let out a chuckle and hear Simon's laugh float down the line, too, the sound welcome.

"Me neither. I love you."

"Love you too."

"And Felicity… remember, you've got this."

I wish I had as much faith in myself as Simon does in me.

I find Nana sitting in the garden. I inhale a deep breath as the familiar aroma from the wild lavender assails my senses. She's looking through an old photo album—one I don't recall having seen before. As I sit down beside her, she begins to speak without looking up. "Lawry was my first love."

Blindsided, I muffle a curse… "What? I thought Papi was your first love?"

She removes a photo from its sleeve. Holding it out in front of us, she points, her hand slightly trembling.

"See that man right there? That's Samuel sitting between Evelyn and me." She points to another man. "That's Lawrence. This photo was taken a few days before Samuel died. He was training in the RAF, God rest his soul. The saddest part was, he never even knew Evie was pregnant."

Still trying to process that my Papi wasn't her first love, I catch up to what she's just told me. "Evie was pregnant? What happened to the baby?"

She drops the photo onto her lap, looking over the field of lavender. "He was born seven months later." Her eyes graze over my face.

I take the photo from her lap and stare at it for a moment. When I see it—the resemblance—it clicks.

"The baby was Nate's Dad? Samuel Junior?"

She gives me one firm nod, as her lips form a straight line.

"But Lawry was his Dad, right?"

"Not by blood, no..." She takes the photo back and carefully places it back in the photo album. "It was a different time back then, and there was no way he would allow his best friend's child to come into the world fatherless. He married Evie—a marriage of convenience. He needed to make sure they'd both be taken care of, so he raised Sami Junior as his own."

I pick at the arm of the garden chair before my eyes find hers.

"But you said Lawry was your first love?"

"Yes, he was, and there was a time he was my everything, when I couldn't see my future without him in it."

"You watched him marry your best friend, though. How did you do that?" Call me naïve—I just thought she was only ever with my Papi.

"It's quite the story, and I'll tell you all about it, but not right now. First, I need to ask, are you sure about this...after everything that's happened?" She takes hold of my hand, giving it a gentle squeeze.

I chew the inside of my cheek before answering.

"I'll be fine. Besides, I want to be there for you, and it's about time I finally faced Nate. I was never going to be able to put it off forever, especially not now." Thinking of what he must be going through—losing the closest thing to a father he had—and knowing how Dad and I rarely make time for one another, makes me feel selfish.

"I never quite understood what happened with you and Nate. You've always loved that boy."

I swallow the lump in my throat. "Well, things change, and I'm different now."

"Not that different." She gives me a warm smile.

If only that were true. Reality sends a shiver down my spine. I try to shake it off before it has time to consume me, pulling me into a pit of darkness with no escape.

It feels like we've been at the airport forever.

I couldn't sample any more perfumes if I tried—duty-free can only keep you occupied for so long before you end up smelling like a tart's handbag. I've read a magazine, and even tried getting into my latest book…to no avail. When I look up to see our flight is finally boarding, I let out a sigh of relief.

Despite my nerves, the flight's been bearable. I even fell asleep long enough to glimpse Nate in my dream—we were in the tree house again, but it was the day the swing seat had been fitted.

"Now it's perfect." I remember Nathaniel saying.

I felt free and invincible while he pushed me. When he sat next to me, his mum took a photo of us together.

It's the one photo I keep on my bedside table. What made it special was he'd always preferred slides. The memory of the swing had my stomach dipping, but it was the flight descending for landing that woke me from my memories.

The stewardess announces our landing, and my hand grips my Nana's. I let go, flexing my fingers to get some circulation back.

"Sorry." Shit, I probably bruised her, holding on tight like that.

"Don't be, how are you feeling?" She moves my hair behind my ear.

"Fine." I shrug like this whole scenario is no big deal. I'm about to see my old best friend—the one I walked away from. The thought makes me feel uneasy. This is going to be a flipping catastrophe.

Chapter Two

I still can't get my head around the fact that she's coming back here with Ana—her Nana. If it weren't for my Gramps, I doubt she would be at all. So, what? We were two stupid teenagers who got a little hot and heavy one summer—blurring lines between friendship and something else entirely.

We were practically joined at the hip growing up. We'd do everything together—whether that was digging for worms or riding Laddie. But then it all went to shit. We crossed an invisible line, and there was no going back. It wasn't like anything *really* happened anyway.

But then what?

She decided to sulk about it and stayed away all because we had a falling out. We were best friends once. Hell, you'd think that would have meant more to her than her stupid pride, for fuck's sake.

In my case, curiosity manifested under the social media category of *"friends"* on Facebook—you know, sending the obligatory Happy Birthday and Merry Christmas post. Just like we're old acquaintances.

How bloody pathetic. Facebook is one of the main reasons she kept away for so long, even though I'd bet my life she'd never admit it.

All I know is, I'm barely managing to keep my shit together as it is, and her coming here, in all honesty, is going to be a complication I don't flipping well need. A goddamn distraction of a cluster-fuck, if ever there was one.

I've been here for over an hour already, waiting. Regardless of what we might have had or not had, I'm not about to let them get a taxi. One, I wouldn't do that to Ana—I was brought up better than that. Two, as I said, curiosity is a bitch, and I'm glutton for punishment. I want to see what has become of my estranged, ex-best friend.

My phone vibrates in my jean pocket. It's Charlie, and I'm grateful for the distraction.

"Hey, man," I say when I answer.

"You all right, mate?"

Well if *that* ain't a loaded bloody question, I don't know what is. I chew on the hangnail of my thumb, which is royally pissing me off.

"Yep, all gravy. Just waiting at *arrivals*." I lean back on my stool, trying to relax.

"What time does their flight get in?"

Thank God for small talk.

"About an hour."

He laughs, and I pull the phone from my ear, looking up at the girl on the table opposite. She's smiling at me. I roll my eyes in mock annoyance at his laughter that's echoing. Bringing the phone back to my ear, I pull—my now third bottle of coke—closer.

"Shut up, man."

I pick at the label to stop myself biting my nails—it's a nasty habit, and I haven't done it since I was a kid.

"You've still got feelings for her?"

"Not like that, no. I mean, she's practically family."

"So, you'd be okay with me asking her out? I'm sure she's all—"

"Don't even think about it." I try to act like his comment hasn't bothered me.

I don't care who she sees...*do I?*

"Just pulling your chain. Honestly, I wanted to check and see how you're doing..."

I feel my throat tighten. Bringing the bottle to my lips, I take a long gulp in an attempt to swallow my emotions.

"I've been better, but you know..." If anyone understands, it's him.

I don't know what's worse: losing someone suddenly, or when someone you love is given a diagnosis that's terminal. When you don't know when their time's up, you have to watch them suffer and deteriorate until death comes for them.

"Anything you need, just buzz me, yeah? I meant what I said—the food and drink are covered."

He wants to pay for the wake, and I know it's his way of contributing. I won't insult him by refusing.

"Thanks, man." I take another swig of my drink.

"No worries. And be sure to say *hi* to Flick for me."

"Yeah, will do, catch you later." Hell. The last thing I want to do is make small talk with her, but it is what it is, nothing I can do about it now.

I've been replaying the last time we were together over in my mind. We were fooling around in the tree house. Damn, that girl used to make me nervous in ways I don't even want to admit now. Sometimes, it was as though my breath had been sucked right out of me—my heart pounding frantically, like a racehorse. How I even managed to put the brakes on that day, I'll never know.

It's laughable now—how me being the *"good guy"* would come back to bite me on the arse. She wouldn't even give me a chance to explain—storming off like a brat out of hell. That girl always could take stubborn to a whole new level. I mean, who leaves their best friend without even so much as goodbye? Who ignores their calls and texts?

I didn't have a lot of time to dwell on that for too long—not when I found out about my Gramps. To say I didn't handle the news well was an understatement. Angry, and with raging hormones, I didn't know what to do with all my pent-up frustration, or myself. I was so upset, and I couldn't talk to the one person I needed the most—her. That was the weekend that changed everything.

I went out on a bender and didn't come home for two days. I got so wasted, I couldn't tell my own earhole from my arsehole.

When I woke up in bed after a one night stand—with someone whose name I couldn't even recall—my only saving grace was the used condom wrapper I found on the side. Thank goodness for small mercies.

I threw up as soon as I got home. My phone had died, so I plugged it in to charge as I dealt with my raging headache and churning stomach. When my phone came to life, I was assaulted with pings of missed calls and messages. I was not ready to deal with the shit, but I was being a dick. There my Gramps was—terminally ill—and I'd gone and disappeared for two fucking days.

Resigning myself to the fact I couldn't hide any longer, I'd scrolled through my messages, and the one that kicked me straight in the gut was from her—the one person I needed.

Flick: I'm sorry. I heard about your Gramps, I'm always here if you need me Xx

She'd sent it the night before—an olive branch—but I was too out of my face to see it. Perhaps my battery had died by then, who knows? All I remember is the bile that rose, causing me to throw up my guilt.

It was the next text that confused me though. It was sent early hours of the morning.

Flick: Never mind I can see you're already taken care of.

I had no idea what that was supposed to mean, at first. It was only after I booted up my computer and logged into Facebook, that everything made sense.

I'd been tagged in a photo. A photo with my tongue down the throat of the girl I'd woken up next to. It wasn't until I saw that post that I'd learned her name—Katie. The worst part? It was *liked* by Flick.

Attempting to fix it, I sent her a text.

Sorry, it wasn't what it looked like.

Her response came quick.

Flick: What it looked like was you sucking face. Did you sleep with her too?

My hands had never trembled so much as I typed my reply. I had to do the one thing I'd never done before—lie to her.

I'm sorry, I wasn't thinking straight. It was a stupid drunken mistake.

It felt like an eternity waiting for her reply.

Flick: Listen, I am sorry about Lawry. I know what you're going through must be hard, but I thought I knew you. Obviously, I was wrong.

I pulled up her number in an attempt to talk to her, but it rung out. Of course, it did. I didn't leave a message.

I made a mistake, and I know sorry doesn't cover it. I wish I could take it back but I can't.

I still needed her. Even though what we had didn't come with a label on it, first and foremost, we were best friends. But I knew. Deep in my gut. We may have been up in the air, but I'd still cheated on her.

For months afterward, I got lost in other girls. They were a distraction, but only for a while.

She never did respond to my last text. As the radio silence grew, I honestly couldn't blame her. Any way you looked at it, I'd fucked up.

It comes back to Facebook. Months later, I saw her status had changed to *"in a relationship"* with some twat called Simon. The irony isn't lost on me. I'm a quick learner that social media is a recipe for disaster.

She'd moved on. I was jealous. I knew I had no right to be—I'd been sleeping around. It's not like I expected her to pine for me, but I was fucking jealous all the same.

I didn't ask after her the first time Ana showed up without her. I was gutted, of course, but in no way was I surprised. After she'd come a number of times without her, though, my willpower cracked, and my curiosity got the best of me.

My Nan and Ana were all-secret squirrel hush-hush, cloak and dagger when I asked questions. I knew she'd been avoiding me, and the guilt it was my fault has never been lost on me, either. I was far from proud of it.

How could she go from being part of everything one minute, then to none of it the next?

Now, I've been sitting here, at the airport, twiddling my thumbs like a loser for the past two hours. When the arrivals confirm their flight has finally landed, my hands begin to shake. I'm sweating. Too much caffeine. Wiping the palm of my hands over my thighs, I stand and pop a mint into my mouth. I feel wired as shit. I take a deep breath and make my way over to a pillar to the left of the place they'll come out.

Nervous doesn't even begin to describe how I feel right now. I need to pull myself together. I run my fingers through my hair in an attempt to tame it, and then scrub my palm over my face. *I should have made more of an effort this morning.*

It's stupid, but I swear, I feel her before I even see her. My eyes wander until they land on her. With her head down, she's pushing—no fighting—with a reluctant trolley. Also looks to me like she's muttering to herself as she veers it one way and it goes the other.

Holding back my inappropriate smile, I give myself a few seconds to take her in from head to toe. She's leaner than she used to be. The way she carries herself is far from confident. Her shoulders are hunched, and she barely lifts her gaze from the task at hand while gripping the trolley like a lifeline.

Ana is next to her, scanning left and right. When she spots me, she scurries towards me.

Closely followed by Flick.

Chapter Three

I shit you not, I want to stomp my feet. This damn trolley has a mind of its own. At least I wore my trainers and not flip-flops, or I would've lost a toe by now. I let out a frustrated sigh as I try to avoid crashing into anyone. Following my Nana through the crowd of people, I look at her—picking up speed and shit. Old age pensioner, my arse.

That's when I hear his voice.

"Having trouble, there?"

Nate. I think my mouth actually falls open. Before I can even gather my thoughts to respond, my Nana is in his arms. That gives me a few seconds, at least, to brace myself. Well, I'll be damned.

"Nathaniel, my dear boy," Nana says.

He lets out a small laugh, stepping into the hug.

It takes me a moment to get my breathing under control. He's still handsome, but not in a GQ magazine kind of way—he's real.

I think that's what also drew me to Simon. He's quirky, lean yet solid, wears glasses when he doesn't have his contacts in, and, boy, does he have charisma. But mostly, I was drawn to his sense of humour.

Same with Nate. He was always funny growing up—it was one of my favourite things about him. He's filled out since I saw him last. A little rough around the edges, but I like this look on him. I shake my head. *Do not go there.*

"Ana, good to see you." He kisses her on each cheek and leans back, as my Nana looks him up and down. I want to roll my eyes—she saw him, what, a month and a half ago? And here she is appraising him. I clench my fist. It's not like his ego needs to get any bigger. Now I sound like a bitch, *great.*

"Flick?" My name—almost a question—drips off his tongue like honey.

The trolley between us is a wall, thank God. He leans over, placing his hands to take hold of my shoulders, and his stubble scratches my cheek when his lips place a soft kiss there. My eyes close. My senses are on high alert, his signature scent—familiar—and all Nate.

I feel him take a step back and open my eyes. I'm met with hazel hues staring back at me. He rakes his hand through his hair—the only tell-tale sign he's nervous—causing it to stick up all over the place.

Angry with myself for being caught in his typical Nate web, I react, my words hard.

"It's Felicity. I don't go by *Flick.*"

He raises his eyebrows and the corner of his mouth twitches—almost in amusement. *Is he freaking kidding me*?

I could slap him. I'd like to say I don't know why I'm so pent up, but I do—it's my anxiety. I force my hand to stay where it is.

"Let me." He comes around, motioning for me to move, taking over the trolley—making it look effortless in the process. *Bloody typical.*

I lag behind, finding myself staring at his butt. I heat as thoughts rush forward of when I had my hands all over him the last time we were together. What the heck is wrong with me? I feel like I'm on a kamikaze.

"How are you holding up?" Nana asks, going straight in for the kill as we make our way towards the elevators.

"Taking it a day at a time, you know?"

She nods in understanding, patting his hand gently. I never thought it possible to miss someone's voice. And what were the first words out of my mouth? Oh, that's right.

I swallow hard—the thickness of my throat suffocating like a Boa Constrictor. I manage to take in enough air to speak.

"I am sorry about Lawry," I say, licking my dry lips.

He turns to me as I enter the lift behind him. My chest tightens. Being here with him has never felt more unnatural, and that thought scares the hell out of me. He nods, his Adam's apple moves up and down, but he doesn't speak. His eyes lock with mine.

I want to look away, but if I do there's a strong possibility I'll freak out—this lift is too small. Sweat slicks between my shoulder blades. It's too hot in here, the air too thick.

His eyes hold me captive. There's always been this intensity about him when he looks at you—like you're all he sees.

The lift comes to a stop. We break eye contact. The doors have barely opened when I rush through them like my arse is on fire. He looks at me quizzically for a moment but doesn't say anything, as we follow him across the car park. When we come to a stop, it's in front of a Lexus RX. Simon and Nate both have a mutual love for cars. He loads the luggage into the boot.

"Felicity, why don't you sit up front?" Nana waves her hand in the direction of the passenger seat…like I don't know where it is.

I want to argue, but she's right. The last thing I need is for him to have to pull over for me to throw up. I smile, then climb in, giving myself just enough time to gain my composure before he slides into the driver's seat…after opening the door for my Nana.

I glance over, taking in his profile. For someone who's only wearing jeans and a t-shirt, he sure looks all kinds of hot. He pauses with the key in the ignition, looking over to me. My face flushes, and I look out of my window. He starts the engine and reverses from the bay.

"Thank you for picking us up, but we could have made our own way," Nana says, breaking the silence.

"Gramps wouldn't have allowed that, and you know it." His voice is pained. His hands clench the steering wheel—utterly devastated at the mention of the man who raised him. And who can blame him?

My heart hurts for him. I want to reach out, squeeze his hand—that's what I would have done when we were kids. But we're not kids anymore. I attempt to focus, intently staring straight ahead. My phone rings, causing me to flinch, knocking my bag off my lap. My head connects with the dashboard as I lunge forward to retrieve it.

"Shit." I rub my forehead with one hand and fumble for my phone with the other.

"Language!" My Nana's voice rises from behind me, admonishing me.

I peer over my shoulder, and mouth the word, *sorry*.

"I just need to take this," I say to no one in particular.

"Hello," I answer, slightly breathless.

"Hey, beautiful. How was the flight? Did you freak out?" Simon asks, and I smile.

"Flight was fine. No dramas. Just leaving the airport now."

"That's good. Let me know how it goes when you see Nate, okay?"

I cough, heat rising in my cheeks.

"Already have, it was fine." A tingling sensation sweeps up the back of my neck and across my face. I use the pad of my thumb to turn the volume down on my phone—Nate in earshot.

"You're with him now?"

"Yes, but I'll speak to you later though, okay?" I can hardly get into a full-blown conversation about it now.

"All right, fine. Make sure you do. And be sure to say hi to that gorgeous Nana of yours. And Felicity?"

"Yes?"

"Love you." My heart warms. He's never been one to shy away from his feelings—even when I'm being an insufferable bitch.

"Love you too." Ending the call, I chance a peek to Nate, then lower my window a smidge—taking in a lungful of air. He looked agitated. I glance over my shoulder to see my Nana.

"Simon said hi."

Nate's grip on the steering wheel tightens.

"Just hello?" she asks.

I turn my attention back to her and smile.

"No, he said, that *gorgeous* Nana of yours."

"Of course, he did. Got to love that boy, he has good taste," she says, chuckling to herself.

I let out a not so lady-like snort, and then quickly hide it with a cough.

Nate looks over to me, causing me to feel self-conscious. Uncomfortable, I stare ahead. I double take when I see a car reversing. We are heading straight for it.

Instinctively, I brace my hands on the dashboard.

"Shit—" I squeal.

Nate presses on the horn in quick succession then slams on the brakes hard. My seat belt pulls me tight, slamming me back into my seat.

I grab hold of my throat, feeling winded, my heart pounding in my chest.

"Damn. Sorry, is everyone all right?" Nate asks.

My hand is over my chest.

"Flick—" His hand touches my shoulder. I flinch.

"I'm fine, and I told you already, it's *Felicity*," I snap again.

He removes his hand, holding it up in surrender. My face heats like molten lava. I just want out of this car, already.

Accident averted, Nate pulls away, leaving a stifling silence that I feel the need to rectify.

"Sorry, it's just …" I'm stammering, no idea what I was about to say, when a not so subtle cough emanates from behind me.

"She was just startled, that's all," my Nana says, trying to diffuse the situation.

I sit on my hands, my knees bouncing, as I look out of my window. When I feel his hand on my shoulder, he squeezes it once before letting go.

"It's fine. So how have you been?"

He's going for small talk. I shuffle in my seat, and then lower my window some more before I focus my attention back to him.

"Same old, how about you?"

He raises his eyebrows, and I quickly cover my face with my hand. *What the hell is wrong with me?* Foot, meet mouth. His Gramps just died. Someone just shoot me now. I drop my hand onto my lap.

"I mean, I didn't mean to…it's just…" I stop, wishing I were anywhere but here.

I hear the distinct sound of him trying to hold back a snicker.

"I know." He smiles, and I'm left speechless.

When my Nana intervenes, I move closer to my door.

"So, Evie told me work has been good. How are you finding being your own boss?"

I've never been more grateful in my life for her ability for small talking.

"It's going well, who would've thought I'd get to have a day job doing something I love?"

I turn my head in his direction. But then it hits me. It's the simplest of questions. Yet, I'm completely clueless.

"Sorry, what do you do?" The question passes my lips before my brain has time to stop me.

"I restore old cars. It's hard work, and I'm constantly covered in grease, but hey, you've got to love what you do, right?"

I nod, settling back in my seat. Yes, that is true, and I'm glad to hear he's doing something he loves, but it's the sound of his voice that keeps doing funny things to my insides.

What's wrong with me?

I feel guilty even thinking like this for more reasons than one. He's grieving, and this whole situation is complicated. More than anything, I'm on edge. Paranoid he'll find out about why I stayed away. My heartbeat begins racing. I clench my jaw tight, grinding my teeth. I close my eyes, my nostrils flaring as I breathe in through my nose and out through my mouth. Clenching my fists, I begin to count. I open my eyes and release my fists. I push away the dark thoughts, and numbly watch the whirring view pass me by.

Chapter Four

Fingers lace over my forearm. I flinch. In an attempt to pull away, the back of my head connects with something hard. I open my eyes, my heart racing. Darting forward with a lurch, I'm held in place by the tightening of my seat belt. A *humph* sound escapes me.

"We're here."

It's Nate—only Nate. I let out an audible sigh, licking my dry lips and swallowing hard.

"Sorry." I look out of the windscreen and take in the sight before me. It looks the same, yet oddly different.

"No worries, I didn't mean to startle you." He's looking me over with concern. I'm fascinated as I watch his pupils shrink, the hazel hues replaced with large, soft streaks of green. His eye colour still changes with his mood.

I clear my throat and look away. I don't ever remember blushing this much around him before. Sucking in a breath, I plaster on a shaky smile and unclip my seat belt.

I turn in my seat, my eyes scanning the wisteria that climbs along the front of the house, weaving above the sash windows like a second skin—the most vibrant colour purple I've ever seen. The green lawn in the turning circle is well tended, the rustic birdhouse pride and place, surrounded by the sweeping gravelled driveway. Either side is lined in pink, cup-shaped roses, woven amongst tall, dark lavender tips and evergreen foliage. This was always a home away from home. I watch on as Nana carefully makes her way up the steps to the large, oak door.

She could have at least woken me. I must remember to thank her for that later.

My fingers have barely touched the door handle when he leans over the centre console to stop me. I feel his warm breath ripple over my cheek, and my pulse begins to race. *Do not panic.*

"I just felt like I should at least thank you, for coming. I mean after everything..."

His thumb brushes over my knuckle, and I'm rooted in place. A warm sensation rises in my stomach, and then, just as fast, he moves away and gets out of the car.

I let out a puff of air. He's always affected me, but something is different. It's alien to me, and I'm not sure how to feel about it. I don't have time to process it now, either. I join him at the boot of the car, reaching for one of the cases, but he stops me.

"I've got this. You go on up and see my Nan." He angles his head in the direction of the house.

"You sure?"

He nods with a small smile.

"Thank you," I say as I walk away.

Nana reaches the door just as Evie comes out to greet her. As I approach, I see their tears, and the sounds of their sobs vibrate right through me.

Evie looks up, motioning her hand toward me. I make up the distance, and they pull me into a hug. I can feel the weight of their loss to my core. It's in this moment I feel more broken than I ever have.

"I'm sorry for not coming before Lawry…" I was being selfish. Bad things happen to good people every day, and I was only thinking of myself. "I feel so ashamed." I wasn't there when they needed me, and that's not how you treat the ones you love.

"Enough. You stop that right now. I know you've had a lot to deal with. We both understood why you didn't come, honey. We missed you," Evie says as she cups my cheek. I feel the faint wobble of her hand.

Nate walks past with our cases in tow, concentrating on getting them up the steps in one go, paying no attention to our exchange.

Nana and I have adjoining rooms. Nothing's changed—the four-post bed, the en-suite bathroom, and the décor is all still so familiar. My favourite part is the window seat. I walk over and unlatch the lock to the window. The heavy glass slides open, and I take a seat, inhaling deeply.

I'm greeted with the earthly aroma of freshly cut lawn as I close my eyes. There's no breeze. Sweat gathers on the back of my neck, but I wouldn't trade this moment for anything. Insects hum, birdsong fills the open space. I open my eyes, and the sight before me is a punch in the memory bank. I'd forgotten how beautiful the mixed array of scattered wildflowers look. How they pop against the vibrant-green backdrop of perfectly maintained shrubs and trees.

I feel grimy from the journey, which only a shower can fix. I turn on the shower and strip. Stepping in, I soak myself under the tepid spray to cool off and wash away the remains of the day. But I don't spend nearly long enough in here. Grudgingly, I turn off the tap, so I can go get ready.

I rap my knuckles on the door in quick succession, it's only when I hear Nana calling out, that I palm the round handle and turn, the door heavy as I push. Pausing, I see her staring out of the window, her back to me, hair in a chiffon bun. I move toward her, engulfed by her signature scent—Coco Chanel.

"Ready?" I ask, placing my hand on her shoulder once I'm beside her.

She covers it with hers, giving it a squeeze. I feel the quiver beneath her fingertips. It's difficult for me to accept, let alone admit it to myself—she's not as young as she used to be.

"As ready as I'll ever be. Thank you again for this." Her voice breaks as she turns toward me. I look down at the hankie she's wringing between her hands, then back to her face, her downcast expression.

My heart stills, missing a beat. This woman has been my constant. She's the reason I need to keep my shit together. "You don't have to thank me," I say gently.

Lunch, is of course, traditional afternoon tea. Evie's the reason I enjoy it as much as I do. Other than the Ritz, I've yet to meet anyone else who puts on a spread like she does.

I'm glad Nate didn't join us—my stomach couldn't handle it. But I'd be lying if I said I wasn't curious as to where he went, instead.

He plays it off cool and collected, but my being here isn't what Nate was expecting. I saw it in his eyes when we were in the elevator. His unspoken question—*why did you stay away?*

Outside, a soft breeze floats across my face. I knew I needed this—to be out here in the open air. It's why I snatched my camera moments ago and left Nana and Evie to talk.

Following the path I've walked so many times before, I head to the paddock. The oak framed stables are open when I arrive, and I shuffle right through without thought. The familiar surroundings are almost comforting—hay, pristinely clean hanging tack, wheelbarrows full from recently mucked-out stools. The paddock is dim—subdued rays of sunlight barely grazing the ground. It smells of sweat, manure, and earth. It smells like home. Measured steps bring me through and to the opening at the other end. I blink, readjusting to the bright daylight. Then I see him. And smile.

Sticking my fingers in my mouth, I whistle, and then call out, "Laddie, here boy?"

He pauses mid graze and swings his head up, his ears flicking back and forth before he goes back to his grazing. I whistle again. He lets out a puff of noise through his nose and trots towards me.

I step up onto the bottom part of the fence, snapping a few shots. Laddie was the horse I learnt to ride on. He hasn't changed—he still has the same three white socks and one white stocking, and his long, black tail swishes back and forth.

"Hello, boy," I say, reaching my hand out, stroking his silky, red side. He pushes his nose against my palm. I stroke him between his eyes, kiss his nose, and then blow on the white star on his forehead. I used to make a wish on that star. He sniffs the air with a contented wobble of his lips.

"Sorry, boy, I didn't bring you a treat. I've missed you. Bet you haven't missed me, huh?"

I can't help but laugh as he continues to push his nose into my hand.

"You missed me a little, then?"

"Of course, he missed you."

I slip, falling backward, my arms flapping around wildly.

Firm, but gentle hands grab my waist. I tense. Now steady, my feet firmly in place, I look up—knowing who it is, but needing to see him, anyway. *Nate.* We lock eyes. His hands tense for the briefest moment on my waist before he lets go.

"Shit," I say. My heart races, a flush of adrenaline tingling through my body.

"Sorry, didn't mean to scare you."

I wave it off, bending forward with a hand on my knee.

Then I feel it. Skin—warm, strong, masculine—grazing my shoulder. Electricity pulses through my body, and I shiver before I shrink from the contact.

"Flick, seriously, are you okay?" he asks.

"I'm fine, you surprised me. Talk about giving me a heart attack. You ever considered a job in the London Dungeons?" I ask between a snort and a giggle. *Well, aren't I just charming*?

"Come off it. I'm not that scary, you're just a wimp," he says playfully, tipping his head, his stare intense.

I look away and straighten my top. Swapping the camera between my hands, I wipe away the sweat from my palms. I must look like an absolute idiot. I begin walking, and he falls into step beside me.

"How are you?" I ask, needing to break this awkward silence. I never minded the quiet before, not with him—but now it's almost deafening.

He shrugs, letting out a sigh. "I'm okay. On autopilot, you know? Just going through the motions."

I nod and turn my head in his direction. His smile is laced with pain. I know he senses me staring, but he avoids my gaze—looking over his shoulder toward Laddie.

I follow his line of sight. Laddie prances about like a show pony—he always did act like a young foal. I pause to take a couple shots of him. The hairs on the back of my neck rise, and I begin to sweat. I sense Nate—staring. It takes everything in me to ignore him, to fill in the silence.

"About Lawry… I hate myself for not coming to see him." God knows if I could change it, I would.

"I don't get it. All because of what happened with us? Seems a little dramatic, even for you," he says, so matter of fact.

Ouch.

"It's not like that… I wasn't trying to be a bitch. Believe me, that's not why I stayed away—" I pause to catch my breath. Even if he knew, he wouldn't understand. I mean, how could he? "But that's neither here nor there, and I'm not here to cause drama. I'd like to think we could at least be civil, yeah?"

He lets out a humourless laugh.

I cross my arms over my chest.

"So, let me get this straight… You say I'm not the reason you stayed away, but you won't tell me why?" he asks, shaking his head.

I clench my fists and avert my eyes. *Please don't push this, Nate.* I turn to walk away when he holds up his hands in surrender.

"Fine. I'll be civil. But one way or another, the truth will come out," he says with a confident smile.

I want to wipe that smirk right off his face. I turn again, but this time he grabs hold of my elbow.

"Wait. Fine…how about we call a truce?" he asks, holding out his hand.

"Truce," I say, and take his warm hand in my cold one. We shake once before letting go.

This time when he smiles, it's less pained, and his eyes have a spark to them.

Ringing sounds from my pocket.

"Sorry, do you mind?" I ask. Seriously, why on earth am I asking for his permission? He shakes his head and reaches for my camera. I'm about to protest, but then, for some reason beyond me, I let him take it. Bringing the phone to my ear, I answer the call from Simon, my eyes still trained on Nate.

"Hey."

"Hi, beautiful. I just wanted to check in…see how you're doing?"

I smile.

"I'm all right, just taking a walk with Nate."

I watch him watching me—his eyebrows rising at my mention of his name, the corner of his mouth turning up. I remember those lips, how they offered so much promise when they were on mine, soft and warm. How he always tasted of peppermint. I take a small step back. *What is wrong with me?*

"Oh right, I see," Simon says.

What does he see exactly?

"No, you don't," I say, raising my voice as I wrap my arm over my stomach.

"Right, if you say so. I'll let you get back to rekindling or whatever it is you were doing," he says, insinuation laced in his words.

I roll my eyes, and turn my back to Nate, putting a little distance between us.

"We're just catching up, that's all. Please stop implying otherwise."

I hear him sigh, then the bed squeak, and the ruffle of the cushions in the background.

I pinch the skin under my elbow, biting the inside of my mouth.

"Shit. I'm sorry. I don't know why I'm being such an arsehole."

"Well, don't be an arsehole, then," I say as I kick at the dirt beneath my feet.

"Duly noted. Call me later?" I can hear the smile back in his voice. That's the Simon I know and love.

"Of course, love you," I say, smiling back.

"Love you too," he says, before ending the call.

Turning back to Nate, I find him scanning through the pictures. It's one of the reasons I still prefer film—the prolonged gratification of seeing how your pictures turn out when you develop them.

"Looks like somebody has a hidden talent," he says, his eyes smiling.

My face heats at his words.

"You know about photography, do you?" I'm sceptical about my photography at the best of times.

"I don't need to. It's obvious," he says, looking me in the eye.

"It's mediocre at best," I say, trying to wave it off.

"Don't be so modest, Flick. Just accept the damn compliment." *Bossy Nate.*

"Thank you." My stomach tingles as I look down at my hands.

I stretch out my arm for the camera, but he holds it out of my reach. I take a step forward. He takes a step back, shaking his head.

He brings the camera closer to him, looking at the viewfinder, holding his finger over the button. The noise of a shutter is what I hear just as I turn away, my face heating. I turn back.

"Camera, please."

He moves toward me, his hand extended. Just as I think he's going to pass it to me, he pulls me into his side instead. His arm wraps over my shoulder, and I fit perfectly under his armpit. I feel like a dwarf—his body towering over mine, but the contact is welcome, and my stomach flutters to attention.

"Say cheese," he says into my ear.

I smile, but I feel my lips twitch as his warm breath spreads over my cheek. He chuckles softly in my ear, snapping a shot of the two of us before letting me go, and handing my camera back.

"A keepsake…so you don't forget about me." All humour is gone with his words.

"As if I'd forget about you," I say, swatting his arm.

"No, you just walked away," he says, blunt and to the point. He might as well have slapped me in the face.

"Come off it, Nate. It wasn't like that, and you know it." I clench hold of my wrist, searching out my hairband.

"Do I? All I know is I was trying to do right by you, and even that ended up being wrong."

I shake my head.

"You were right, though. At the time, I mean. I wasn't ready," I say on a breathy admission that leaves me feeling vulnerable.

"Maybe not, but that's not why I put the brakes on." He pulls at a leaf and picks at it.

His response throws me, and now I'm curious.

"So, why did you?" I shift from one foot to the other.

"Does it even matter now?" He flicks the remains of the leaf into the bush.

I sigh.

"Yes. Of course, it does," I say. I don't know why I'm pushing him. I don't even think I want the truth, but I appear to be on a roll.

"Fine. I was worried that once we did it, that it would change our friendship, and I didn't want to rush you. But I lost your friendship, anyway." His words feel like a paper cut—so quick until the sharpness of the sting comes to life.

"Okay…granted I haven't been a stellar friend. But I reached out to you, come on you know I did. I'd never *not* be there for you," I say, licking my dry lips.

He takes my hand in his. Warmth stirs low in my belly.

"So, why didn't you come back?" he asks, squeezing my hand, his eyes begging me to answer.

I look past his shoulder, unable to make eye contact.

"I was embarrassed. Rejected, so *that* Christmas I avoided coming back. Then it wasn't long after you moved on." *Why am I opening up a can of worms?*

"Yeah, well, I wasn't in a good place back then. I messed up. And then to add insult to injury, it was plastered all over Facebook," he says, his lips forming a grimace.

"I wonder, though, if the cat hadn't been let out of the bag…would you have told me?" I ask, summoning my strength to look him in the eye as I wait for a response.

He looks to his feet, then back to my face.

"Yes. I don't like secrets, you know that—even when they hurt," he replies, and I believe him.

"I wonder if we had…you know? Do you think things might have worked out differently?" I ask, stepping from one foot to the other.

He shrugs. "Who the hell knows? Besides, in hindsight, I was more experienced than you," he says with a shit-eating grin.

Boys.

"Come off it, you were hardly an expert," I say, trying to hold back my smile.

"No. But it was enough for me to know. Your first time should be special." His hand covers my shoulder—it's gentle, yet firm.

Why does he have this effect on me?

"It's a moot point now. You're with Simon," he says, removing his hand, that small moment of familiarity now gone.

"Me and Simon…it's complicated. We're not together–together," I say, using air quotes.

"So…what? You just hook up?" he asks, raising his eyebrows.

I feel unsettled at how quick this conversation turned. Do I look like the kind of person who hooks up? To each their own, but that's not me.

"What's that supposed to mean?" I ask, trying to keep the wobble out of my voice as I cross my arms.

He looks up, tilting his head back before making eye contact with me again.

"Oh, come on. You aren't stupid, you know? Late night booty calls…fuck buddies…"

His tone is condescending. Disdainful. He couldn't be further from the truth if he tried.

Who does he think he is? It's hot, too hot—I can feel sweat dripping between my shoulder blades.

"You think I'm promiscuous?" My mouth feels dry, and my chest tight—I try to swallow. I clutch my fist tight, my nails dig into my palm, and then I grab at my wrist.

He shakes his head.

"Now you're just putting words in my mouth. I never said you were a slut—I'm not judging your relationship with him. I just don't see the point in beating around the bush. If you're fuck buddies, and that's all…" he says, his chest rising and falling.

I blow out short, deep breaths—my heart palpitating, the erratic beat feeling like my heart is going to pump out of my chest.

This is not good.

"I didn't mean it like that. Come on—" he reaches for me, "—are you okay?"

I hold up my palm, shaking from adrenaline. He needs to back off and give me space. I shake my head in warning, my hair falling from my messy bun. He steps closer.

"You're freaking me out. What's wrong? Do you have asthma or something?" His voice sounds desperate now.

I shake my head, but it adds to my dizziness. My legs feel like heavy weights. I slump to the ground hard and put my head between my knees.

"Shit, just breathe." I hear the concern in his voice, as he begins to rub my back.

I want to scream at him...*shut up and stop touching me*. But I can't catch my breath—the air won't come.

He says something, but I can't hear it. It's drowned out. Too far away. Everything slows, though my heart races. White spots pepper the world. It's cloudy, shifting, hazy.

And then it all goes dark.

Chapter Five

"Shit, are you okay?" It's Nate—he sounds worried.

Smooth, cool fingertips skim over my brow and brush away the hair stuck to my face. I still his hand, lightly moving it away. Bringing the back of my trembling hand to my forehead, I try to regain some sort of decorum, shaking off my disorientation.

"Did I pass out?" I ask. It's a rhetorical question—my head is in his lap.

I am mortified.

I sit up too quickly, lightheaded and off balance, but his hands steady my shoulders. I breathe in deeply, waiting before getting to my feet. Then without another word, I walk away.

I can feel him close as I frog-march myself towards the house. Even if I couldn't see him from my peripheral vision, I'd know the weight of that stare anywhere. The intensity of it burns my skin. I'm hoping like hell I can make it back to my room without any further embarrassment.

But the powers that be clearly have other ideas.

Standing in front of me, are our Grandmothers. Nana has her phone clenched in her grasp as her eyes flit between Nate and me with a wrinkled brow. Evie fingers her necklace mercilessly as she moves from one foot to the other.

I stop mid-step, and turn on Nate.

"They know?" I say, my voice trembling.

His eyes give him away before he answers me.

"What was I supposed to do?" he asks, throwing his hands in the air.

I shake my head and cross my arms.

He takes a deep breath, running a jerky hand through his hair. "I thought something was seriously fucking wrong. I thought you were having an asthma attack," he says, the heat from his words radiating through him before he clenches his jaw shut, and stuffs his hands into his pockets. His eyes darken and tense as they try to hold my stare.

I turn away and come face to face with my Nana. She takes hold of my hand, and I close my eyes, taking a deep breath before looking at her. She brings the back of her hand to my forehead—checking my temperature. It's all for pretence. She knows what happened.

"Felicity, dear, you should go lie down. I think the news of Lawry, and the flight caught up with you," she says, more for Nate's benefit than my own.

I'm grateful for the pretence, but Nate isn't an idiot. He knows it's more than that, and right now I don't have the inclination or the strength to worry about it. I need space, and I need to get away from him so I can breathe. I nod in agreement and head towards the house.

"I'm sorry!" Nate calls after me. He sounds genuinely apologetic. I close my eyes.

"Nathaniel, what did you do?"

I stop walking. My stomach clenches when I think of the scolding he got for making me bleed all those years ago. Turning around to gauge the trouble he's in, I falter in my steps. Evie's scowl is fixed on her grandson, the lines on her forehead and the ones around her eyes stark—like they're slicing through her fragile skin in an attempt to quell her anger at Nate. She's never looked older—more exhausted—than she does at this moment. The weight of losing the love of her life, and the stress of what I'm bringing them with my bullshit, is sucking her dry. I close my eyes and clench my fists. If I don't get my shit together, I'm going to do more damage, and add to the crap that life has already dealt her.

"Nothing," I call out to her. "He didn't do anything. It was a misunderstanding, that's all. Please just forget about it." I feel light headed. To steady myself, I press my palm against the doorframe and turn back around.

Nate rushes to my side, and before I have a chance to realise what he's doing, an arm goes behind my knees—the other around my back—as he knocks me off my feet, lifting me into his arms. A *whoosh* of air escapes my lips. *What the hell?*

"Oh my God, Nate, put me down," I say, clinging to his top, worried the idiot will drop me. *What is wrong with him?*

He shakes his head.

"No can do. You looked a bit peaky like you were going to faint again," he says, too close to my face.

"I'm fine. Put me down, already." I lean back, trying to wriggle free. He shakes his head...again. *Stubborn arsehole.*

I squeeze my eyes shut. My body is at war with my head and heart. It should feel wrong, being held in his arms like this, but for the first time in a long time, this gives me a small reprieve—a sense of safety. His grip doesn't falter or wane as he holds me securely in his arms.

He pushes the door open with the tip of his boot, not releasing me until he lowers me onto the bed, only inches from my face. Everything slows around me. But my heart rate speeds as my throat dries. I divert my eyes, and see my bra, hanging off the handle on the bedside table. I am officially done.

His head turns, and I know he sees it—in all its glory…the most unflattering thing you've ever seen—the one with the huge hole in it.

His face gives nothing away, except for the twitch of his lips, as he heads over to the window to pull the curtains closed.

My Nana enters, carrying a glass of water.

"I thought you might need this," she says. I sit up as she hands me the water. I take a huge gulp, savouring the cool, refreshing liquid as it slides down my throat.

"Can I get you anything else?"

I chew the inside of my cheek.

"Maybe some headache tablets?" I say, ready to swing my legs off the bed, but she stops me.

"I'll get them. Where are they?" she asks, scanning the dressing table.

I point to the ottoman

"In my toiletry bag."

She rummages through it, and as she pulls out the packet of tablets, out flies a tampon.

Somebody, please put me out of my misery and kill me now.

When I do manage to swallow the tablets, an urge to retch grows in my belly. I hate taking medicine.

Leaning down, she kisses me on my forehead—stroking away my loose hair. I feel like a little girl again as her lavender scent envelopes me.

"Sorry, I didn't mean to make a scene—"

She shushes me.

"Felicity, stop it already. I love you...now rest," she says, before kissing my forehead, then retreating to the door. She pauses her hand on the handle, staring at Nate with her eyebrows raised.

It's a silent warning. My eyes meet his, our gazes lingering, his face torn.

"I just need a minute," he croaks out.

I look at Nana. She gives me a resigned shrug—a silent agreement.

"A few minutes. Try not to upset her *again,"* she says in warning.

I feel bad for him—it's hardly his fault what happened. The sound of the door clicking shut is his signal to speak.

"I'm sorry about what happened. I mean shit…I didn't even know you have anxiety attacks." He's standing at the foot of my bed—his head down—but his eyes look up to meet mine.

"Nate, it's fine. Can we please forget about it?" I ask.

I rack my brain, trying to think of some excuse to try and smooth this over—anything but the truth.

"I don't understand. We were talking, and everything seemed almost—normal, and then… I would never have upset you like that, not intentionally. It scared the shit out of me. You looked like you couldn't breathe, and then you just blacked out," he says, breathless, fisting the bedframe.

"I haven't had one in a while if it makes you feel any better," I say, fidgeting with the cover.

"Not really. I know whatever it is, you don't want to tell me, and I get that. I mean…it's not like I expect you to come back, everything like it was, you sharing all your deepest and darkest secrets," he says, as he comes around the side of the bed. He reaches a hand out, as if to touch my leg, but thinks better of it—instead, stuffing his hands back into his jean pockets.

I squeeze my eyes shut, take a deep breath, then open them. His focus is solely on me, his eyes wistful as he searches my face.

"I've been struggling with my nerves. It wasn't so bad at first, but then it got worse. Believe it or not, it's been getting better. I guess you could say I've…changed since you saw me last," I say. This sounds so bloody mundane even to my ears. There is so much more to my words than I'm willing to let on. But right now, I couldn't tell him even if I wanted to—I'm exhausted, and my eyelids are becoming heavy.

"That's evident, but you look tired. I'll let you rest."

I watch him walk away, letting the door close behind him. Eyes heavy, it's not long before darkness takes hold, and I'm being pulled back into the shadows.

Closing the door behind me, I lean back and close my eyes. I know something is wrong…more than what she's letting on. And I know one thing for sure—it bothered me earlier when she took those calls from Simon. It wasn't lost on me the way her throat flushed, the red sprinkling in her cheeks when we were on the drive back from the airport.

I made a point to keep myself busy and out of the way when we got back here. The last thing I wanted to do was sit around, playing happy families—like she didn't go AWOL for two years.

She's different, though, and not in a good way. I noticed how she kept twisting the hairband around her wrist, pulling it back until it pinged back against her skin—tight enough to leave a mark. *Does she even realise she's doing it?*

We were best friends once. I could pretty much always tell what she was thinking, but...now it's like she's there, but no one's home. Even the conversations we've had have been stilted, strained—like she's overthinking what to say. Not to mention how jumpy she was when I woke her up, and when I touched her. She either flinched or tensed up.

I was perfectly fine engrossed in my work. But when I heard her whistle to Laddie, I couldn't stay hidden. And look how that ended up—her having a full-blown panic attack.

I need to find out what the hell is going on, and I know just the two ladies who have the answers. Pushing off the door, I go search for them. And find them right where I thought they'd be—the drawing room.

They don't hear me as I walk through the doorway. They're huddled together as Ana wipes away a stray tear. My Nan squeezes her hand while fingering her necklace.

"But didn't you say she was getting better?" Nan asks.

I take another step into the room, my ears perking up.

"She is...I mean, she was."

Nan turns to Ana. "Well, what did the doctor say?"

My heart jumps into my mouth. "What the hell...please tell me she isn't sick?" I blurt out. *God, don't let her be sick.*

Ana stands, her hand covering her chest. "Goodness, no, she isn't sick. Calm yourself down and watch your mouth." She waves me over, then sits back down and pats the empty seat beside her.

The last thing I want to do right now is sit—I'm too wired. I shake my head.

"What is it, then? Because quite frankly it scared the shit out of me," I say.

Ana avoids eye contact with me, smoothing out her skirt. I think I hear a *tsk* sound escape her lips, but I can't be sure.

"Language. You need to learn to harness that tongue of yours," Nan says. I curse internally. Is she kidding me right now?

Something's clearly going on, and I'm being reprimanded over my choice of fucking words?

I watch Ana and Nan look to one another, an unspoken conversation—one I'm not privy to.

"Care to explain to us what happened?" asks Ana.

Wow! Well deflected. They won't tell me what's going on with Flick, but they expect me to tell them what triggered her panic attack? I look away in an attempt to avoid the question, but the weight of their stares burns into my skin like a hot poker prodding me. Sure enough, they have zoned in on me like a pair of hawks. It's like they're a tag team. *Talk about making me feel like I'm seven years old.*

I clear my throat.

"Oh, for Pete's sake. Don't look at me like that…all right fine. We may have broached the subject of her relationship with Simon," I say, and throw my hands up in surrender.

"*Nathaniel.* You haven't seen her for how long? And then you decide to interrogate the poor girl? I take it from your lack of words, you're giving us the edited version. You really should think before you speak," my Nan says.

"Back up, so let me get this straight. Flick tells me she and Simon aren't really together, then by me asking her what that entails, is what?" I ask, dumbfounded. I don't understand women.

"Well, it sounds to me like that's kind of private, and a moot point…is it your place to ask?" my Nan replies, raising her eyebrows.

I grab the back of my neck, squeezing it hard to release the pent-up tension. Maybe I did come off a bit of an arsehole, implying they were basically fuck buddies. Hypocritical of me considering that's what Rachel and I are—*were.*

Fuck. Maybe I'm jealous.

"So, are either of you going to tell me? Or do I need to find out by myself?"

My Nan is tight-lipped as Evie speaks up. "There isn't anything to tell, and even if there was, don't you think it would be for her to say?" she says.

I look up.

What a load of bullshit!

This shit right here confuses me even more. I could do with my Gramps on my side. Since losing my parents, it had always been Nan and us against the world. I miss him so much, my chest constricts. Accepting he's gone is still hard for me to comprehend. I swallow down the lump in my throat.

"You're right. I'm sorry," I say, as I kiss my Nan, and make to leave the room.

"Nathaniel, hold on one second dear," Ana calls out.

I wait as she approaches me and takes my hand.

"I understand how what happened may have been a shock, but please try to keep the drama down to a minimum. For your Grandmothers sake," she says as she stands on her tiptoes and kisses my cheek. "And as you can tell, the less stress for Felicity, the better."

I'm tempted to run my mouth, but then think better of it. She's right, my attitude isn't helping anyone.

But one way or the other, I will find out.

Chapter Six

Nathaniel

I rap my knuckle on her door but hear no answer, so I enter her room. I can tell from the sound of her breathing that she's asleep. Granted me being in here is kind of stalker-ish—even by my standards—but something is really wrong with her.

I take a seat in the overstuffed armchair. Might as well be a *comfortable* stalker. I've made a point to avoid this room. Every time I passed it after she first left, the sweet apple scent of her perfume would creep up on me and overwhelm me with all those times I was close enough to her to practically taste it.

Her eyes are squeezed tightly, crinkling around the edges—worry lines. It reminds me of when she was thirteen.

That's when I knew my feelings for her had changed.

Past - 2000

"I don't know if I want to kiss Leroy," she says, swinging her legs back and forth over the balcony of the tree house.

"So, don't," I say, hoping like hell she won't.

She turns her head, squinting her eyes from the sun.

"But I have to kiss someone, sometime, don't I?" she says, as she bites her lip. She looks away, head bowed.

"Technically, no, you don't. Besides, you've already had your first kiss, with me..." I say before I have a chance to stop myself.

What the heck? Where did that just come from? *I look away. The truth is, I've wanted to kiss her for a while now—she's all I can think about—but that's all kinds of wrong. First, she's practically family, and second, I'm older—more experienced. And she's so unashamedly Flick.*

I nudge her, and she looks over at me.

"Nate, I was ten. It doesn't count. Besides, I want it over with. All my friends have kissed—even Sophie. What's wrong with me?"

"God. Flick, there's nothing wrong with you. When the time's right, you'll know. You sure as hell won't be up here with me talking about doing it, you'll be doing it."

"Is that what it was like for you?" she asks, picking at the skin around her fingernail.

I tap her hand for her to stop—if I can't bite mine, she can't pick hers.

"What do you mean?" I ask her.

A blush creeps up her throat, and over her face. I feel something deep in my gut, she has my insides in knots—and yet she's completely unaware.

"Your first kiss," she says.

I'm not sure what she's more embarrassed about—asking about my first kiss or talking about kissing.

She rubs at her eyes.

"You're not old enough to know about the kind of kissing I get up to," I say with a smile.

She glares at me, her face almost comical.

"I'm not a bloody kid, Nate."

I swallow my discomfort. No, she's not. Every time I've seen her lately, she's different, and that's why I want to be there to look out for her. If I lived closer, I could keep little shits like this Leroy kid away.

"I know you're not. I just don't want some idiot kid taking advantage of you," I say, unable to stop myself.

"He isn't a kid, Nate. He's older than me."

"What? You have got to be kidding me!" I clench my fists.

"No, he's fifteen."

*I shake my head. Nope—no way—*not happening. *The thought causes my stomach to dip, and it leaves a sour taste in my mouth. I swallow hard.*

"In that case, no. You most definitely *should not be kissing him," I say.*

"You're being stupid. It's just kissing." She waves her hands about.

Is she trying to piss me off?

"I should think that's all it would be, too," I say, trying to stay calm.

Thirteen going on fourteen my arse. She might as well be sixteen the way she acts. I should know. I'm seeing someone that age, and we get up to plenty. My stomach plummets at the thought of her doing any of those things with Leroy—or anyone else, for that matter.

"Maybe I shouldn't be talking to you about it...if you're going to be an idiot. But you're my best friend," she says, shrugging.

"That is why you should listen to me..."

She rolls her eyes and puffs out air through her nostrils.

I clear my throat as I continue. "You deserve special, Flick...not some sloppy kiss at Saturday morning pictures, or over a park somewhere."

She raises her eyebrows. Shit, am I giving her ideas—scrap that.

"Special?" she replies, smiling.

I nod.

"Yes, you geek. Special," I say, and elbow her.

"I think that only happens in Disney and shit," she says, sighing.

I let out a chuckle. "Such a cynic for someone so young." I put my arm over her shoulder and pull her into me, kissing the top of her head.

She jabs me with her elbow, and I release her.

"Fine. How about you kiss me*?" I say, almost choking on my own Adam's apple. I can't believe I just said that.*

"What?" she whispers as she leans back to look at me. Her face contorts in what looks like confusion. "You'd kiss me?"

The way she says that agitates me. But it's what she didn't say—I can see the wheels turning—she thinks it's a pity offer.

"Yes... I mean, better than you kissing that Leroy kid." I look away, licking my dry lips.

"He's the same age as you, Nate. Not a kid." She attempts to punch me, but I swat her away like a gnat.

"Whatever you say." I don't care what she says, he's a prick, and he doesn't have her best interests at heart, I'm sure of it.

"I don't want things to be weird between us," she admits, swinging her legs.

"It won't be. Geez, it was only a suggestion." I pull at the collar of my t-shirt, and push myself up on the palms of my hands—ready to get up—but she pulls me back down.

"You promise you won't think differently of me?" She nibbles at her bottom lip.

"Why would I think differently of you?"

God, *if only she knew about the dreams I've been having about her. I'm pretty sure she'd be out of this treehouse, and down that ladder faster than Linford* bloody *Christie.*

"Because I don't know what I'm doing."

I want to laugh—is she for real right now?

"You're overthinking this. It's just a kiss."

She nods, wringing her hands together.

I feel like a prick for suggesting it, now. I want her to want to kiss me as much as I want to kiss her, but it's an ulterior motive—I just don't want her kissing someone that isn't me.

The air is thick between us—filled with uneasiness. It's foreign and unwelcome.

I hate that I'm the one who put it there. I begin to tickle her, and like I knew she would, she lets out a snort, and wriggles around like an oversized worm, trying her hardest to tickle me back.

I hold up my hands in surrender. Her face flushes, and she laughs as she leans her head against my shoulder. I kiss the top of her head. She turns, smiling up at me.

My chest feels like it's shrinking. I bring my hand up, cup her cheek, and shift slightly. I watch as she sweeps her tongue over her bottom lip.

I lean down. Her eyes dart to my lips, and then—as I close the distance between us—her eyelids flutter shut.

My lips descend upon hers until they're met with a soft gasp that passes her lips the moment before they connect with mine. Neither of us moves—I don't think I even breathe— until I pull back slightly. Her eyes are still closed, her fingers gripping my t-shirt.

My lips gravitate back towards hers. When I lightly stroke her lip with my tongue, she lets out a small breath of air. Slowly, our tongues collide, and we explore each other. I feel it everywhere.

Reluctant and breathless, I pull back. Her breathing is heavy. I kiss the tip of her nose, then her forehead, before her eyes flutter open.

"Wow," she exhales.

Her cheeks are rose coloured, and her green eyes sparkle—lighting up like evergreen. I pull her into my chest to stop myself from kissing her again.

Wow *doesn't even begin to cover it.*

"Nate?" she whispers

"Hmmm?" I don't want my voice to betray my over-driven hormones.

"Was that okay? Did...did I do it right?"

I'm not used to hearing her sound so unsure of herself. I pull back to look at her—big mistake, I want to kiss her again.

"Yes, you did. It was great."

I look away. I want to tell her it was perfect, that if I died tomorrow, that kiss would be the best thing that's ever happened to me.

"You're just saying that."

I laugh, but it's humourless.

"No, I'm not..." I've opened Pandora's box now. "I need to ask you something?" I cough, trying to hide my unease.

"Okay..." she responds. Her eyes have a buoyant light about them, as if they are smiling.

"Promise me you won't kiss Leroy?" I look her straight in the eye. I know I'm being a selfish bastard.

"Don't worry. I don't feel like kissing him now, anyway," she says, matter of fact.

I squeeze her a little tighter.

Good. *I don't feel like kissing anyone else either.*

I wake with a start and sit bolt upright, clutching my chest. From the corner of my eye, I see a silhouette. Someone's sitting in the armchair. My heart rate picks up speed, but my eyes don't shy from the figure as I draw in a deep breath.

"It's just me," Nate says.

I drop back onto the bed, my head thumping against the plush pillow.

"Shit, Nate, you nearly gave me a flipping heart attack."

I forgot where I was for a moment. I wipe my hand over my face—my skin feels clammy. *Nice.*

"Sorry. I needed to make sure you were okay after what happened earlier." He sits forward, his hands hanging between his knees.

"I'm fine, but Nate, watching me sleep is creepy." I raise my eyebrows.

He only shrugs his shoulders while looking down at his watch.

"How long was I asleep?" I swing my legs off the bed.

"A couple of hours. I was about to wake you." He looks at his feet.

"I'm awake, so all good." I pick up the glass beside me and take a sip, trying to ignore the shake of my hand. I get the impression he's leading up to something—I just don't know what.

"Flick, I wanted to ask you about earlier…" he says, watching me as I set the glass down.

"What about it?" My stomach plummets.

"Why did no one tell me about what was going on with you?" He tilts his head to the side, waiting on my reply.

I stand, twisting my head from side to side, trying to release the kink in my neck.

"I asked them not to, and believe it or not, it's not something I make a habit of telling people."

I make my way over to the window, pulling my fingers through the knots in my hair but give up.

"I'd like to think I'm not just people. God, Flick, I've known you my whole life," he says, his voice pleading as he approaches me.

I pull open the curtains. The sun hangs low on the horizon in rich waves of ambers and oranges. It's so beautiful, and I itch for my camera—this would make such a gorgeous shot. I take a deep breath, relishing in the fresh air blowing through the open window. This always was the perfect reading spot.

How many times have I sat in this very spot contemplating life? What I wanted to be when I grew up, who I was going to marry? What shoes to wear? Skittles or peanut M&M's? It's all so insignificant now.

"I never said that, Nate. But people change."

I breathe in deep and release it through my nose. A small whistling sound escapes, and I squeeze my eyes shut—I should just be grateful I haven't farted in front of him yet. Nate plonks down beside me, his knee brushing against mine. I concentrate on the view out of the window.

"Yeah, but we were best friends once." He says it so low I almost don't hear him.

"Yes, Nate, and I also used to want to be a beekeeper. Like I said, people change. I don't know…maybe we need to get to know each other again." I wrap my arms around my middle.

“That’s obvious, seeing as I’m the only one who appears to be in the dark where you’re concerned.” He squeezes my knee, and I turn to catch him looking me straight in the eye.

It’s a challenge—one that says, *it’s because of what I did to you, you don’t trust me.* Yes, Nate, you hurt me—you slept with another girl—but we weren’t even together. It was a lifetime ago, inconsequential now.

This is going to hang over us like a brewing thunderstorm if I don’t give him something. Like it’s not going to be difficult enough getting through the next couple of days.

“Fine. I’ll try to explain.” I pull my legs underneath me.

He shakes his head, but I put my hand up before he can try to talk me out of it—typical Nate behaviour.

“It was around the time of my eighteenth birthday. My confidence took a serious knock. I became withdrawn, depressed. I didn’t want to go anywhere or do anything. I was pretty low for a while. But as you can see, I kind of worked through it. I took up photography—it’s like a coping mechanism. Don’t get me wrong, I have support, but this is something I can do on my own. I know that probably sounds weird…”

I leave out the details of how some days I wish I wasn’t here, or how every time I closed my eyes in the weeks following *it,* all I’d see is that bloody room, and the smell felt like it would never leave me.

Nate pulls gently on my arm, until I release my waist, and takes my hand in his.

“Flick, you should’ve called me. Damn it, if I’d known, I would have got my shit together.”

I shake my head, even if he had, I wouldn’t have wanted him to. Not at first…not even now.

“I think, sometimes, we have to work through stuff on our own, you know?”

He rubs his thumb back and forth over my knuckles.

"You weren't alone, though. You had your Mum, Ana, Simon. What I said about the two of you, it was out of order. It's none of my business, and I'm sorry."

I feel something strangely like disappointment. Deep down, maybe I don't want him to be sorry. Maybe I want it to be his business.

"Simon is one of the good ones, Nate. Believe it or not, you two have a lot in common, and you'd probably get along."

"Easy tiger, I don't know about that. I'd like to think I was one of the goods ones. I've missed you, Flick."

My chest physically aches with his words. I've missed him too.

"Listen, the last thing I want is to cause drama, but me being here has been long overdue. And I have, too—missed you."

He looks up from our joined hands, a smile lighting his face. I can't help but return it with mine—he's always been infectious in that way.

"So, friends?" He cocks his head to the side, a goofy look on his face.

I nod.

"Yes, friends," I say with a roll of my eyes.

"Pinkie swear?" He lets go of my hand and holds out his little finger.

I look at it and laugh before I link it with mine. He gives it a little shake. Feeling awkward, I let go and stand. He does the same, running his hand through his hair. I'm just about to turn away from him when he moves towards me, pulling me into a hug.

Stunned, my arms hang limply at my sides. I feel his hold soften. Worried he'll let go, I wrap my arms around his waist and rest my cheek on his chest.

I feel his shoulders relax, his chest moving as he lets out a breath. My heart is drumming heavy in my chest. I'm both elated and terrified. I've built walls, and yet, in the space of less than a day, he's managed to climb right over the top. And I don't know how to process it.

"Nate…"

"Hmm?" I feel the vibration through my cheek.

"I did call you," I whisper into his top before I lose my nerve.

"What, when?" Hands on my shoulders, he pushes back slightly to look me in the eyes.

"Ages ago. A girl answered—said you were in the shower. I left a message. I just figured…" *That he didn't want to talk to me.*

He shakes his head, his eyebrows pulling together. He never got my message.

"I would have rung you back." He looks frustrated.

"It doesn't matter, I don't even know why I told you."

I'd be lying if I said I never wondered about her—if they're still together. Why does the thought of him being with someone rile me up the wrong way?

Ignore it.

He places a gentle kiss to my forehead before stepping back.

"Well, it matters to me. I'm going to give you a minute. I'll see you downstairs for dinner?"

I nod. Feeling cold as he walks away, I wrap my arms around myself, trying to recreate the warmth from his touch. The door clicks shut behind him, and I'm left alone. But for the first time in a long time, things don't look quite so sepia.

Chapter Seven

Dinner without Lawry isn't the same. I've spent the whole time trying to avoid, looking anywhere but at Nate. After he left my room, my mind went berserk, going over our conversation. I do that—over analyse every minute detail, every touch. I wish I didn't, but I can't help myself.

I take it upon myself to clear the table. Nate joins me, and we carry out the task in silence. The only noise is the hitting and clinking of cutlery, the clanging of plates as we carry them to the kitchen. I scrape the leftovers into the bin, rinse, and load them into the dishwasher.

Nate sits down at the kitchen table, his head low. Fidgeting, he looks like he has the weight of the world on his shoulders. The air feels thick as I swallow.

"I need to ask you something?" Nate says, elbows on knees, his hands hang between them.

"Okay…" I stop what I'm doing and sit opposite him.

"I have an appointment with the funeral director tomorrow. Nan hasn't said it, but it will crush her going, and she won't let me go alone…" He clears his throat, clearly uncomfortable. I'm not stupid. It's obvious what he's asking.

"You want me to come with you?"

He looks up. "Would you? I know it's a big ask, I figure she's more likely to agree if I'm not going alone." His vulnerability is palpable. The only time I've ever seen him look like this was when his parents died.

"It's fine. Besides, I can order the flowers for Mum and me while we're there."

"Thank you. I don't know what else to say except…thank you." He lets out a gush of air.

"What are friends for?" I reply.

I begin wiping down the worktop to keep busy, but when he doesn't respond I peer over my shoulder and catch him looking at my backside. He averts his eyes, but not before I notice. The thoughts I've been having of Nate recently are anything but platonic. Feeling discombobulated, I sit down again and rub at my wrist. What I did to Nate by not coming back was no better than what my dad did when he left mum and me and started a new family.

"I'm sorry I stayed away. I'm messed up, I know."

He looks me straight in the eye, stretching his arm across the table. He takes my hand in his, and I let the hair band ping against my flesh.

"I don't think you're any more messed up than the rest of us."

The dryness in my throat itches as I swallow.

"Believe me, I am. Just count yourself lucky you aren't stuck in my messed-up head," I say as I shrug my shoulders.

"I wouldn't mind knowing what goes on in that pretty little head of yours."

He winks, and I can't help but smile. If I didn't know better, I'd think he's flirting with me. I cough—time to change the subject, me thinks.

"How are you feeling about tomorrow?"

I'd like to think I still know him well enough to know he's struggling. His shoulders slump—the weight of my words heavy on his resolve.

"Barely holding my shit together. It's hardest in the mornings. When I first wake up, for the briefest of moments, I feel fine. Then it hits me full force that he really is gone. It's like everyone I love ends up leaving me." His eyes are glassy. He looks so lost. My insides twist with torment.

"I can't tell you anything you don't already know about loss. But take some solace in the fact they didn't leave you, not by choice. My Dad, he left my Mum and me by choice. Lawry and your parents… Them passing wasn't a choice."

He works his jaw, his eyebrows scrunching.

"I know the only guarantee in life is death. It's inevitable, I get that, but it sure as hell doesn't make it easier to accept. Not when you're the one left behind." His voice cracks on the last word. His head drops to his chest, silent tears only betrayed by the movement of his shoulders.

I stand, unsure what to do. It's the fear of intimacy that tries to hold me captive, but I force it away, making my way to his side. Placing my nervous hand on his shoulder, I squeeze.

A small sob escapes him as I move my other hand up and down his back, rubbing it gently. He shifts. I freeze. His arms wrap around my middle, and he buries his head into my stomach.

I slowly breathe in through my nose. *Steady, steady.* I don't know how my hand finds its way to his hair, but I rake my fingers through it like I used to when we were younger.

It's all I can do to let him know he's not alone. The first time I saw him after his parents died, I didn't know how to process it. Didn't understand the magnitude of the situation. It wasn't until I saw his face, and the pain mirrored there, that I knew—they weren't coming back.

I'd given him my beanie bear, the one I used to carry with me everywhere. He shook his head, but I'd kissed his cheek, and told him it was his. I cried that night, missing my bear because it was the last present my dad gave to me before he moved out. But I knew he would be missing his parents more. They were never coming back…at least *I* would still get to see my dad.

Chapter Eight

I've been awake long enough now to know that's all the sleep I'll be getting. I twist and turn, looking for a cool spot amongst the sheets. I think about last night, how Nate crumbled, how once upon a time we felt invincible. But now life lets us know just how vulnerable we are.

I need to run; clear my head. It's the only time I feel free from these prison walls encased around my busy mind—a constant loop that only stills in the eye of the beast when I run. Workout clothes on, iPod in hand, I make my way through the house, as quietly as I possibly can.

I stretch my arms and calves, then set off into a jog. Earbuds in, music on shuffle, I pick up the pace. I forget all about the shittiness of the world, I let it all go.

There's this moment—right in the build-up to the burn—when I think my body can't take anymore, and I consider quitting. But my instinct to stop morphs into an obsession to carry on. And just like that, I push. Harder. An all-out sprint before I slow and come to a stop. I feel it everywhere.

Hands on knees, I lean over to catch my breath. I hear something and stop my music. It's a clanking noise—like metal on metal, coming from the garage. I walk over, my footsteps light as I peer inside the open door. His legs peek out from underneath the bonnet of a car, and I watch him work. When Nate slides himself out on a trolley, he's shirtless.

As if by magic, he must sense me. He looks up and catches me mid-gape. The corners of his mouth twitch.

"Morning," he says, wiping his hands on a rag hanging from his jean pocket. He pulls himself up, his jeans riding real low. *I wonder if he's commando...*

I choke on thin air—*what the fuck*—my eyes springing back to his face while I cough away my embarrassment.

"You're up early, have you been out here long?" I hope the fact I'm already hot from my run covers up my embarrassment. My sweat-stained face, and a bird's nest on the top of my head, are small mercies. At least I brushed my teeth. I bite my lip. Since when did Nate fill out so much? I want to smack myself in the head because I'm gawking again.

"A while. So, you run?" He tilts his head, watching me, waiting for my response.

I wonder if that look works on *whats-her-face*, or any other girl for that matter. He manages to carry it off, and I know how easily it could be misconstrued for arrogance, but I think he's just confident—unassuming, even. I blink. *Shit, he asked you a question. Answer him.*

"When I can." My voice sounds strange even to my ears, but he doesn't seem to notice.

"Well if you fancy a partner while you're here, let me know." He says it with a wink, and my body reacts, sending a flutter to my stomach. *What's wrong with me?*

"Okay, I'm going to go grab a shower."

He smiles playfully with a wiggle of his eyebrows. I roll my eyes. This is the flirtatious side of Nate I remember, and I can't help but smile.

"I'll see you at breakfast. Are you still all right to come with me today?" That boyish look he had seconds ago vanishes with his question.

"Of course."

His relief is evident, and I turn to leave before I do something stupid like hug him…or worse, lick that sheen of sweat from his neck. A tingle comes to life deep in my belly.

"Hold up, is that a tattoo?"

He catches me off guard, stopping me in my tracks. I turn back to him. Looking down, I realise my tank top doesn't quite cover much of my mid-drift—my ink visible. I feel self-conscious. If I could pull my top down lower, I would. I'm more modest than I used to be, but I need calm down. It's not like I'm standing in my bra, for fuck's sake. It's just a sports top.

"It is." I wrap my arms around my middle, my fingers squeezing me on either side.

"Can I see it?"

I pause and take a few breaths.

"I guess so." I drop my arms, turning to an angle so he can see.

"Wow, that's beautiful. Did it hurt over the ribs?" he asks, looking back up to my face.

"A little… Well, a lot, actually, but it was worth it. You forget about any pain afterward, and I'm pleased with it."

I designed it myself—a Japanese-style cherry blossom. I suck in a quick breath as his fingers trail over the outline, his touch tickling, causing me to let out a laugh.

"Still ticklish, I see?"

I wince and step away, but he grabs hold of my waist with one hand, continuing to tickle me with the other, his assault relentless.

"Nate, stop. Please!" I squeal like a baby pig, trying to wriggle free.

He stops tickling me but keeps a hand on my waist. He moves closer. My breath catches as he brings his other hand up to my face, tucking the loose hair behind my ear. I lick my lips before swallowing nervously. I bite my bottom lip. He is so close—too close. If I move just a fraction, I could lean in and… I glance over my shoulder, trying to focus my attention somewhere else when I spot it—something familiar.

"Is that one of the cars you're working on?"

He looks over his shoulder, which gives me the perfect opportunity to slip out of his touch. I walk towards the car.

"Yep," he replies, popping the p.

I smile, touching my chin with my thumb and forefinger, as if in thought.

"Let me guess, a sixty-seven Chevy Impala?"

His jaw drops, his eyes going wide as he nods.

"Damn. There's something seriously sexy about you knowing what car this is."

I walk around it, my hand gliding over the smooth finish of the paintwork, then laugh at his comment.

"Well, Nate, it just so happens that this car right here—" I place my palm on the bonnet, tapping my fingers for emphasis, "—is one of my favourite cars."

His smile is wide as he steps in front of me. Instinct tells me to take a step back, but my body comes to a stop as the backs of my calves touch the car. I go to step to the side, but he extends both arms around me, caging me in, his palms now flat against the car.

"No shit. Really?"

There's this look in his eyes, which if I'm not mistaken, looks something akin to lust. It causes me to suck in a quick breath, my lower region clearly affected by his proximity.

"Yes, really," I say, feeling a burst of bravery.

He leans into my ear, his breath warm against my neck as he whispers.

"In that case, once I finish, I'll take you out for a drive."

I close my eyes, my body trembling slightly. We always had a connection, but this is something else entirely. I've never felt this kind of attraction. My breath quickens when his lips brush a feather-light kiss on my neck. I move just a little when his lips touch my collarbone. I place a hand on his shoulder to steady myself, something like a whimper escaping me. *What the ever-fucking God?*

I feel a vibration against my pelvis coming from his jeans. He looks to the ceiling, letting out an audible groan.

I take a breath. My heart feels like it's running a marathon. There's no denying my attraction to him. He moves back and pulls his phone from his pocket to silence it. His eyes drift up to my lips, which now suddenly feel so dry, I sweep my tongue over them. I swallow as I watch him—his stare burning my skin, causing goose bumps to rise on the nape of my neck.

"Nate?" I say, breaking the silence.

He shakes his head. A small, tender smile crosses his face as he clears his throat.

"Sorry, we should go get ready."

I nod before walking away. And make sure not to look back.

I can't believe I let his lips touch my skin. My willpower evaporated. What if his phone hadn't brought me back to reality? I wonder who it was—I'd ask, but it's none of my business. All I know is I'm left feeling confused.

I shower as soon as I return to my room. I can still feel his lips on my skin, and I get this warm feeling deep in the pit of my tummy. I try to ignore the pulse between my legs, squeezing my thighs together. My skin flushes. Shit, I'm totally turned on. I can't let myself believe it's anything more than just pent-up frustration on his part *and* mine. One thing I do know for certain—I'm not emotionally stable to go there, the whole no strings attached. *No can do*.

Now I'm getting ahead of myself, but for the first time in a long time, I have a burning desire for something more to happen. But it's not just anyone. It's Nate. My hand slips between my legs of its own accord, and I squeeze my eyes closed. Biting my lip, I think back to the feeling of his lips on my skin.

Chapter Nine

Looking over at Nana, I realise her skin no longer holds the olive glow from hours spent tending to her garden. It's taken on a lighter tone, her wrinkles now more prominent, the crow's feet around her eyes are set now deeper. Her hair used to have a silver sheen to it, but now it's a lacklustre grey, hanging limply. The halo of light that once surrounded her is beginning to fade. Her posture is frail, brittle even, her shoulders slump, and a small hump rests between her shoulder blades.

"Morning, how did you sleep?" she asks, her voice weak as I give her a kiss on the cheek.

"Not bad. I went for a run earlier, cleared my head. How are you feeling?"

Her shoulders slump. "Overwhelmed. It feels like a lifetime ago that Samuel Junior was born, and I went to France as a Special Operations Executive. But it also feels like it was only yesterday."

"Wait, *what?* Hold on…you were a female spy?" I'm flabbergasted. This woman has always been someone I aspired to be growing up, but even now, she never ceases to amaze me. *Talk about a dark horse.*

"Something like that, I guess."

"You're a war hero?" My heart is warm.

She shakes her head. "No. The men and women who never made it home—they're the heroes. It's tragic so many died to give us the freedom we have today. I remember when I first met your grandfather. He was part of the resistance. Handsome. Of course, but believe me when I say our relationship was far from plain sailing, God rest his soul." She smiles at the memory. "By the time the war ended, he already had my heart and soul. Of course, I wanted to be wherever he was, and I knew he was happiest in France, but he understood I wanted our children to have the best of both worlds. My family was here in England, so we compromised—traveling back and forth.

"He always believed that home is where the heart is, and his heart was wherever I was. It sounds cliché, but it's the truth. Finding our happily ever after took hard work and sacrifice on *both* parts. Love doesn't come easy, or without seeing the other at their worst. I think that's why I feel closest to him when I'm in France—especially now that he's gone." She casts her gaze.

I take her hand in mine. The weight of her fingers as they squeeze mine is welcome and familiar. "Yes, of course it does."

"I never told anyone this—not even your mother. He was married before me, you know? She died during childbirth. He lost both her and the baby. I tried to avoid my feelings toward him, but he stirred something in me that not even Lawry had, and I refused to accept it."

She lets go of my hand, and then makes her way over to the window while spinning her wedding ring with her thumb—a habit I don't even know if she is aware of.

"I tried to ignore the attraction, but one day I had an epiphany. I came to understand that you can't choose who you fall in love with. When I thought I'd lost him, I knew he'd always have my heart. God, I wasn't even sure if his feelings ran as deep as mine. He'd already lost the woman he loved."

She turns back to me, melancholy in her eyes. “But he *did* love you. I can’t imagine finding a love like that.” My thoughts flit to Nate as an ache rises in the back of my throat.

She smiles, her dimple present, and returns to sit beside me, wrapping her hand in mine.

“He did,” Nana continues, “With a raw passion. He was just as flawed as the next man, and our relationship still had issues, but I loved him fiercely. Still do. Don’t be mistaken, there were times I didn’t particularly like him, and times he was lucky I didn’t strangle him. But I wouldn’t change it—not for all the tea in China. You love, who you love,” she says, and shrugs, matter-of-fact.

Yes, you do.

My pocket beeps. I pull out my phone, “It’s Nate asking if I’m ready.”

I type my reply.

“Thank you for going with him today.” Her hand squeezes my shoulder.

Unease weighs heavy in my chest, but I force a smile.

“It’s the least I can do—to make myself useful.” I fiddle with my phone.

“You being there will mean more to that young man than you’ll ever know.”

She pulls me into a warm embrace. Overcome with melancholy, I squeeze her tighter, not ready to let go just yet.

I don’t notice her come in the kitchen until her scent washes over me…right before she sits down, reaching out to take my hand in hers. She interlaces our fingers, squeezing gently, causing my thoughts to freeze momentarily. Fidgeting in my seat, I take a sip of my now cold coffee and shudder.

"Ready to make a move?" she asks, tentatively.

"You're not eating?"

She nods, grabs an apple from the fruit bowl, and takes a bite.

I give her a quick smile and glance around, checking my pockets for my car keys before we head out.

The drive there is filled with static—the atmosphere almost palpable, my muscles tense. But she leaves me to my thoughts, and it's only when I park the car that I break the silence.

"I can't do this." Heaviness settles in my stomach as I tighten my grip on the steering wheel.

"You can, and you will...you're not alone. I'll be right there with you. You're stronger than you realise."

I shake my head, rubbing the back of my neck.

Let's get this over with.

I unfasten my seatbelt and exit the car. Meeting her at the passenger's side, I take her hand in mine. She doesn't question it, just squeezes a little tighter as we make our way to the funeral director's.

A wave of heat swamps me as I push through the entrance, my insides quivering when a lady called Eleanor greets us. She seats us in a private room. It's beige—boring, neutral. A large box of tissues and a couple of binders sit on the coffee table that's centred in the room. On one side of it, there's a grey sofa and two matching armchairs. Maybe it's designed to make you feel more comfortable or less distracted, *I don't know.*

Eleanor is friendly enough and empathetic to a fault as we work our way through the uncomfortable details. It's not lost on me that Flick hasn't once let go of my hand…even though my palm is slick with sweat.

When the subject of the coffin is broached, nausea engulfs me, a sour taste rising in my mouth. I struggle for air.

"Sorry, do you think it would be all right if we stopped for a break, please?" Flick asks.

It's only when the door clicks shut that Flick speaks to me.

"Hey, you okay?" she asks, her tone perturbed.

I shake my head. "No, not really. I have it all here—written on a damn list. I never considered I'd be here discussing coffins. I can hardly comprehend the fact he's gone."

My voice cracks on the last word, my throat becoming tight. I press my palms into my eyes. I can't lose my shit. Her hand is on my back, moving in small circular motions—like how Nan used to do it when I was upset.

"Nate, there's no time limit on these things, and you're allowed to grieve. This is all so raw. I know Lawry would be proud of you—stepping up this way—like the rest of us are."

I want to laugh. *Proud? She has no fucking idea.*

"Hardly. I'm a poor excuse for a grandson. I could've had more time with him when he was first diagnosed. But no, instead, I fucked off out of the country when the shit hit the fan."

It's my burden to bear.

"Nate, you were scared. Who wouldn't be? But you came back when he needed you the most. That's what's important," she says with conviction, taking both my hands in hers.

"I just never thought he would die. Even after we were told it was terminal… I thought he'd beat it. I still had hope—" The ache in the back of my throat intensifies. "When his pain became unmanageable, I felt completely powerless. That's when I knew. If I could change one thing, it would be that he didn't have to suffer like he did." I can't look at her, so I concentrate on her thumb as it rubs circles over my knuckles.

"Nate, you were being positive. It's what he needed. I'm sorry he suffered… God, I feel so ashamed, not being here for any of you. I know this isn't about me, but you're not the only one who feels guilty. You're a good person, Nate, and a good grandson."

She cups my cheek. I close my eyes, taking a deep breath. Soft lips place a chaste kiss to mine. I open my eyes, and they're greeted with hers. I've missed her, and now that she's back, I understand by her being gone, I was missing part of myself. She's always been my conscience, and here she is again, right when I need her the most—in all her open vulnerability.

It's in this moment I crack under the pressure of it all. Emotions I've reserved for the privacy of my room at night break free, releasing an onslaught of tears. Without a word, she pulls me into her body and holds me with reverence.

I let out a soft sigh, and then inhale deep when we leave the cool confines of the funeral director's office. A swift summer breeze floats across my skin, my body weary. I could so easily sleep.

"I wouldn't have been able to do that on my own. Thank you." Nate says, taking my hand and squeezing it.

I'm just glad I held my shit together. I stare at our hands, the feeling so…*normal*.

"I'm sorry you had to go through it at all."

He turns towards me, pulling me in for a hug. I tense—*instinct*—but then relax into his arms, trying to recall if he was always this tactile.

All I know is, being like this with him makes me feel conflicted and somewhat confused. He steps back and grips my upper arms gently.

"I don't want to push my luck, but I have another appointment. I didn't realise how long this would take—" He nods his head towards the building. "I guess there's no time limit with things like this. It's up to you if you want to come with me, or you can take the car… I can catch a cab when I'm done."

He's speaking a mile a minute. It's been a long time since I've seen him like this—almost excited. I'm intrigued.

"I might as well come with you. Besides, what kind of sidekick would I be if I deserted you now?" I say with a smile, the reference so clear in my head, though it was ages ago when Nate used to call me the Robin to his Batman.

A rumble of laughter escapes him as he nods and starts walking. I fall into step beside him as we head up the high street. When we come to a stop outside a tattoo studio, he smirks before he pushes the door open, waving his arm for me to enter in front of him.

"After you."

Greeted by the smell of surgical spirit and latex gloves, I scan the reception area. Apart from two large binders on the coffee table, two black leather sofas, and a water dispenser in the corner, its décor is minimal.

"I wanted to get something in memory of him…and my parents."

Maybe that's why he was so inquisitive about mine.

"I think that's lovely."

"I'm not looking forward to the pain. You know how I feel about needles—hence my virgin skin."

I try not to snicker. The word, *virgin,* and him don't go together. A pang of jealousy sparks as I think of all the faceless girls he's been with. I'm not even sure where that came from.

"It's not the same as an injection, Nate. Do you need me to hold your hand?" I ask, joking when I nudge him in the ribs with my elbow.

"Since you're offering."

I can't stop the heat that rises over my body when he bends his head, turning my hand as he places a soft kiss on the inside of my wrist. Shit, if that doesn't do things to my insides. He promptly pulls me towards the tattooist and signals for me to sit in the spare chair.

It turns out Lenny has been tattooing here for over ten years and happens to know the tattoo artist who did mine—small world.

After a couple of hours, the buzzing of the gun comes to a stop—it's finished. Nate stands, twisting his neck to look in the mirror behind him as he examines it.

"So, what do you think?" he asks, smiling. From his reaction, it looks like I don't need to ask him his thoughts.

"Honestly, it's beautiful."

A cluster of roses with grey and black shading—symbolic, but not overstated. The sentiment behind the design is lovely.

"Yeah, I think Lenny got the exact idea of what I was looking for." Nate has the sweetest smile. It's been too long since I've seen him look like that—happy.

I excuse myself and wait for him outside. The air is heavy without the breeze. I fan my face and check my phone. Voices interrupt me as a group of guys walk by. It's clear almost immediately they've been drinking—they're rowdy, intimidating. I clench my jaw.

"All right, darling?" one of them slurs, wobbling unsteady on his feet, sending a waft of alcohol in my direction.

I take a step back, pretending to be engrossed in my phone.

"Don't be shy, Sweetheart. How about your number?"

My heart picks up speed as I look around, my pulse racing through my ears.

I cough to clear my throat. "No, sorry, I'm with someone," I stutter. This right here is the reason I choose to avoid pubs or clubs. You always get one who can't handle his drink. Attempting to keep my breathing under control, I count in my head—*one, two, three, four, five.*

"I'm sure there's nothing he can give you, that *I* can't." He edges closer. A whiff of tobacco makes me want to gag. I step back again. I see in my peripheral vision that his friends are halfway down the street. I'm alone. My body becomes tight with tension, dread settling in the pit of my stomach, a cold sweat pooling between my shoulder blades.

"No, sorry, I'm not interested."

Why is it I feel like I have to apologise?

"No?" He cocks his head, his eyes sliding up and down my body, causing my skin to prickle.

I rub at my wrist, trying to breathe. *Just breathe.*

I shake my head.

"I'm not sure I believe you." He smirks, baring his yellow teeth.

I step to the left, but his arm comes up. I try for the right, but he's quick for someone who seems half-cut. I lean away, connecting with the wall. He's in my personal space—*trapped.* I rack my brain. What was it they taught Sophie and me in that self-defence class? My mind draws a blank.

I'm barely able to catch my breath when the guy is yanked away.

"Back the fuck off, man," Nate growls.

The guy looks stunned before his lips turn up at the corners.

"No harm no foul?" he says, hands in the air as he backs away…like he didn't just try to accost me in the middle of the street.

What the fuck?

"Flick, are you okay?"

I shake my head, my chest tight.

"Look at me. Just breathe, okay?" His hand is on my shoulder, his eyes filling with concern as he studies my face.

I breathe in through my nose and out through my mouth. When I can get enough air into my lungs, I nod. Gently, he pulls me into his chest, and I wrap my trembling arms around his waist. My fingers grab hold of his t-shirt. I can feel his heartbeat pulsing as he strokes my hair.

My face and neck now clammy—a sign I've almost had a panic attack. Embarrassment takes hold. I release my grip and step out of the security of his arms.

"Panic over," I say, a crack in my voice.

"Not funny. You sure you're all right?" He searches my face. I look over his shoulder when I nod.

"Well, you sure know how to pick 'em," he says, taking hold of my hand.

A snort of laughter escapes through my nose, though I try to conceal it with a cough.

He looks away with a smile. "Come on, let's get back before they think I've gone and done a runner with you."

If only I were that lucky.

Chapter Ten

"Hey, sleepy head. Wake up," Nate says close to my ear, his breath tickling my cheek.

I rub my shoulder against my ear. A warm shiver runs through me as I blink myself awake. It takes me a few seconds to grasp that I'd dosed off…again.

Oh my God, please don't let me have snored, or worse—dribbled. I quickly wipe my palm over my face, sighing with relief when it comes away dry.

"Sorry," I say, pulling down the sun visor to check my reflection.

I attempt to pat down my hair, but curly bits stick up all over the place as I finger-comb it. I sweep it into a bun instead, using a band from my wrist—an indentation of a red ring remaining.

I peer beside me to find Nate staring, an amused look on his face.

"What?" I ask, wiping my palms over my leggings.

"My company clearly seems to have an adverse effect on you," he says with a lazy smile.

I swallow, the roof of my mouth dry.

"I didn't want to say anything and risk offending your ego," I say, unclipping my seat belt. His laugh echoes behind me as I get out of the car, stretching my neck from side to side.

He joins me, leaning back against the car with one leg crossed over the other. I lean back beside him.

"Hey, can I ask you something?" He turns his head towards me.

"Depends on what it is," I say, smirking.

"No, serious. All jokes aside," he says with a smile.

I mirror his smile, remembering how we would piss about when we were younger—bantering back and forth, answering a question with a question. It would drive our grandparents potty.

"Go on, ask me something," I say.

"What happened to you that was so bad, it knocked your confidence enough to bring on anxiety?" he asks, then bites the inside of his mouth.

I don't know what I thought he was going to ask, but that wasn't it. I come over a little queasy, the back of my neck damp. He reaches for my hand, stirring something in me— something I haven't felt in a long time. If I told him the truth, he wouldn't look at me the same, and I can't deal with pity. Not from him.

"What happened to me is hardly important in the grand scheme of things. Not when you look at the reason for me being here." I know it's harsh—using Lawry's death to deflect from his question.

"You're important to me."

His words catch me off guard, my stomach fluttering to life.

"I can't talk about it. I'm still a little messed up, to be honest," I say, exhaling.

"Come on, Flick. Who isn't?"

I pull my hands away and wrap them around my middle. "I'm not stupid, Nate, I know everyone has their fair share of issues."

My heart is racing. *I can't do this.* I push off the car, trying to walk away, but he stops me. Coming face to face, he looks me straight in the eye. I'm unable to look away. I purse my lips together. For the first time in a long time, I find myself wanting to be kissed. I glance between his lips and eyes.

His face comes towards me.

My eyes slip closed when his lips meet mine.

I release a breath, his tongue darts out, and my lips part in invitation as his tongue meets with mine. The world slows on its axis. The kiss is slow and full of purpose. His tongue retreats as he sucks on my bottom lip. I bring my hand up to the nape of his neck and squeeze.

The kiss shifts, becoming more intense—greedy—but it's just not enough. In one swift movement, he lifts me by my waist onto the hood of the car. My heart drums to a frantic beat as I suck in a deep breath.

Hands on my thighs, he pushes them apart, and steps between my legs. His fingers stroke up and down my thigh before he lifts my left leg, and I wrap it around his waist. He places his other hand over my thumping chest. Then his fingers move, trailing a feather-light caress over my breast...before inching down toward my stomach. His mouth doesn't leave mine. A sound vibrates through his throat, and I pause, my eyes open.

I still his hand on my stomach, leaning back so our lips part. I place my other hand over his chest to push him away, then slide off the car, my breathing laboured. He grabs my elbow.

"Please, wait—" he says on a ragged breath. "Shit...sorry, I don't know what came over me. I mean...you're gorgeous.

Please don't walk away, I can't handle you being upset with me. Not right now."

I shake my head. "God, I'm not upset with you. I'm annoyed with *myself*. Things are already complicated enough."

Emotions are high, that kiss proves it. I'm not ready for whatever that was. Kisses we've shared in the past pale in comparison, and I'm sure as hell not ready to deal with that right now.

"Listen, I'm sorry. I admit it's selfish—me needing you. I haven't been there for you, and that kills me. I should have been a lot of things, but mainly I should have been a better friend."

I inhale before I reply. "Let's be clear on one thing. No matter what, we'll always be friends. But with everything that's going on, we don't need to further complicate things. Agreed?"

He nods.

"Agreed," he says before he pulls me into a hug.

My stomach grumbles.

He snickers as he pulls back and checks his watch.

"Dinner will be ready in thirty," he says.

I smile. Maybe some things don't change.

I'm so famished when I enter the kitchen, that the aromas greeting me make my mouth water.

"Is there anything I can do to help?" I say, kissing Evie on her cheek.

"Yes, can you please go see what's keeping Nate?"

"Okay, I'll be right back."

I opt for the back staircase; it's the quickest route to his room. I keep thinking that maybe he's already on his way down, but that's disproven when I get to his room, and he still hasn't materialised.

I rap my knuckles on his door. It feels weird—knocking. I've never knocked before. I clear my throat.

"Nate, it's me," I call out but get no response.

I wait before twisting the handle. My eyes scan over the contents of the room. Everything is so familiar—even the scent of his aftershave. I pause when his voice travels from the direction of his bathroom. I gravitate closer, trying to listen.

"I don't give a shit if it was yesterday or a year ago." He pauses before speaking again. "Well, there won't be a next time." He lets out a gruff sound. "It was sex—nothing more. You and I both know that."

I should probably feel guilty for listening, but I can't seem to stop myself. I'm uneasy at the mention of sex, but he's so brazen about it.

"Whatever. For the first time, I think I actually pity your boyfriend."

Oh my God. I cover my mouth with my hand.

"Of course, I have a fucking conscience. It looks like you're the one who doesn't."

Nate comes strutting out of the bathroom, phone to his ear, spinning a tube of cream in his free hand.

I forget why I'm here.

The room becomes smaller as every inch of my body tingles to life. Swallowing hard, I look him over…standing in front of me in only a towel. Nate stops dead in his tracks.

"Rachel, I have to go." He places his phone down and cocks his head.

It takes me a moment to gather a coherent thought—undecided if I'm more embarrassed about eavesdropping or that I blatantly just checked him out. My face heats.

"Sorry… I did knock. Evie sent me after you," I say, as I scan the length of his body. How does he manage to look better every time I see him? I fan my face—it's really hot in here. "I'll let you finish getting ready," I say, and turn away.

"Actually, can I ask a favour?" he says.

I look over my shoulder. "Okay."

I'm so quick to answer, he lets out a small laugh.

"Would you just rub some of this cream on my tattoo, please?"

I let out a breath. "Yeah, just let me wash my hands."

I brush past him, entering the bathroom. I'm flustered, and my upper lip is sweating. His blurry reflection is what I see when I look up to the partially steamed mirror—he's leaning against the doorframe. I dry my hands on the nearest towel.

I hold my hand out for the tube of cream and signal with my finger in the air for him to spin around, pushing his back enough for us to get out of the bathroom. I make quick work of rubbing the cream in. "All done."

I'm twisting the cap back on, and when he turns to reach for it, his towel drops. My eyes dart down. He's as naked as the day he was born—his manhood standing to attention.

"Whoa," I blurt out before looking away.

"Oh shit," he says, laughing as he steps around me, tucking the towel back into place.

"Shut up, you," I say, my face burning as he continues to laugh, which becomes infectious. Maybe it's my nerves, but before I know it, I'm laughing, too. I shove at his shoulder, but he grabs my hand, pulling me towards him, raising his other hand to wipe away the trail of laughter tears that have escaped my eyes.

I inhale a sharp breath, mesmerised by his eyes. He clears his throat.

"Could you tell them I won't be a minute?"

I nod, not trusting myself to speak. All I want to do right now is kiss him, but I don't move. It isn't until he speaks that I realise I'm still standing here like a moron.

"Err, Flick, you're killing me here."

Looking down, I see what he means, and I cover my mouth as I retreat from his room. Out on the landing, I lean against the wall in an attempt to compose myself.

"Felicity are you all right? You look a little flustered," Nana asks when I enter the kitchen. Why does she have to be so observant all the time?

"I'm not, I'm fine."

"And Nate?" she asks.

"What about Nate?" I fiddle with the glass in front of me.

"Is he coming down?"

Shit did I leave my brain in his room?

"Yes, sorry. He got caught up in the shower. I mean when he got out of the shower, he was getting dressed…" I smack my lips together to stop talking. Neither Evie or Nana quite know how to respond to my babble. Instead they continue to potter around and make room for plates and server platters.

Then Nate appears.

"Hey sorry," he says sitting down next to me.

I feel my face heat, *damn it.* "That was quick," I say, leaning towards him so he can hear me.

"What was?" he asks, coming even closer.

My eyes land on his lips.

"You, getting dressed," I say on a whisper and wave my hand up and down his body for emphasis.

He knows what I meant, and he lets out a small rumble of laughter.

"I just threw on jeans and a t-shirt," he says with a shrug.

"Commando—" I say out loud, and then slap a hand over my mouth as a blush creeps over my face. I peer towards our grandmothers who seem oblivious.

The corner of Nate's mouth quirks up before he lets out a sexy laugh. His eyes gleam with mischief as he reaches for his glass. I don't know where that even came from.

His hand rests over my wrist. I look down, eyeing the indentation marks from where I've been pinging my hair band. When he removes it, I look up. Nana's eyes are trained on me. I give her a half-smile then make myself busy with my knife and fork.

During the next few hours, I try hard not to look at Nate. Instead, I retreat into my own head. I begin to relax as we listen to my Nana and Evie reminiscing. Nate insisted on clearing up, so I left him in there to do it. I retreated to the sofa giving me time to compose myself.

Nate joins me. "You've been quiet. What's up?"

"Just tired." It's only half-true. I can't un-see him naked. Or ignore the kiss we shared. It's sitting there, in the back of my mind—haunting me.

"Sorry. It was a long day, and me dragging you to the studio was selfish." He flicks my arm.

"Don't be daft—"

Nana interrupts us. "Good night you two, we're off to bed."

"I'll come up, too," I reply.

"Dear, you're in your prime. Enjoy it," she says with a twinkle in her eye.

"Okay, goodnight." I stand and give her and Evie a kiss before they make their way out of the living room.

Left alone with Nate, a weird weight settles over the room. I squirm in my seat.

"Drink?" Nate asks as he stands, pointing his thumb towards the door.

I nod. "Why not?"

We make our way to the kitchen.

"What would you like?" he asks, opening the fridge.

"Hmm…a beer is fine."

He tilts his head.

"Beer, huh?"

"Yeah, sorry." I shuffle from one foot to the other, unable to keep still.

He gives a lopsided grin. "Why are you apologising? Last time I checked, it wasn't the nineteenth century. Women can even vote now, too. Who knew?"

He pulls out two bottles. The caps rattle as they hit the counter before he passes me one. The coolness from the condensation on the glass is welcome.

"Cheers," he says, clinking his bottle with mine.

I take a nice, long gulp. Nothing beats an ice-cold beer. Simon says it's not very attractive—girls who drink beer. But it's not attractive when men stand there with their hands down their pants, either, but there you have it.

I peer over my bottle to catch Nate watching me.

"Who knew drinking beer could look sexy," he says, his mouth turning up into a smirk.

I let out a snort of laughter. My stomach sparks to life.

"Fancy watching a film?" he asks, rolling the bottle between his hands.

I rub the back of my neck. "I don't think I could manage an entire film, but I'll give it a go."

Truth is, when I'm with him, an image of what *could be* flashes through my mind. I feel my pulse quicken in my throat.

We leave the kitchen, but he continues past the living room. I stall, mid-step. He looks over his shoulder, and I slant my bottle towards the living room.

"DVD player's in my room, but if that's not okay…" His face drops.

I clear my throat. "Yeah, it's fine, why wouldn't it be?" *Because we would be alone together, that's why.*

I take a swig of my beer.

"It's been a while… I don't want you to feel uncomfortable."

Typical. Now he's the one giving me an out. Or is this reverse phycology—a test?

"Nate, it's fine." He doesn't make me uncomfortable, well not in the way he might be thinking.

"Good to know," he says with a wink. *Cocky bastard.*

In his room, he wanders over to the cabinet, thumbing through the dvds.

"Got it," he announces. Waving the box in the air, he strides over to the TV and loads it into the DVD player.

He places his beer next to him on the bedside table, and I do the same with mine. I glance at the couple of photos. One is of him alongside his parents, and the other one is of us two in the tree house. I reach for it.

"That was taken the last time you were here." His eyes dart to the picture in my hand.

I glance around, noticing the beanie toy. "I didn't know you still had this." I place the framed photo back down and pick it up. It's soft and squidgy.

"Why wouldn't I? Besides, it means a lot to me. I love that damn bear."

"You big softy. What do the girls think?" I ask, raising my eyebrows

"I wouldn't know. I don't have girls in here."

I'm strangely relieved to hear that.

"Ready?" he asks, tossing the remote in the air then catching it. He does that—he did it with the cream and his car keys—it's his tick. I put down the beanie toy and grab my beer, picking at the label.

He switches off the big light and turns on the lamp before hopping on the bed.

"Come sit." He pats the bed.

I swallow the lump in my throat, my heart beating in my ears as I sit on the edge of the bed.

"Get your backside up here already." He grabs all the pillows, stacking them against the headboard.

I hold my breath as I shuffle closer, then reach back over for my beer before sitting back. I see him from the corner of my eye, smirking before he hits play.

"The Goonies?" I say, snorting—unable to keep the smile off my face.

"Only the best for you," he says with a shrug.

It warms me from the inside out. I haven't seen this in years. I relax, and then as if on cue, we both adlib the opening scene word for word.

I feel like I'm home.

Nate is on his side, facing me. The soft hum of his breathing, and the buzz from the TV trickles across the room. I try to move as quietly as possible, so not to wake him.

I turn off the TV and pull the throw over him. I take him in for a moment, the crinkle he usually wears on his forehead is smooth, his eyelashes so long, they'd make any girl jealous. I'm so pre-occupied by his scent, I lean closer, itching to touch him. My breath quickens. His lips separate. His head moves in my direction. I tense, needing to leave before I do something stupid. Like kiss him.

The house is silent—with the exception of the grandfather clock—as I head back to my room. I take my phone off charge. One missed call from Simon, and a text from Sophie.

I send her a quick reply, promising to call her tomorrow.

I text Simon that my phone was on charge. Moments later, his name flashes on the screen. I let out a breath.

"Hey. you."

"Hi, it's late, why you still up?" I ask

"I couldn't sleep. What about you?"

"Nothing, just getting ready for bed."

"How did it go today?" he asks, stifling a yawn.

"It was…let's just say…emotional."

"Why do I get the impression there's more to that than you are letting on?"

I chip away at my nail polish.

"What are you talking about? I've barely said like five words."

He laughs before replying. "It was more like six, actually. Besides, your tone is a dead giveaway," he drawls in an American accent.

Not only is he talented, he's super smart—photographic memory smart. I found him a little intimidating when we first met.

I cover my face with my arm, even though he can't see me blushing. I mumble my reply.

"Fine, we may have sort of…kissed. There, you happy?"

Simon practically squeals.

"Whoa, what do you mean, *sort of kissed?* Where did he kiss you exactly?"

I choke on my saliva—I need to wash my ears out. He's such a saucy little shit. I stifle my laugh, but cave. I need to tell someone, so I do, omitting the fact that Nate made me feel things I haven't in so long, it's foreign to me.

Simon stays on the phone until I fall asleep. It's a thing he started doing when I was at my lowest—even if no words were exchanged. There's something about listening to his breathing as I begin to doze off that I find comfort in.

I feel a deep sense of unease. Pulling the cover up to my chin, I clutch it between my fingers. I used to feel like this when I'd think about dying when I was younger. I'd be paralysed to my core, wishing I were brave enough to run to my Mum and Dad's room to make sure they were both still breathing.

Of course, it would pass, but not before it filled me with dread—the uncertainty of what's to come.

Chapter Eleven

It's been a peculiar couple of days. Nate and I have fallen into a routine of sorts, always ending the evenings chatting over a bottle of beer and watching a film. But for some reason, unbeknownst to me, I'm yet to keep my eyes open long enough to watch an entire film. I can't wipe the smile off my face while I stretch. There's something self-satisfying about waking free of my usual nightmare.

"Well, that's a sight for sore eyes."

I cover my chest with my hand and look to the side. I straighten. Nate approaches, holding out a bottle of water towards me. Why does he have to be so damn charming?

"Thought I'd join you for a run."

I nod as I take the bottle—grateful he's wearing joggers…not shorts. I don't need the added distraction.

"It's your garden." I shrug with indifference.

He takes a sip of water. "You snuck out on me again. What time did you go to bed?"

I look away. "Just after twelve. We fell asleep again."

A cocky grin crosses that smug face of his. "I noticed."

I turn to look at him. "What do you mean?"

He doesn't even try to hide his smirk. "I watched the rest of the film while you snored your head off."

I squint my eyes at him. "You should have woken me."

"Why? Your snoring wasn't that bad," he says with a laugh.

I elbow him hard, but from his lack of reaction, you'd think it was a butterfly kiss.

"Ha, bloody, ha. Come on then, shall we run?" I ask, waving my hand out in front of us.

He smiles and nods. We head off, falling into a comfortable rhythm. The sounds of our feet drumming the ground mix with birdsong.

Sweating, our breathing heavy, I am ready to call it a day when he speaks.

"How about a final sprint? First one to the lake wins?"

Before I have a chance to answer, he darts off ahead of me. I break into a sprint, trying in vain to catch him.

I can't help but smile when we run under the cover of the green branches. Overhead, arches intertwine hands, the light breaking through the slits of their fingers, casting hundreds of lightning shadows—like an old black and white silent movie. I blink as we make our way into the clearing—the light a brilliant white—until my eyes adjust to the perfect seaside-blue sky reflected in the calm, crystal lake. When I was small, I used to reach out my arms as wide as they'd go, imagining I was a giant and this was my lake.

"I win," he shouts, jumping up and down like a big kid.

I raise my eyebrows. "Only because you cheated," I reply, breathless. I slump on the damp grass, then collapse on my back, chest heaving.

Nate joins me, leaning back on his elbows, a smug grin on his face. "Always so competitive, Felicity."

"Yeah, well, you've always been a show-off," I say, sitting up and shoving his shoulder in an attempt to knock him off balance. But he's fast. In one swift movement, he has me on my back—pinned beneath him, his legs straddling me.

The air literally knocked right out of me, I take a deep breath—panic about to set in— when he begins to tickle me.

"Nate, *stop*. Shit, please pack it in," I squeal. It's like some sort of weird torture technique. I swear, who actually likes to be tickled?

"Seriously… I'll wet myself," I burst out.

He stills, giving me just enough time to wriggle free. But where he has me in such a fluster, I'm wobbly on my feet. I step back and lose my balance, but my feet only connect with air. As I begin to fall backward, my heart jumps up into my mouth.

Nate's on his feet as he reaches for me, but I only manage to grab a fistful of his t-shirt, my other arm waving around like crazy as we both hit the water with a huge splash.

I suck in a mouthful of water before my head surfaces, where I splutter to catch my breath.

"Fuck, that's cold," Nate says when his head appears.

"No shit, Sherlock," I stutter, splashing my way back to the edge.

"Where do you think you're going? You can't just pull me in here and then get out."

I turn on him, my eyebrows shooting up to my hairline. "I bloody well can. It's your fault, tickling me, what are you, *twelve?"*

"What are *you,* like twelve?" he mocks.

My hand snags on my earphones from my iPod in my pocket. It's ruined.

For fuck's sake.

Tossing it on the grass, I'm about to hoist myself out when warm arms wrap around my waist and pull me away from the edge. A very un-lady-like snort escapes me.

"It's not that bad. Quite refreshing, actually," he says, pulling me with him.

"Don't even think about it, Nathaniel. I swear to God."

The water is slimy, a sheen of green covering the surface. A shudder escapes me—it looked so much cleaner from a distance.

"Think about what?" he says, smiling. As I spin towards him, his expression changes into a serious frown. He moves closer, keeping his eyes glued on mine.

I don't move. "Nate," I say in warning, unsure what he's about to do.

"Calm down, already. Lack of trust much? You have…something on your face."

I wave my hand around. "What is it?" I ask, breathless.

"Calm down, it's just a weed," he says, amusement lacing his voice as he wipes it away.

Yuck. I let out a shiver as he flings the weed off his fingers and it floats off.

"Is it all gone? Is anything else on me? That's so gross."

My body tingles all over as adrenaline runs through my veins.

Nate whispers my name. "*Felicity*."

I look and see how close we are.

"What?" I reply, licking my lips. I regret it almost instantly, tasting the lake water.

"I forget," he replies, bringing his hand to my face, eyes on my lips.

His mouth crashes down on mine. A whimper escapes me, my body responding in kind as I kiss him back, losing all inhibitions. I place one hand around his neck, the other on his shoulder to steady me. Our teeth clash in desperation, but it doesn't slow us down.

His fingers squeeze my hips. Then slide down. He lifts my thighs, and my legs wrap around his waist. His hands are under my butt cheeks supporting me as I push my centre into him. His chest is flush with mine, my nipples hard. I feel a vibration from deep within his throat, and it turns me on— knowing it's me that's having this effect on him. I can feel his hard length strained against me, right where I need him to be.

I grind myself into him, desperate, the build-up intense. As I find my release, my head falls back, and I bite my lip.

"Flick," he says, exhaling. His tongue works along my neck, followed by tiny kisses. It feels so intimate. "Do you have any idea how much I want you?"

I tense and pull away. If he even knew, he wouldn't be saying that. He leans back to look at my face, but I can't meet his eyes.

I do the only thing I can think of in the moment. I press both my hands on the top of his head, and push. Hard. When his head is dunked under water, I push away, scrambling to get out. I grab my iPod and storm off.

"Shit, Flick, wait!"

I hear the slosh of his wet clothes when he pulls himself out behind me, followed by the squish of his wet trainers as they hit the ground. He catches up and grabs my shoulder. Instinct takes over. I raise my hand, squeeze his fingers hard, and jab him with my elbow.

A whoosh of air escapes him as he bends over. "What the fuck, Flick?'

"Sorry—" I take a step away from him. "Nate, I can't do that, whatever this is with you… I just don't—" I wave my hands between us and the lake like that explains it.

"Do what, Flick?" He straightens to his full height. His shadow engulfing my body, I take another step back.

"Hook up."

I'm furious with him. Myself. With everybody. My body is telling me one thing, yet my brain is telling me another. I don't know what to think, or what to do.

"God, Flick, really? You think all I want from you is to just *hook up*?" He shakes his head in disbelief.

"I don't know, Nate. I'm confused," I say, squeezing my eyes shut.

"Well…pretty sure you were just as into it back there as I was. You were right there with me, Flick. Damn it, don't do this to me. Don't shut me out." He lets out an exasperated sigh.

"I can't help it, Nate. I told you already I'm messed up. What did you expect?"

His shoulders slump. "I don't have any expectations, but *God*, how can you not see how much I care about you? I've always cared about you."

My heart drums in my ears. I turn, power walking back towards the house. I don't know what to say or do, but I *know* I can't leave it like this. *It's not healthy*, my counsellor says. *Communication is important*.

I don't need to turn to know he's following me. Even if I couldn't hear his footsteps, I'd feel the weight of his stare anywhere.

I spin on my heels. "Listen, Nate. I'm sorry. I don't mean to give you mixed signals, it's just…complicated."

He shoves his hands into his wet joggers. They slip lower on his hips. I look up at his face.

"It's not you. I can't seem to think straight when I'm with you. I know the score, Flick. You have something with Simon, and I don't claim to understand it. But I *should*, at least, respect the fact."

Maybe what Nate and I have is unfinished business, but if he knew…I mean *really* knew, he wouldn't want me…not in that way. The evidence—I can't even open up to him about it—only proves I'm not ready. I just never anticipated these feelings he would conjure from within me.

I clear my throat. "There are things…you don't know about me. I want to try to explain it, but I'm not ready. I'm sorry."

His reply is on the tip of his tongue when Evie walks out. She gasps when she looks us both up and down

"What on earth happened to the two of you?"

I peer down at my dishevelled appearance. I have no words. Nate however, doesn't hesitate.

"Flick pushed me in the lake," he says, so matter of fact, I almost believe him.

I let out a shocked laugh and shove his shoulder, squinting my eyes at him before looking back to Evie.

"No, I didn't. I grabbed hold of him. It was an accident, but now that I think about it, you kind of deserved it," I say, turning my head towards him.

He lets out a loud boom of laughter, which eases the recent tension, and reminds me of the boy I grew up with—the carefree, unassuming version of Nate.

"Maybe," he says with a wink.

I just shake my head.

"Well, in that case, go sort yourselves out. You're acting like twelve-year-olds."

With that, Nate and I burst out laughing. We pull off our wet trainers and socks and head into the house.

I glance up as Nana leaves her room.

"What the—" she covers her mouth with her hand to stifle a laugh.

"Don't ask," I say. She follows me into my room and grabs the towel off the back of the chair.

"I have to. You're wet, and smell like wet dog." She covers her nose.

"Nate and I had a little accident," I say, trying not to smile.

"Hmm, an accident, really? So, what's going on between you two anyway?" she asks, sitting on the ottoman.

"Nothing…it's complicated. God, I don't know?" I shake my head. Wet strands of hair stick to my mouth, and I splutter, *disgusting.*

"I know I'm old, but I'm not blind. I see the way you look at him when you think no one is watching, and I also see the way he looks at you."

I let out a sigh. "I don't know what to think, honestly. All I know is, he makes me feel things. Why is it so complicated?"

"It's only as complicated as you allow it to be."

"Well, he kind of thinks I'm still with Simon, and before you start… I should tell him the truth, I know. But I don't think he's ready. Not with everything that's already going on." When he learns the truth, he won't look at me the same.

"I think maybe you're the one who's not ready. You're just prolonging the inevitable. If you ask me, you're meant to be together."

"I'm not ready to put my feelings on the line," I say, pacing back and forth.

Nana stands and approaches me. "He is a good man, just like his grandfather. You can't let the past dictate your future. Concentrate on the present, and live for today."

I know what she's saying, but I've just got my friend back. I'm not sure I want to jeopardise that. Sometimes, it's like I need him to breathe—co-dependency comes to mind.

"I'll try."

"You only live once, Felicity. If it means taking a chance, then do it. What if he is who you need to finally help you heal here?" She places her hand over my heart.

"Who was it who said get busy living or get busy dying?" Nana says with a wink.

I smile, is there any film this woman hasn't seen? I'm positive my love of film is her influence.

"I'll leave you to shower... But think about what I said. God knows you'd be making two old ladies very happy." With another wink, she leaves me alone in my room.

My damp clothes cling to my body as a cold shiver rolls over me. I have a bad feeling.

A buzz from my bedside table forces my feet to move. Five missed calls and a voicemail. All from Simon. I don't hesitate to dial his number.

"Felicity, thank God! Did you get my voicemail?" he asks, breathless. He never calls me Felicity. My stomach drops.

"No, I rang you straight away. What's wrong, Simon?"

I tug at my clothes.

"God, shit I'm sorry...I know you have a lot to deal with, but I didn't know what to do, She's not herself—"

My heart begins to race. "Sophie?" I say, interrupting him. It's a rhetorical question.

"She's a complete mess. She just rocked up at mine around four this morning, she hasn't even been to bed yet. I've been up with her, you know...trying to talk her down. She's not making any sense it's beginning to freak me out."

She hasn't been on a bender for a while. She's been doing better. Something must have triggered this. I know she's been avoiding home like the plague—out before her family is up, and only goes home when they're in bed. But they started setting the alarm, so she's been staying out.

"What the hell? Put her on the phone."

"I can't, she's locked herself in the bathroom—I don't know what to do."

I clench the fist of my free hand.

"Shit."

"She told me not to call you, but she's unhinged. I've never seen her like this."

"I'm coming to you."

I feel my breathing speed up, a nervous energy overtaking my body. I perch on the edge of the dressing table, my legs weak.

"Breathe, Baby Cakes. Why don't we see how she is in a few hours?" I hear the tension in his voice—he's as worried as I am.

"No, I'll see if I can borrow a car, or I'll call a cab."

"Please be careful."

"I will. See you soon."

Just as soon as I can sort out getting there. I need a car. I'll ask Nate.

As soon as I hang up, I put my hands on my knees, bending over to take a deep breath. I have a really bad feeling about this. I shake my head and straighten, typing a text to Nate. Then rush to take a shower.

Chapter Twelve

Attacking the chest of drawers, I pull out the first items of clothes my fingers come in contact with. A knock sounds at my door, and with no time to be modest, I call out. "Come in."

Nate enters, halting as soon as he sees me, and letting out a small whistle. I tilt my head and raise my eyebrows—any other time I'd probably feel embarrassed about standing in only a towel, but not today.

"Two minutes," I say as I rush back into the bathroom.

I think I hear him mumble under his breath, *no need to rush on my account.* I dry myself off and pull on my clothes. This will have to do.

Nate is sitting on the edge of my bed when I come out of the bathroom. I tie my hair into a quick bun and let my arms drop to my sides.

"Sorry about that," I say.

"Don't be, I'm sure as hell not. Anyway, what's up?" He smiles up at me.

"I hate to ask, but it's kind of an emergency. Is there any way I could borrow your car for a few hours…maybe the day?" I ask, biting my thumbnail.

"Yeah, of course. Or I can give you a lift… Where do you need to go?"

I can't accept a lift—that would involve an explanation.

"I need to go to Simon's house. He rang me, and I can't get into it, but I wouldn't ask if it wasn't important."

He stares at his feet. When he looks up, his forehead crinkles.

"Shit, I hope it's not because of what happened with us?"

"God, no…it's my friend, Sophie. She needs me," I say, pacing.

Nate stands in front of me, placing his hands on my shoulders to stall me. I look up into his eyes.

"Stop and take a breath. It's not a problem—my car is yours for as long as you need it. I know you wouldn't ask if it wasn't important."

My heart softens with his sincerity.

"Thank you," I say, and wrap my arms around his torso. I give him a quick squeeze, and lift to my tip-toes, kissing his cheek before I take a step back.

"I'll meet you in the garage in ten. Let me go grab my keys," he says

"Thank you."

He nods before leaving my room. I grab my bag and go in search of Nana and Evie so I can tell them what's going on.

Nate is waiting for me when I walk into the garage. "So, I rang my insurance company and had you added to my trade policy. I wasn't sure if your insurance covered you."

I smile at his thoughtfulness.

"Thank you. I didn't even think of that. Let me know how much I owe you, and I'll sort it out when I get back."

"Don't be silly, it's fine. You sure you're okay to drive?" he asks, rubbing my arm.

I stand there for a moment, finding comfort in his touch.

"I'll be fine. Nate, I just want to say—" I swallow the lump in my throat, "—thank you, for this," I say, but it was not what I was going to say.

"No worries. There's almost a full tank of diesel, so you should be all right for fuel. Do you need any money?" He pulls out his wallet.

I shake my head. "No, I'm good," I say, patting my bag.

I'm a little overwhelmed right now—over his kindness.

"Drive safe." Handing over the keys, his hand brushes mine, and my skin heats from the contact.

I step past him and get into the car. But just as I'm about to pull the door shut, he grabs hold of it. Kneeling, he leans over me to fasten my seatbelt. I close my eyes, breathing in the familiar scent that is all him.

"Promise me you'll be careful?"

I can't help but smile. It's not like I'm skipping the country. If it weren't for the serious look on his face, I'd probably say as much.

"I promise."

"If you need anything, just call me." He leans in, giving me a chaste kiss before stepping back and closing the door.

Breathing deeply, I take a moment to compose myself as I adjust the mirror and seat. Before I start the engine, I smile to him, then put my foot on the accelerator, and slowly pull away. I see him in the rear-view mirror, watching as I drive away.

Chapter Thirteen

The drive here has been torturous. Being stuck in my own head for near on an hour is not where I wanted to be. Simon is waiting for me as I step out of the car. I take the steps two at a time, and when I reach him, he pulls me into a big, bear hug. I don't have a choice where he's concerned—it's a given—the boy is going to hug.

He closes the door behind me. I kick off my shoes and drop my bag on the table in the hallway.

"Where is she? Is she all right?" I ask, looking up the stairs.

"Loaded question. She came out of the bathroom to get her bag but then locked herself back in there. She's been quiet for a while now," he says, rubbing the back of his neck.

"Right. You go get the kettle on, and I'll go talk to her," I say, heading up the stairs.

I brace myself before knocking, taking in a deep breath. "Soph, it's me. Can you open the door?"

She doesn't respond. A chill rolls down my spine. Goosebumps run up and down my arms. I knock a little harder. *Something's wrong.*

"Sophie, open the door," I say, louder.

Simon runs up behind me. "What's going on?"

"She isn't answering me."

"Sophie, this isn't funny. Can you open the door?" he hollers.

No response.

He crouches down to try and look under the door, but it's useless. He shoots to his feet and grabs the corner table, pulling it in front of the door. He grabs hold of the doorframe as he stands on top of the table. My hands shoot out to steady him as he peers through the glass pane at the top of the door.

"Shit!" he hisses as he jumps down, causing the table to topple over. I pull it out of the way, my pulse racing heavy in my ears.

"What? What is it?" I ask, afraid to hear his answer.

He shakes his head, his face morphing into fear.

I swallow hard.

"Move," he says, as he starts to kick hard at the door.

My insides are in knots. I hold my breath with each grunt he lets out as he kicks harder. Just when I think it's no use, there is a creak of wood followed by a crack. The lock gives, and he forces the door open.

"What's wrong?" I ask, but he doesn't answer.

I peer round him and let out an audible gasp. My hand flies to my chest.

She is lying on the bathroom floor.

I push past Simon, and rush to her side, landing hard on my knees. Her face lies in a pool of her own sick.

"What the fuck?" I say aloud.

I scan the bathroom. *A pill bottle!* I grab hold of her face and turn it towards me.

"Sophie, can you hear me?" I yell, tapping her cheek for a response. *Nothing*. I bring my head down to her mouth.

"Please tell me she's breathing?" Simon asks, the worry lining his breathless voice.

I nod. "Yes, but it's shallow." My voice cracks.

"Thank fuck for that. Should we make her sick?" he asks, panic-stricken.

"God no, that's dangerous. Besides, she's already been sick. I need you to call for an ambulance."

I tap Sophie's cheek with a little more force.

"Soph, come on. Wake up! Please don't you do this to us!"

Remembering my first aid training from years ago, I move her into the recovery position. I scamper off the floor and grab the dressing gown.

Simon asks me questions, relaying what the operator is asking, and I answer best I can. But everything is fuzzy. My hand is unsteady each time I touch her back to feel her breathing. The smell of her vomit makes me even more nauseous.

Simon has been pacing the whole time, talking to himself. I block him out, trying to keep my shit together. I don't notice him leave until he returns with two paramedics in tow. Everything else happens in a blur—questions, radios buzzing, Sophie being loaded onto a stretcher, Simon following the ambulance to the hospital.

He hands me my shoes before we get out of the car. I didn't even notice I'd left his house in my bare feet. We sit, anxiously, in the waiting room. Everything is so clinical. Hospitals make me think of death, and all I want is to be out of here.

Unsurprisingly, Sophie has had to have her stomach pumped. They also put her on a drip for rehydration and gave her activated charcoal for her stomach. People shuffled in and out for hours, asking her questions. She even had a visit from someone in mental health who suggested she seek out support, to which she agreed, and they discharged her just after three this afternoon.

Simon asked if she wanted to go home, but she said she couldn't face *them*. That this would only make everything worse, so we drove back to his place in silence.

Sophie and I sit on the sofa when we get back. Simon rushes off upstairs.

"It was an accident, you know that right?" she asks, her voice hoarse.

I nod and take her hand in mine. "Of course."

She leans her head on my shoulder, her legs tucked beneath her. We sit and say nothing as we watch a blank television in front of us—the only sounds coming from Simon moving around upstairs. My stomach finally begins to settle.

"Hey, baby girl, I've run you a bath in my en-suite," says Simon, re-emerging.

He holds out his hands and pulls her to her feet. She wraps her arms around him, muffling a *thank you.*

I follow her up the stairs—her body movements slow, lethargic. I close the door behind us and sit on the floor beside the bathtub once she's submerged under the cover of bubbles. She pulls her knees up to her chest.

"I'm so sorry I put you both through this, but it really was an accident...you do know that, right?"

"I'm not going to lie, Soph, it looks like a cry for help," I say, skimming the bubbles onto my fingertips, and blowing.

"I had so much going on inside my head. No matter what I do, I always seem to mess up. I'm worthless," she says, choking back her tears.

"What the *fuck?* You are not worthless. Don't ever think like that, do you hear me?" I say, determination in my voice.

"Don't say the F-word," she reprimands, sniffing back her tears.

Sophie isn't a swearer—she has always chastised me over my use of language. It's not like I go around swearing nilly-willy, I just don't believe in sugar coating some things.

"Fine, but you're not worthless. Do you think *I'm worthless?"* I ask, unblinking as I look in her eyes.

"No, of course not. I just can't seem to get my crap together. I mean look at me—" she waves her hand in front of her, "—the guys I sleep with… I pick the wrong ones every time."

"Do you want to know what I think?" I ask, but don't give her a chance to respond. "I think you choose the wrong guys on purpose. You know it won't go anywhere with them, but in that moment, it fills the void."

"I think I just want to feel connected you know?" She rests her forehead against her knees.

"We both handle what happened to us differently, but I think you're the bravest person I know. I'm terrified to put myself out there. At least *you* try." I look away, unease settling in my stomach.

"I like to take back the control, but it's all a front." She looks up, tears in her red-rimmed eyes.

I feel an ache at the back of my throat.

"I understand about wanting control, Soph. I hate that my body conspires against me, that my head and my body aren't synced like they used to be."

She reaches her hand out for mine, and I take it.

"But you're doing better, and that's what counts." She gives me a pensive smile and my hand a gentle squeeze.

She's right. I was withdrawn for so long, but I'm moving past that now, and that's because of Sophie and Simon.

"I have a good support system, that's why. You will find someone worthy of you. You're way too special not to."

She releases my hand and rolls her fingers over the remaining bubbles.

"I thought I had, with...*you know who."* She won't speak his name, and I don't blame her. When things got tough, he dropped her like a hot potato.

"Well, he showed his true dick colours, that's for sure. But this path you're on...it's self-destructive, Soph. And it hurts us to see you hurting because you deserve better."

"I'm sorry, I know you're right."

I know why she does what she does. After what happened to us, there are times I want to completely block out the world round me, too.

A tap on the door breaks me from my thoughts.

"Are you okay, Baby Girl?" Simon asks through the door.

She nods, wiping her face with the sponge she grabbed off the side of the bathtub.

"Yeah, she will be," I say, "Can you grab something for her to wear, please?"

"Yeah, course."

When he comes back, he cracks the door open, dangling a handful of clothes from his hand. I take them and place them on the toilet seat.

"Kettles on, how about some tea and toast?" he asks, hand hanging limply in the air.

"Sounds good," I reply as he pulls the door closed.

I find a towel and place it on the sink.

Sophie laughs. "Whoever said tea solves everything clearly didn't know a thing," she says, shaking her head.

"Come on, you. Get out," I say, passing her the towel. "What's the point of Simon spending thousands of pounds on a new sofa, if we aren't going to abuse it?"

She smiles and takes the towel. I leave her to get dressed.

I head downstairs of Simon's freshly decorated townhouse—it's like a bloody show home, his self-made interior design expertise evident.

Sophie joins me on the sofa, and I pull the throw over us both. I'm glad to see she has some colour back to her face—I've never seen her skin look so pale. Simon hands her a mug of tea. She wraps her hands around it, peering over the rim.

"Si, I really am sorry. I'll pay for the bathroom door," she says before taking a sip.

"*Behave*. Don't even go there." He twists in his chair to give her a stern look.

Her eyes go wide as she looks towards me and lowers the mug.

"You left Nate's to come here. I'm so sorry. When is the funeral?" Her eyes cast downward.

"It's fine. It's not for a couple of days. You need to stop beating yourself up—you'd be here for me if the roles were reversed, wouldn't you?"

"Of course…but I do think I do need to reconsider having some counselling. I don't want to wake up in the hospital like that again." A shudder runs through her.

Simon moves to sit on her other side, wrapping his arm over her shoulder.

"I think that's a good idea, baby girl. You need to stop bottling it all up. Listen, I've been thinking… I want you to come and move in with me. At least until you find somewhere else to live."

She's been saving for a deposit so she can move out of her parents'. Their relationship is as dysfunctional as they come. They've never been big on public displays of affection, but they *are* all about image.

"I may take you up on that offer," she says, gratitude in her voice.

We talk for hours until she ends up drifting off to sleep. Simon and I fall silent as we watch her for a moment, her breathing heavy as she falls deeper.

"Bunny, get the door. I'll carry her," he says, scooping her in his arms like she weighs nothing.

I pull back the duvet as he lays her on the bed.

"Thanks, sweet cheeks," he whispers.

I pull the duvet over her. "Do you really think she'll go back to counselling?" I ask.

"I do. It frightened her—what happened. You were amazing, by the way. I was the one who almost had a panic attack when I saw her through the window…"

He rubs at his face.

"I didn't feel calm. I thought she was gone—" I choke on the word and swallow. He puts his arm around my shoulder, pulling me into him.

We leave the door ajar, then return to the living room.

Simon looks up at the clock. "Are you going to stay?"

"No, I think I should head back. Do you think that makes me sound like a shit friend?" I ask, feeling conflicted.

"No. Shit friend, You. Are. Not. I already rescheduled my diary while you guys were in the bathroom. I'm off for a couple of days. I'll take her to go pick some stuff up from her parents'. Damn, they make mine seem normal."

"Nothing strange as folk," I say, my eyes round.

"Will you at least stay for some dinner?" he says, fluttering his eyelashes. My stomach grumbles. I smile with a nod as I rifle through my bag, coming back empty-handed.

"Shit, can I borrow your phone, please?"

He hands it over and heads to the kitchen.

"Hello?" Nana says loudly into the receiver.

"Hi, it's me—Felicity."

"Is everything all right, dear?"

I slump back into the sofa and let out a long breath.

"Yes, it is, but it could have been so much worse. It was dreadful—we had to call an ambulance. For a brief moment, I thought she was gone… It was an accidental overdose, but I'll tell you all about it properly when I get back."

"Thank the heavens, she's okay. I hate to see you girls like this… She will get there—you both will. In time, you'll learn to adjust."

I rub at the tightness in my chest.

"I hope so. I'm going to stay for dinner before heading home."

"If you need to stay, we'll understand."

As much as I want to stay, I need to be near Nate. There are things I need to say.

"No, I'll see you later."

Simon pokes around at his food, loading his mouth as he tries to speak. I raise my eyebrows, watching him swallow before he continues.

"So, about Nate?" His eyes peer up.

"What about him?" My face flushes.

"What's going on?"

"Nothing," I say, unable to hide my smile.

"Cookie, I can tell something else has happened, so you might as well tell me."

I drop my knife and fork with a clang. "Fine. We may have kissed…*again*. You know, I've always liked him."

"So, what are you going to do about it?" he asks, raising his eyebrows.

"I don't know. It's so complicated." I take a sip of water.

"No, it's not. You need to start living. It's been what? Almost two years?"

I know it's been long enough. I don't need him rubbing salt in the wound.

"Listen, I know you and Soph think you're handling what happened to you, but *newsflash,* neither of you have a healthy way of dealing. You both gave up on everything you loved doing. She stopped going to church, and you became a hermit. I know you've come a long way, and if there was a way for me to fix it, I would."

"I get it, but it is what it is." I fidget in my seat as he watches me playing with my food.

"I know you don't need someone to make you happy, but it does make a difference when you find your special someone."

I stare at him. His grin widens. I raise my eyebrows. What's he not telling me?

"Spill," I say, then take a bite of my food.

"I met someone," he says, nonchalantly, with a shrug—like it's no big deal. His eyes actually sparkle.

I swallow my food as quickly as I can before I speak.

"What? When?" I ask. A buzz of excitement shoots through me, and I wriggle in my seat.

"About two months ago."

I drop my cutlery on my plate and push it aside. Whoa…back up. He managed to keep it a secret from me for two months? Damn, he must really like him.

"And you didn't think to tell me, you sneaky bastard. I want details."

This boy doesn't know how to keep a secret—he couldn't if his life depended on it. That's how I know this isn't some passing crush.

"His name is Ryan. We met through a mutual friend at an exhibition. He was working security. Once it was closed, we got talking… I didn't know he was gay, not until he asked for my number, so he could call me to arrange a date. And the rest, as they say, is history."

His dimpled smile tells me all I need to know.

"Damn, your radar was off. So, is he a good kisser? How many dates have you been on?"

"I told you, just because I'm gay doesn't mean I have gay-dar. We see each other as much as we can and talk every day. I really do like him."

"Oh, you're smitten. I'm just surprised you kept it so quiet."

"I didn't want to jinx it, you know? Like if I told you it wouldn't be true."

I take his hand. "I understand."

He grabs his phone and pulls up a photo.

I fan my face. "Wow, he's *hot*. He looks like a bodybuilder."

He actually blushes. "I know, right? Like I said, he works security, so he can take care of himself. There's something else I wanted to talk to you about."

"What?"

"Ryan and I have talked about it—a lot, and I've decided to come out to my parents."

I push my chair back and lean over, slinging my arms around his neck.

"I am so proud of you." I give him a kiss on his cheek and sit back down.

"I think he was the push I needed…besides we want to be exclusive, no sneaking around. It's not like my parents can threaten me with material things. I work enough to look after myself, now."

"That you do," I say, my grin so big, my jaw aches.

"Just means the façade between us will need to come to an end. I'm sorry," he says, worry crossing his features.

"So be it, we're still best friends, and that's all that matters."

He smiles and points upstairs. "Always. You two are stuck with me…the three amigos."

It seems like fate has well and truly intervened this time. All I have to do now is work out how the hell to explain this to Nate. I get a heavy, sinking feeling in the pit of my stomach. The thought alone scares me, so how the hell will I even manage to get the words out?

Chapter Fourteen

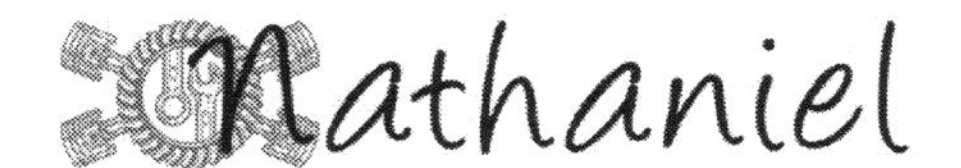

To say it's been weird—Flick being gone—is an understatement. I know she's only been back in my life for a few days, but I feel her absence now more than ever. Even when she's quiet, her company is welcome—a comfort I never knew I needed.

She's so guarded now. I always saw her as an introvert who played the good extrovert, but now that side of her has diminished. I know I pushed my luck—getting swept away and kissing her like that. She's unsure of herself, it ripples off her like waves of summer heat.

If my Gramps were here, I'd confide in him about it, but I also now know they were privy to whatever went on with her. They might have acted as though everything was fine, but they knew.

I've kept myself busy all day. When I hear the familiar sound of a bike pull up, I don't need to see Charlie to know it's him—always so heavy with the clutch.

"Hey, mate," he says. He pulls off his lid, stuffs his gloves inside, and leaves it on his seat. He comes into the garage, takes off his leather jacket, and grabs my hand, pulling me in for a pat on the back.

"How are you holding up?" he asks, wiping the sweat from his brow.

I grab him a bottle of water from the fridge and toss it in the air. He catches it with one hand.

"Fuck knows it's hard, that's for sure."

"It will be. He was great man."

"True."

"Is there anything I can help with?" he says before downing half the bottle of water in one huge gulp.

"No, you're already doing enough with covering the wake."

I still don't feel comfortable—him paying out of his own pocket—but I'm not going to argue with him about it. It'll be a losing battle anyway.

"So, where's Felicity?" he asks, looking around like she's hiding behind one of the cars or something.

"She had an emergency. She had to rush off to Simon's."

He raises his eyebrows with a smirk. "Dude, you're going through a lot. Are you sure she was even here, and she wasn't just a figment of your pretty imagination?"

I punch his arm. "Very funny. If I hadn't kissed her, I might have questioned that myself."

"Come again? You kissed her?"

"Yeah…it's fucked up, right? My gramps just died, and I'm hitting on Flick," I say, scrubbing my hand over my face. My chin is scratchy. *I need a shave*.

He shakes his head. "Nah, mate, there's always been *unfinished* business there." He wiggles his eyebrows, and walks around the car, eyeing it up.

"It will never be finished."

"What?" he asks.

I've never admitted my feelings about her to him, but he's not stupid. *I need a drink.*

"Hey, do you fancy a beer?" I ask, grabbing a bottle and twisting off the cap.

He holds his hand out, so I pass him one. "Cheers," we say in unison and clink our bottles. I take a long, hard pull, and sit down in one of the chairs.

Charlie follows suit.

"Is it safe to say she's the one?" he asks, hanging his leg over his other knee.

I shrug. "I can't speak for her, but if I had my way she would be… But she's different. I can't explain it…it's like she's holding back. Could be this guy Simon, but she said they're not '*together-together*'," I say, using air quotes.

"Are they in an open relationship?" he asks.

See, I should have asked *that* instead of saying *fuck buddies*. I'm a grade A arsehole.

"I wish I was more like you, man."

He coughs, choking back his beer. "What, why?"

"You at least have a filter… I should have said that instead of asking if they were fuck buddies."

One of his eyebrows shoots up, and then he lets out a gruff of a laugh. I kick the leg of his chair, but he doesn't budge.

"That doesn't sound like you at all," he says around a sarcastic smirk. "Don't beat yourself up about it. Come on, I have issues, too."

Now it's my turn to grin. "Yeah, well your commitment issues are your own, but at least you're upfront—they know the score."

"The last thing I need is to end up like my dad. No. Thank. You."

I squirm in my seat. *True.* He doesn't need to go through the same bullshit his dad has gone through where women are concerned.

"Don't you ever see yourself settling down? You know, have the kind of relationship my grandparents had?" I ask, leaning forward, my arms hanging between my legs as I roll the bottle between my palms.

"No disrespect to your grandparents, but what was right for them, isn't necessarily right for everybody. I just can't see it for myself."

"I've only imagined spending my life with *one* girl…and she just so happens to be at her boyfriend's as we speak."

"Casual sex partner," he interjects.

I nearly choke on my beer. "Don't say that, man. The thought of her being with him, or anyone else, riles me up the wrong way."

"That's a bit strong coming from you. You're hardly celibate—how do you reckon she feels about the girls you've been with?"

"Shut up, man. That's just sex. Don't make me out to be worse than what I actually am. I'm not that bad, am I?"

"Depends what our perception of *bad* is. I can't really talk, but at least I think I can still keep count. Can *you*?"

Of course, I can. I'm pretty sure I can count on both hands, but I refrain from answering as I see Ana approaching.

"Charlie," she says. He stands to greet her, and she looks him up and down, a huge grin on her face.

"Hi, Ana," Charlie says, pulling her into a big, gentle hug. *Soft bastard.*

"Well aren't you as dashing as ever?" she says as she cups his cheek.

A blush creeps over his face. I cover my mouth with my fist to stifle a laugh.

"Nathaniel, I just wanted to let you know Felicity rang. She'll be back later. Her friend, Sophie, wasn't in a good way, and those three are as tight as a lid on a pickle jar."

"No problem. As long as she's okay, that's all that matters."

She pats my shoulder with a wink.

"Charlie, you're staying for dinner?" It's a question that leaves no answer as she heads back towards the house.

We crank up the radio, and Charlie helps me work on the Impala. I still can't believe this is her favourite car. I must ask her about that. I'm distracted, I keep replaying the kiss from this morning—the look of unbridled passion as she came hot and heavy around my waist. How I shot my load pretty much as soon as I stood under my shower when I made it back to my room. I move from one foot to the other, now uncomfortably tight in my jeans.

All I know is, if I only ever kissed one woman for the rest of my life, it would be her. Gramps always said when you know, you know—you can't choose how you feel.

I look at the dashboard. A quarter after twelve, no wonder I'm so tired. I take it slow as I hit the gravelled driveway, which is lit by LED solar-powered lanterns. I haven't seen them before, but they look marvellous.

I come to a stop and switch off the engine, resting my head against the headrest. Yawning, I think of what Simon said about letting go of my insecurities. I'm the kind of broken that can't be fixed—no matter how much counselling I have, fragments will always remain fractured.

Nate has a way with the ladies. Facebook is testament to that. Could I really trust him with my body? With my heart? I'm over-analysing—I know this.

I shake my head as I unclip my seatbelt and step out of the car. I feel Nate before I see him sitting in silence on the steps.

"Hey, I was starting to think you were going to spend the night in the car," he says with a soft smile.

"No. Just trying to get my head together."

Is it possible to miss him for only a few hours?

"You came back," he says, matter of fact.

"Yeah, I wanted to get your car back." *And I wanted to see you.*

He raises his eyebrows. "You do know I have more than one car, right?"

"I know that…I don't…know."

I'm rattled with guilt now for leaving Soph so I could see him. Maybe I should've stayed. I wrap my arm around my middle.

"Didn't Simon want you to stay?" he asks.

"It's complicated," I say, and sit beside him.

"He's a better man than me. I wouldn't have let you go."

My stomach flutters with a new sense of life, the dread from moments ago gone.

"He understood why I wanted to get back."

"And that is?" he asks.

"We have no secrets," I say like that will explain it all.

"Your friend, Sophie…is she okay?"

I nod but then shake my head. "She's been better…I'm worried about her. I should have stayed—I feel guilty for leaving."

I hand him back his keys, and his fingertips brush mine, causing goosebumps to appear over my arms.

"If you need to go back, I'd understand."

He doesn't though—that's the thing. I shake my head.

"What were you doing out here anyway?" I ask in hopes of changing the subject.

"I lost my film buddy, so I worked in the garage…lost track of time, I guess. And then I heard you pull up," he says, spinning his keys.

"How are Evie and my Nana?"

"We kept busy. You missed Charlie, by the way. He stayed for dinner and asked after you."

"It's been too long. I remember when I thought you made him up, that he was your invisible friend."

He lets out a laugh. Who knew laughing could be sexy?

"He asked if you were even really here or if I made it up, so you two kind of have that in common."

"What can I say? You have good choice in friends."

"That I do," he says with a genuine smile.

"I wish I was a better friend. Me leaving Soph…it's hard because I know how she feels—what she's going through. At least Simon took off work tomorrow to be with her."

"He sounds like a good guy. Not many boyfriends would be there like that for their other half's friends.

"Nate, there's something I need to tell you about Simon and me."

He stands abruptly.

"Please don't tell me you're engaged…or something like that. I couldn't deal with that right now."

I'm so surprised by his words. I can't contain my laughter as I get to my feet.

"What's so funny?" he asks, giving me a dirty look.

"You're overacting. We're not engaged."

He wipes his sleeve across his forehead. "Sorry, of course, it wouldn't be a bad thing for you…"

He couldn't be further from the truth if he tried.

"Do you fancy a walk?" I ask. I talk better when I'm moving. I don't wait for him as I walk off. When I hear his feet connect with the gravel, I start talking.

"I'm not with Simon. He isn't my boyfriend. What we had…it's ancient history. We're best friends, that's all."

"I'm confused. When you said you weren't *together-together*, I thought you meant you were in an open relationship."

Well, that's an improvement from fuck buddies—I'll give him that.

"No, he's gay," I say, and come to a stop once we hit the grass.

"But Facebook says you're in a relationship."

I push my head back looking at the clear night sky.

"Do you believe everything you see online? We never changed it, that's all. It was just easier that way."

"Why? Because he's gay?"

It's only part of the reason. I take a deep breath as I pick up my speed and answer his question.

"No, because of what happened to Sophie and me."

I need him to understand why I am the way I am.

"Come on," he says, taking my hand in his.

"Where are we going?" I ask as he pulls me along beside him.

"You'll see."

We come to a stop at the foot of the tree house. I look up. It seems bigger if that's even possible.

"Are you coming up or what?" he asks as he climbs the ladder.

I shake my head, *is he serious?*

"Come on, get your cute butt up here."

I begin to blush so hard, even my earlobes begin to heat. Before he can embarrass me further, I grab hold of the ladder and climb.

"Sit with me," he says from the balcony, patting the floor beside him.

I join him. "It's even more beautiful up here than I remember."

"I come up here a lot—I imagine what it would be like watching my children play down there on the grass. Like we used to."

I turn to look at him. "I didn't know you wanted kids."

Children, who would have thought it?

"Of course. One day. What about you?"

I swing my legs back and forth. "I don't know, maybe. Never say never, right?"

I don't know how easy it would be to bring children into the world, even more so with how messed up my life is. I shiver, but it's not from the breeze of the cool, night air.

"Talk to me. You're holding back."

"I'm afraid when I do, you'll see me differently…you'll see me for the broken person I really am."

"Not going to happen. Listen, we may have been out of touch, but I see you for exactly who you are…which is a beautiful person—both inside and out."

His words stroke my ego, but it only makes what I need to tell him that much harder.

"A drink wouldn't go amiss right about now," I say.

"Hold that thought." He jumps to his feet, heads back inside, then reappears with a bottle in hand. "Ta-Dah."

Vodka. In his other hand, between his thumb and forefinger, he has two glasses.

I shake my head.

He nods his head over his shoulder. "Renovations…mini fridge." He pours us each a small shot. He hands me one and clinks his glass with mine. Before I can chicken out, I bring it to my lips and knock it back.

"Shit," I choke out, the afterburn of the liquid attacking my throat.

"You okay?"

"Yep, just not big on spirits. I don't know how Sophie can drink this shit."

He laughs, but it dissipates when I hold out my glass again.

"Really, you sure?"

"No," I say, but he pours me another. When I swallow this one, it's not as bad as the first one.

Dutch courage running through my veins, I know it's now or never—flight or fight—I need to tell him, I need to fight.

Here goes nothing.

Chapter Fifteen

Two years earlier.

The tempo from below pulses through my body as we descend the poorly lit stairwell. People pass us from the opposite direction—some looking worse for wear, others laughing as they talk over one another.

Chloe grabs hold of our hands, leading us in the direction of the nearest toilets. She's been busting to go the whole cab ride over. I told her to go before we left, but she never listens to me.

She pushes through the large door. The lighting in here doesn't fare any better than the dim hallway we just walked through. Probably a ploy, an attempt to keep people from spending too much time in here.

A woman sits over by the end basin, head down as she reads, paying no attention to us what so ever. Laid out beside her, is an array of stuff. I move closer to get a better look—there's everything from tights, to plasters. A girl exits a cubicle and washes her hands. It's only now the woman looks up and passes her some hand towels. She makes quick work of drying off the excess water and then tosses them in the bin. She eyes the contents laid out in front of her before grabbing a bottle of perfume, giving herself an overzealous squirt, and almost blinding herself in the process. Dropping a couple of quid in the bowl, she prepares to leave while the other woman nods her thanks, then goes back to the Woman's Weekly in her lap.

"I can't believe we all got in," Sophie says as she smacks her lips together. That shade really suits her.

"It's all right for the two of you. You're old enough, but if they asked me for ID, I'd be on my way home right about now," I whisper, eyeing the woman.

Sophie spins to look at me and shakes her head. "Never, we came together, we leave together. Besides, you're eighteen in a week."

Chloe reappears from the toilet and washes her hands. "Who's up for a drink?" she asks over her shoulder, already half-cut. The two bottles of wine we shared before we got here are clearly kicking in. The woman holds out some hand towels for Chloe, but she declines, shaking her hands in front of her.

"Why not," I say with a shrug. I look in the full-length mirror one last time—here we go.

The dance floor calls to me. The more I drink, the more I want to be free. Bass pumps through my veins—an iridescent wave coursing through a crowd of nameless faces. Raising my arms in the air, I let myself go and get lost in the rhythm.

I bump into something hard, and stumble, turning my head—dark eyes smile back at me.

"Easy, tiger," he says, holding onto my elbow to steady me.

"Sorry," I reply, my ears beginning to burn. I'm not sure if it's from all of the dancing or falling over a complete stranger.

He says something else, but the tempo of the song playing drowns it out. I wave in the direction of my ears and shake my head. Smiling, he leans in close, cheek to cheek

"I said, my name's John." He holds out his hand.

I wipe mine before taking his. “Felicity,” I reply, trying to calm my erratic heartbeat.

“Can I buy you a drink?” he asks.

“Hey, hey, hey,” Sophie says, handing me my drink.

John introduces himself to Sophie and Chloe and then invites us to go join him and his friends in the VIP area. He introduces us all, but I know I’ll never remember their names. The girls are sweet from the off, asking where we got our shoes or about Sophie’s hair. The guys are loud, a little rowdy, but otherwise entertaining as they make up some dance moves and the complementary drinks flow freely.

John hasn’t removed his hand from my lower back. My body tingles with appreciation and is flattered by the attention. I watch him as he watches Sophie with his friends. He catches me, and his lip tilts up.

I shake my head, and his arm wraps around my waist as he pulls me into his body.

“What?” he says loud enough so I can hear.

“She’s taken,” I say, feeling deflated from moments before.

“Well, I’m not interested in her. I was just making sure to keep my boys in check.”

I pull back to look at him, his eyes smile back at me.

“Please, tell me the same doesn’t go for you?”

Smiling, I shake my head.

“Good to know.” He squeezes my waist, causing my stomach to flutter.

I laugh, watching Sophie and Chloe doing the running man. I don’t think I’ve laughed this much in ages—not since I stopped seeing Nate. I could scold myself. He is the last person I want to think about right now.

"They've invited us back to a party," Sophie whisper-shouts from the cubicle beside me, as I fight to pull my trousers up.

"What did Chloe say?" I call back, before flushing.

"She's easy."

I laugh and wash my hands.

"I'm game if you are," she offers, joining me at the sink.

"Why not," I say, smiling. I'm not ready for tonight to end, not yet anyway.

She jumps up and down then pulls me into a hug. Drunken Soph is all about the love.

Shivering, I reach for my cover. My fingers connect with an unfamiliar texture—the sheets beneath me feel odd, foreign. A scratchy material rubs against my bare legs. I suck in a deep breath, and my senses are assaulted with a damp musk, which settles in my nose. It's as though someone hasn't opened the window in here for a long time.

My breathing increases as confusion sets in. *Tick-tick-ticking* of a nearby clock thumps through my head. I swallow what feels like tiny razor blades sliding down my throat. I feel so…off.

I hold my breath and strain my ears. I don't think anyone else is here with me, but it still takes me to the count of three to open my eyes. Remnants of sleep blur my vision as I try to focus on my surroundings. The room is cast in dim lighting, but not enough to hide the yellow-stained ceiling above.

Turning my head just a fraction, I flinch. My body rejects the movement, the clock ticking now replaced by the fierce drum of my heartbeat as it pounds mercilessly in my ears. My stomach lurches. I squeeze my eyes shut, waiting for it to pass.

Sometime later, I risk a slow look around the room again. The window is covered with a sheet—a makeshift curtain—and the window ledge is covered with crushed-up beer cans and an overloaded ashtray. But what makes my breathing halt is when my eyes stop on the torn-open condom wrappers. I sit up too fast. My head thunders at the back of my eyes in retaliation.

I scan down the length of my body—covered with bare threaded sheets, and only dressed in my bra. My hand flies to my mouth as I try to control the bile threatening to escape. My arm goes over my chest. I feel exposed—like I'm being watched. My breathing comes in short, rapid bursts.

The mattress beneath me is without a bed frame and pushed up against the wall in the corner. The only other furniture is a cabinet opposite, with a dusty portable TV on top. From the corner of my eye, I see a pool of material. I crawl towards it. My knees chafe on the rough carpet as I lunge for my clothes.

Frantic, I dress. My fingers are unsteady as I pull up the zip of my trousers, and my nail snags, ripping off the tip. I ignore the sting to pull my top over my head. Something buzzes around my bare feet. *My bag.* Grabbing it, I scramble amongst the contents but keep my eyes on the door as I approach on my tiptoes. Holding my breath, I listen for sounds of life before I begin to turn the handle. It clicks open, and I step out.

Four doors adorn the distance of the hallway, including the one I came from, with another at the end—which I can only presume to be the front door. I bring my phone to my cheek and shoulder—I want my hands to be free.

"Hello?" I whisper, my voice hoarse.

"Felicity, where are you?" Soph whisper-shouts.

I have no fucking idea.

"I don't know," I croak out.

Floorboards creak. A door opens.

I grip my bag, and raise it up, ready to swing. When Sophie appears, my body lurches in surprise. I throw myself at her.

Her arms are limp at her sides, so I pull back. Her eye makeup is smudged, hair a matted mess. I probably don't look much better.

"Where's Chloe?"

I shake my head.

She types into her phone. Moments later, we hear the echo of a ping. Soph takes the lead. Grabbing my arm, she creeps in the direction of the noise. We pause. She opens the door with trepidation, and the only sounds I can hear is our heavy breathing.

Chloe is sitting up on a sofa, phone in hand, rubbing her forehead. She looks as confused as I feel. Sophie rushes forward, grabs her bag off the floor, and flings it towards her.

"We need to go. *Now,*" Soph says in a tone that leaves no room for argument.

Chloe drops her legs to the floor, leans over, and pulls on her shoes. I look around the living room—I have no recollection of this place. *How the hell did we end up here?*

My brain is foggy as I try to recall exactly what happened last night, but no matter how hard I try, all I remember is the club, climbing into a cab, and then—*nothing.*

Sophie scans the room, her eyes trailing back to me, eyebrows raised.

"What?" I ask

"Where are your shoes?"

I look down to my feet, and then back to her face. Yet another fucking question I do not have an answer to. I throw my hands up. She grabs my hand and pulls me back into the hallway. For a split second, I think she's going to direct me back to that room, but instead, she swivels and heads for the front door. Chloe is hot on our heels.

We step out into an alcove-shaped hallway. The faint scent of urine fills the air, and my stomach heaves. I cover my mouth and nose as we descend the stairwell. Two sets of stairs later, we encounter the exit. I squint from the light, holding my palm over my brow. Blinking, I try to find my bearings. *No fucking clue*.

We head towards a bus stop. Soph takes a seat as I look at the post to see what stop this is. I hear someone suck in a deep, pained breath and look over my shoulder. Any colour Soph had, which wasn't much, has completely drained from her face.

"Are you okay?' I ask, taking a seat beside her. I shudder as I pull my foot over my leg to wipe the discarded cigarette butt from the ball of my foot.

"I don't feel so good," she says through clenched teeth. Her face takes on a weird expression before her eyes roll into the back of her head. I have no time to react when she slumps to the ground with a loud, hard thump. I scramble to my knees. Chloe and I try to coax a response from her, but we get nothing.

"Chloe, call an ambulance, tell them the name of the bus stop."

Her eyes spring to mine, panic evident.

"For *fuck's sake,* Chloe, just do it. I don't care if we get into trouble."

She fumbles with her phone and dials.

I don't see it at first—it's concealed by the dark shade of her trousers. At a glance, I think maybe she's wet herself, maybe she's had some kind of fit, and when she passed out, she lost control of her bodily functions. But no—it turns out, its blood.

It's not until I'm waiting for my Mum to arrive at the hospital that I throw up. My body shakes heavily. There's nothing quite as disgusting as being barefoot in hospital toilets, of all places. I'm sore when I urinate—I want to ignore the sting, pretend it's normal. But I know it's not.

I'm laid out on a hospital bed. The tissue paper beneath me feels cheap. Dressed in the hospital gown I was told to put on, I wait, staring up at the florescent light. Two nurses enter, both wearing the same expression of pity. They're kind and reassuring while they explain to my mum and me what they're about to do. It's for my benefit, my mums a nurse, she's not stupid. I zone out.

In my head, I retreat to a far-away place. I cocoon myself with memories of Nate—us playing dungeons and dragons in the tree house. Like this is all a dream. *Just a really bad dream.* When I open my eyes, all will be right with the world—all will be as it should be—none of this ever happened. I can pretend Sophie isn't currently in surgery due to haemorrhaging. Or Chloe and I aren't both being examined and tested for traces of Flunitrazepam, otherwise known as the date rape drug—Rohypnol.

Nathaniel

The cold, night air blasts my body but all I feel is white-hot rage. The moon is full, the sky clear, casting a glow on the deserted country roads.

I'd do anything right now to have Flick with me, riding on the back of my bike, her arms wrapped around me. My fingers clench the throttle hard, her broken voice echoing in my ears.

Her face became vacant as she retreated inside herself when the words began spilling from her lips. I saw it in her eyes—a brief moment when the light went out—a shift—and then her whole aura changed. She began shutting down.

When I walked her back to her room, the air was thick—

heavy with melancholy. Flick once told me how a photograph speaks a thousand words, but in that moment, her silence said so much more.

I wanted so badly to hold her, but even taking her hand in mine caused her to flinch. It made my gut twist. All I wanted was to take her in my arms and carry the burden. But she wouldn't even look me in the eye. It was written all over her like a coat of badly made armor—shame, humiliation, lack of self-worth. Her shoulders hunched, struggling to carry the weight of her head. She wrapped her arms around her middle, squeezing her waist tight.

If anyone should be ashamed, it's the monsters responsible for doing this to her. And me, for not being there.

When she closed her door, I couldn't contain my rage. I needed so badly to hit someone or something. I was wired yet exhausted. Needing to let off steam, I grabbed my leather jacket and keys. With no destination in mind, all I knew was if I was going to lose my shit, it wouldn't be at home.

Eyes brimming with tears, I release the throttle and come to a stop.

How can I make her see that what happened to her was not her fault? Deep down, she knows it's the truth. This in no way changes my feelings towards her, although it does consume me with a self-loathing I've never felt before.

I was meant to be her best friend, but my ego and pride let her slip through my fingers. I could live a thousand lifetimes and still not find a way to forgive myself.

Tomorrow, I had planned to write my eulogy for my Gramps, but now I know I need to take her somewhere away from here, so she doesn't try and fester away inside her own head.

Chapter Sixteen

Violation. Having no recollection of an incident—but knowing it happened—doesn't make it any less real or humiliating. Revealing this to Nate hasn't lifted the heavy weight I still carry. Unveiling the tragic truth hasn't miraculously made me feel liberated.

My sleep has been torturous, broken. I wake wrapped in my sheets, soaked in sweat. I shower in the hottest water my body can tolerate as I scrub myself raw. Although I don't think I'll ever feel completely clean, it'll have to do. I strip my bed and then cocoon myself in a throw. I sit on the window seat. Pulling my legs underneath me, I stare blindly out at the view as I retreat into myself.

Knocking interrupts me. I'm stiff when I move, with no idea how long I've been sitting here. I ignore the knocking.

"Flick, I know you're in there. I'm coming in. Hope you're decent."

I don't answer or watch as he enters. His footsteps falter before they continue and grow louder as they approach me. I see a tray from the corner of my eye as it's placed beside me.

"I made you some breakfast."

"Thanks, but I'm not hungry. I don't feel too well, sorry." I can't look at him. I won't. I don't want to see the look of pity.

"Well, can you at least try and eat something for me?" he says, moving from one foot to the other.

"Leave it there, I'll try some in a bit," I say, hoping it will placate him into leaving me alone.

"Okay, but we don't have long. We have errands to run."

I look over to him. Is he serious?

"I'm not really up to it, sorry."

He moves towards me and brings his palm up to my face. I move back, but it doesn't deter him. He places it on my forehead. I swat his hand away.

"Well, you feel fine to me. Be ready in half an hour."

I don't have a chance to argue as he leaves me alone, shutting my door behind him.

Another knock, followed by the door opening, disturbs me again. I turn my head, ready to give Nate what-for, when I'm caught short.

"For fu—"

"What was that, dear?"

"Sorry, I thought you were Nate," I say, with a sigh.

She comes and sits beside me. Picking up the milk, she pours it over the Coco-Pops, then hands me the spoon and the bowl. I scoop a small amount and place in my mouth, but it tastes like cardboard. I put the bowl down and look back out the window.

"I heard you last night in your sleep. It's been a while since that's happened. Do you want to talk about it?" she asks, taking my hand in hers.

"I don't know. After I left Soph last night, I came back here and told Nate about what happened to us—" I feel an ache in the back of my throat, "—I don't know…maybe I thought I'd feel better, but if anything, I feel worse."

"You listen to me, and you listen to me *good*. You are a brave young woman. Every day you get up, and you *fight* to be the best version of yourself. Even when you feel like giving up. So, do not let this right *here* give up on you now," she says, pointing to my heart.

Some things are easier said than done. It would be so simple for me to retreat into my head, shut out the world around me—I should know, I've done it once before. But empathy is the one thing that keeps me moving forward, putting one foot in front of the other. It's about making the effort for those around me, to keep pushing forward.

I make my way through to the garage, and pause, mid-step, at the sight before me.

Nate is leaning on his car—adorned in his leather jacket—one leg crossed in front of the other. Tight jeans show off his thick thighs, and his boots are laced up over the ankles.

He smiles when he sees me. "Good, you wore jeans."

I look down and wipe my palms over my thighs. He *so* caught me looking. "And that's good why?"

Pointing his thumb over his shoulder, he replies. "Because we'll be going on that."

I go to back away, but he takes hold of my elbow.

"No, I'll pass. But thanks." I shake my head.

He tilts his head. "Come on. You used to love coming out on the bike."

I raise my eyebrows. "So…that was then, and this is now."

"Oh, come on, you trust me, right?"

"Yes. It's other drivers I don't trust." I pull at the band on my wrist.

It's funny how the things I used to get a kick out of don't thrill me the same way as they used to. He pulls me closer, so we are almost touching. My breath gets caught in my throat.

"If you're too chicken, we can just go in the car," he says with a wink.

I cross my arms over my middle. "Fine, let's just go on the bike."

He laughs. Rubbing his hands together, he walks over to the locker and pulls out a ladies' leather jacket.

"Good girl. Here put this on." He drops the jacket into my hands.

"Whose is this?" I ask, slipping my arms through it.

"Yours." He shrugs.

"What do you mean, *mine?"* I ask, zipping it up.

His head disappears as he peers inside a box, his reply muffled. "It was a present that I never had the chance to give you."

I stroke my hands down the front. *Mine.*

He comes to stand in front of me. His forefinger lifts my chin to close my mouth, and my stomach warms from his touch.

"And your lid." He holds it out to me.

I take it with a smile. Something I do recognise—the black Arai crash helmet he insisted on buying for me if I was going to be his pillion.

I clear my throat. "So, how many girls have you taken on the bike?"

"None."

"Really?"

He looks up. "Yes, really. Are you stalling?"

"No, but now you mention it, that's a good idea," I say with a humourless laugh.

"Come on, it will be fine." He holds up a rucksack in one hand, and motions with the other for me to turn around. I do, and then he pulls the straps up my arms. "I just need to drop my suit at the dry cleaner."

By the time he pulls up next to the dry cleaner, my death hold has eased off, and I've relaxed into his back—holding on with my thighs leaning with him like he taught me. He kicks down the stand, and I climb off, removing my lid. There's no movie moment. As my hair snags, I finger comb it and tie it into a loose plait. He takes the bag with his suit in it from my shoulders and runs into the dry cleaners.

I check to see if Simons messaged me back. It makes me feel better knowing Sophie will be moving in with him.

"Everything all right?" Nate asks.

"Yeah, fine. Where to next?"

"I thought we could go for a ride. Maybe grab an early lunch if you fancy it?"

"Might as well," I say, pulling my lid back on.

I get lost in thought as he rides. Closing my eyes, I think about everything that's happened over the past couple of days. It's only when he stops and turns off the engine that I see we've arrived at our destination. High Beach in Epping Forest. I can't help but smile. It's been so long since I've been here, and the Kings Oak Pub does the best club sandwiches.

Sitting outside, on a worn, wooden table that's seen better days, I find myself looking over the sand-dirt path, which leads to the lush, green fields and hills and beyond. We eat in a comfortable quiet. The only noises overhead is from local birds chirping away, or the humming of engines as the occasional vehicle passes us by.

After we've eaten, I lean back and inhale, closing my eyes and turning my head in the direction of the soft heat from the sun.

"I've missed you," he says from beside me.

I turn to look at him, but *his* eyes are closed, his face tilted upwards.

"I've missed you, too," I say. I watch as his dimpled smile spreads across his face.

"That's good to hear, I did wonder..."

I elbow him. He squints his eyes in my direction.

"I just know how big your ego is, and I didn't want to stroke it."

He lets out a chuckle. My ears burn—that could have been so easily misconstrued.

"If you say so. Did you want to make a move back? Or are you okay?"

"I'd like to stay a little longer."

It's beautiful here. I feel stupid, now, thinking back to when he first brought me here. I was disappointed that it wasn't actually a beach. But one of the many walks through the forest quickly made up for it. If I had known we were coming here, I would have grabbed my camera—taken some shots of the church. I always thought it strange how this was off the beaten track, but it made sense when he explained the rear of this pub was the venue for Britain's first motorcycle speedway meeting.

It's almost easy to get caught up in the tranquillity of this place—ignore the fact that the funeral is the day after next. I just want to soak this up, even if only for a little while.

"Shall we walk?" He stands, holding out his hand.

I nod as he pulls me to my feet. He lets go of my hands, grabs the lids, and leaves them with the bike. When he returns, he reaches out and takes my hand in his. We walk in a comfortable silence—apart from our feet meeting with gravel and the crazy bird chatter. I inhale deeply. My eyes flicker closed. Rays of light sneak between the branches, dancing over my eyelids. A gentle breeze whispers on my skin. *Bliss.*

He nods his head in the direction of a bench, and we take a seat.

Playing with his hands in his lap, he coughs before speaking. “How long do you think you’ll stay here after the funeral?”

I chew on the inside of my lip. I hadn’t thought about it. “Depends on my Nana, I guess,” I say, with a non-committal shrug.

“I wanted to know how much time I have with you before you leave again.” He turns to look at me.

My heart picks up speed as I see the pained look in his eyes.

“Nate, it’s not like before. We’ll stay in touch, I pinkie swear.”

He lets out a small chuckle. Holding out his little finger, I link it with mine and give it a tiny shake.

“Do you regret telling me about what happened to you?”

I let out a sigh. “No, but at the same time I don’t like you knowing why I am the way I am.”

“You’re fine the way you are. I’m glad you trusted me enough to tell me. But I’ll always feel guilt that I wasn’t there for you.”

“I don’t think it would have made a difference back then. But you’re here now.”

He attempts a poor excuse for a smile. “Do you think my gramps would be ashamed of me?”

“Of course not, why would he?”

He begins listing off his fingers. “I let him down. He was ill, and I pissed off—went travelling with Charlie. Who the hell does that?”

I know he’s carrying around a lot of regrets, that’s more than evident after the other night, but he needs to let it go.

"You didn't know it was terminal then. We can sit here saying *what ifs* until we are blue in the face, but believe me, it doesn't change anything. It just makes you crazy from the inside out. What if I'd waited until I was eighteen before going out that night? I beat myself up about it all the time. It was one stupid decision that changed my life. I only had to wait one more week." I stare at the robin bopping about on the path in front of me. I can't hide my smile. Nana always says when a robin appears, it's someone you've lost paying you a visit. I take comfort in that.

"It's taken me a while, but I'm trying to get some sort of structure back into my life. I know better than anyone that there's no such thing as perfect, but I also know we can't let the past dictate your future," I say, looking back to Nate.

It's in this exact moment I have an epiphany. It's everything Nana and Simon have been trying to tell me.

Nate smiles, I mean really smiles. "Damn, Felicity grew up," he says, pulling me into his side and kissing my forehead.

I feel a moment of calm. I haven't felt this way in such a long time, it's foreign, and I don't trust it. I'm waiting for the other shoe to drop.

Chapter Seventeen

I've been in a constant state of unrest since we got back earlier today—even more than usual. I've been over-analysing everything I'm feeling for Nate. I've always cared about him, but something has shifted—it's more than that.

"Penny for them?"

I blink. "Huh."

Nate hands me a beer with a warm smile.

"Thanks."

Clinking my bottle against his, I stare as he takes a sip and licks off a stray drop from his upper lip. My belly comes to life—a warm sensation in my lower region. I clench my legs together.

"Film?" he suggests. It's become our thing.

"Why not?" I reply.

Like he even has to ask—any time I can spend with him, I'm going to take it. I'm not even as bothered if my legs brush up against his, now. Any contact with him, whether accidental or not, is welcome.

In true tradition, I fell asleep. Waking, I find my arm is slung over his chest. I can feel him touching my hair. Opening my eyes, I see him gently twirling a section around his finger, his eyes focused on the TV, the volume low.

"Sorry," I say, sitting up.

"Don't be."

I stretch, but a twinge causes me to wince.

"You all right?" he asks, sitting forward.

"Just a crook in my neck."

He moves to his knees. "Here let me."

He takes me by my shoulders, moving me so my back is towards him. I perch on the edge of the bed. His hands begin to knead the back of my neck, and then he works over my shoulders. My heartbeat increases when he moves my hair to one side. I tilt my head as his hot breath tickles my ear. If he doesn't stop, I'm worried I might do something to embarrass myself. I put my hand over his to still it.

"That's better, thank you."

Letting go, he comes to sit beside me, his arm brushing mine.

"I should go," I say, my voice hoarse.

"Why?"

"It's late." It's a feeble excuse, but it's all I can come up with.

The moment my eyes meet his, I'm lost.

"Don't go. Stay with me."

"What?" I strangle out, my heart pumping in my ears.

"You know I'd never hurt you, right?"

No, not intentionally he wouldn't.

He takes my hand in his. "I know I've got shit-poor timing, but if I don't say this now, I don't know if I'll find the nerve. I like you, a lot. Way more than friends."

My breath catches in my throat. My face flushes. He says that, but this is Nate. He's a player.

"I understand if you think it's too much, too soon. But life's so short. If you only see me as a friend, I'm not going to lie,

I won't like it, but I'll accept it. If it means not losing you again." His stare doesn't once falter.

His words speak to my soul, hitting the very heart of me. Who am I kidding? I can't deny my attraction towards him, I never could.

"Can I ask you something?"

"Anything," he replies.

"Will you kiss me?" I stumble over the words.

"Kiss you?" His eyebrow rises.

I nod. Embarrassment sets in, and I look away when his fingers catch my chin and turn my face towards his.

"I want nothing more than to kiss you, but not if that's all you think I'm after. It's not. Yes, I'm a man with basic needs, the same as anyone, but I need you to want me…like I want you."

I watch his face. It's open, with honesty, and I answer him the only way my heart will allow.

"I do want you," I say.

He leans his face towards me, pausing centimetres from my lips. My breath catches but in a good way. He doesn't move, and it's in this moment that I know I need to be the one to close the gap.

My lips connect with his like an implosion. It begins soft and slow, then increases with an intensity I've never experienced before. Every sound that escapes him, my throat reacts with a whimper of my own. Heat pulsates through my body as it tingles to life.

He lies back, pulling me with him, rolling me on top. I don't move at first, but soon my inhibitions escape me, and I grind into his hardness. I lose all sense of control as I gyrate over him. He meets me, move for move, and something begins to build between my legs, only the thin fabric of our clothing between us.

I contemplate stopping, but Nate holds me tight, whispering into my neck.

"It's okay, Flick. You're allowed to feel. You have the control."

With that, his hand rolls over to my arse and pulls me closer. The friction sends me into a spasm of complete ecstasy. I can't help the moan that escapes me as pleasure ripples through me.

As my body begins to calm down, reality sinks in. *I just came from dry-humping Nate.* But I can't prevent the satisfied smile on my face, either. If it's that good with clothes on, how much better would it be without?

A nervous giggle escapes me.

"That has to be one of the sexiest things I think I've ever seen," Nate says, his eyes dark, hazel hues reflecting off the lamp.

I swat his shoulder before sitting up. Bravery overtakes me as I straddle him. Still throbbing with a warm ache, I move my hands to the waistband of his shorts and dip my hand under them. He pauses my arm, but not before I touch him. A hiss escapes through his teeth.

"Flick, you don't have to do that. I don't want you doing anything you're not ready for."

"I want to. I'll say if it's too much."

I see him weighing my words. He sits up slightly, and, raising his hand, he pulls my head to meet his, claiming my lips. His arousal sparks a new awareness within me. I stroke my hand down his long length.

"Flick, stop." He says it like a warning.

"Why?" I ask, removing my hand. I rock into him. In what feels like a split second, he lifts me and rolls me onto my back. Air rushes from my lips.

"Why? Because I want you. I've never wanted anyone as much as I want you."

I lean up and nip his chin.

"I want you, too," I say, with an honesty I wasn't expecting to share.

"Do you mean what I think you mean?"

"Yes."

I pull him down on top of me. Dragging his hands to the waistband of my leggings, his fingers slowly caress my skin before he slips a hand underneath. My breathing becomes heavy. He lowers his hand to the thin fabric of my thong.

"Take them off," I whisper.

Slow and deliberate, he sits up to pull my leggings down, planting soft kisses over the material of my thong before moving them to one side. He trails his fingers over my sensitive folds before inserting one finger, moving it slowly inside me before inserting another. I gasp at the contact. It feels so good.

"You're wet," he says.

I reach inside his shorts again. He's so hard. I stroke down his warm length, the tip moist. I love the weight of him in my hand.

"Take these off," I say letting go, and pinging the waistband.

He slides his fingers free to take them off before he continues to familiarise himself with my skin. Pushing my top up and over my stomach, he spreads tiny kisses over my belly. His fingers are welcome when they slide back inside me. My body rises off the bed at the contact. I pull him closer, so we are face to face, and take hold of his hard length again. Moving my hand up and down, I tighten my grip as the rhythm of his fingers inside me intensifies.

"Don't stop," I say, breathless.

"Wasn't going to," he grunts out.

My hand tightens around him. I don't know if it's too tight, but I can't help it.

"Fuck, I'm not going to last much longer," he groans.

I take that as a good sign. My hand speeds up, as do his fingers.

"Nate I'm going to—" I gasp out.

His lips smother my mouth—blocking out the sounds I can't hold back—as I experience the most intense and satisfying orgasm. My hand becomes clumsy around his length, but he doesn't seem to mind. A tremor vibrates through him as he comes hard—all over my belly. Strangely, it doesn't gross me out; if anything, it turns me on.

"Don't move," he says, in the sexiest voice I think I've ever heard, taking himself in his big strong hand. As he struts to bathroom, I cover my eyes with my forearm, trying to regain control of my breathing.

"You okay?" he asks. The bed dips.

"Yeah." I move my arm to look at him, my face flushed as I chew on my lip.

"Sorry about this," he says, as he wipes over my stomach with a warm flannel.

"Would it be weird to admit that I kind of liked it?" I say, biting the tip of my thumb.

"Do you know what you do to me?"

My eyes scan down the length of him. He's getting hard again. He stands to toss the flannel into the sink, his length bouncing as he walks. Grabbing for a pair of shorts, he slips them on, tucking himself in. They hang loose on his hips. He grabs a t-shirt and throws it at me.

"Here, put this on."

I pull off my top and catch him eyeing my bra. The way he looks at me makes me feel like I'm the most beautiful thing in the world. I slip it on over my head and inhale—all Nate.

"Flick, I'm not letting you leave after that. You're staying with me tonight."

"But we didn't have sex."

"No, but we did have excellent foreplay," he says, kissing my neck.

"You're okay with us not having sex?"

"I waited this long, I can wait a little longer."

My chest squeezes. This is the moment my heart opens, and I accept I'm falling for him.

He pulls me down onto the bed, opening his arms. I cuddle into him. The sound of his heartbeat lulls me into a careless sleep.

I wake to find him fast asleep. His breathing is heavy and deep—there's no way I'll be able to get back to sleep now. According to his stereo, it's still early. I'm quiet as I leave him in bed. Grabbing his hoodie from his chair, I slip it over my head and make my way through the quiet house towards the kitchen.

Evie is sitting alone, wrapped in her dressing gown when I enter.

"Felicity, couldn't you sleep either?" she asks with a sad smile.

"No." I walk towards her.

"Do you want to join me for a hot chocolate?" she asks, standing.

I place my hand over her shoulder. "I'll get it. Do you want another one?"

"Yes, please."

I heat the milk in the copper pan on the stove before pouring it into two mugs and adding a generous spoonful of drinking chocolate. I join her on the cushions covering the kitchen bench. She's turning an envelope over in her hands. It's Lawry's handwriting—he always did have excellent penmanship.

"You miss him?"

"Yes, immensely. I know I can't complain—I had a long and happy life with him. And I was fortunate to have a second chance at love. Falling in love was unexpected for both of us, but it's *Nathaniel* I worry about."

I blow on my hot chocolate. "I do, too. Nana tells me how time helps to heal, and if you'd asked me that a year ago, I wouldn't have believed it. But now I have hope things can get better as we learn to cope."

"I hope so, too. I keep questioning how I'm going to find the right time to give him this letter from Lawry. I know he would have preferred to tell him in person, but his health just deteriorated so suddenly." She lays it flat on the table.

"I don't think there's ever a good time for something like this."

She pulls a hankie free from her sleeve and wipes at her nose with trembling fingers. It scares me—accepting her and my Nana are both getting older. I place my hand over hers.

"I know Ana told you about Lawry not being his biological grandfather. His parents would have told him, but after they passed away, it just didn't seem that important…not in the grand scheme of things—"

"Wasn't important!"

I knock my cup, hot liquid sloshing over the sides. I grab the envelope, saving it just in the nick of time. I toss it to Evie as I reach for a tea towel to wipe up the mess. My eyes flit between the table and Nate's dark silhouette filling the doorway.

"Nathaniel, it's not what—"

He doesn't give her a chance to continue. "Nan, what the fuck?"

I flinch as his voice booms through the quiet kitchen.

Evie covers her mouth as she attempts to contain her sob.

"Nate, just take a breath and calm down," I say, raising my hands slowly.

"*Calm down?* How the fuck do you expect me to *calm down*? And better still, you knew, and you didn't fucking tell me?" he asks, coming into the room.

I can smell his disdain—it radiates off of him like a kettle kept on the hob too long, whistling wildly. His pupils are deep and dark—his mood smothering the hazel hue of the irises I've grown to love. I want so badly to turn away, to leave, but I can't. I'm rooted where I stand, knowing he has every right to be angry. I kept the truth from him—an omission…but still, I knew. From the corner of my eye, I see Evie's body rattle with her quiet sobs.

"It wasn't like that… I mean, Nana told me something before we flew out here, and I put two and two together, but I found out by accident," I say, squeezing my arms round my middle.

"Accident or not, you should have still told me." His voice raises another octave; my body begins to shake.

"I'm sorry," I say. And truly I am. My breath quickens as I find the courage to move towards him.

"I don't know why I'm surprised. I mean, you let me think you were with *Simon.* What was that? A sick ploy to make me jealous? Don't even get me started on you not telling me about what happened to you when even my *grandparents* knew. It all makes sense now," he says, placing his hands in his hair and pulling at it.

I pause. That was a low blow—even for him. My throat tightens, and I feel a pain rising in my chest.

"Nathaniel, that's enough. Do you hear me? Do not take this out on Felicity," Evie says around her tears.

He throws his hands up in the air, causing me to flinch.

"You're a fine one to talk. How the hell would you feel if you were in my shoes? The man I looked up to, who I was in awe of…turns out not to be my grandfather at all."

"Don't you dare say that, of course he is—" Her words break off.

"Is or *was*…he's not here to explain himself. All of this is fucking horse shit," he says, waving his hands around the room.

Everything about his body language causes me to tense. I watch him getting more frustrated, fists clenching and the veins in his neck coming to life.

"Nate, please will you just—" I try, but he cuts me off.

He points his finger at me. "Don't you dare, *Nate, please will you...*" he says, mimicking me.

The sting is like salt in a wound—a slap in the face—from how I felt so close to him a few short hours ago. He turns and storms away.

"Nathaniel, wait. I have a letter from your grandfather, it explains it all," she says, holding it up to his retreating back.

He peers over his shoulder, eyes so dark they are alien to me.

"Burn it. I don't want it."

"Evie, I'm sorry," I say, feeling at a loss for words.

"Oh, come on now. It's not your fault," she says as she wipes at her face.

I can't let him walk away, not like that. Who the hell does he think he is treating Evie that way?

"I'm going to try talking to him," I tell her.

"I don't think he'll listen. He's hot-headed just like his grandfather. If he would just calm down enough to see reason..."

I nod and give her a hug before jogging off to Nate's room.

I tap on his door but don't wait for an answer. I walk straight in. He's already out of his shorts and dressed in jeans and a jumper, sitting on the edge of his bed, lacing up his boots.

"Nate, please can we talk about this?"

He doesn't bother to look up when he answers. "No, we cannot. You fucking knew, Felicity, and you said *nothing*." He tugs the last knot in his laces.

I move towards him. I need to make him understand. "It wasn't for me to say. I only found out by accident." I know it's a lame excuse, but still, it's the truth.

"I couldn't give a shit how you found out. You should have told me."

"No, Nate, I shouldn't have," I say, standing my ground.

Springing to his feet, he slips on his leather jacket and pulls up the zipper before grabbing for his wallet and keys. I put my hand out to stop him, but he swats it away like I'm nothing.

"Nate, please don't leave like this. Talk to me," I say, pleading. I know he's angry, hurt, and he has every right to be, but he shouldn't leave—not like this.

"I never thought I'd say this, but you are the last person I want to talk to right now." His admission is like a punch to the gut.

"I'm sorry," I say, my body trembling with tension.

"Save it for someone who gives a shit."

My heart is hammering like mad as I try to control my breathing, shifting from one foot to the other.

"You don't mean that," I say. I try to take his hand, but he snatches it back. *This* is what I was afraid of—letting him in so he could push me away.

"Oh, but I do. And don't think the waterworks will work, either. I need to clear my head."

I bring my fingertips to my face, I didn't even realise I was crying. I'm stunned.

He hits me with a look, that for the first time, I can't decipher. Then he turns and, without looking back, walks away.

I slump down on his bed, holding onto my chest—feeling a pain I've never felt before. Not even with the panic attacks. I begin to sob. I don't know when Evie comes in—she doesn't say anything when she sits down, cradling my head in her lap as she strokes my hair. I cry for all the times I haven't been able to. For myself, Evie, and my Nana. But mostly, I cry for Nate—the one boy who I've ever truly wanted.

Chapter Eighteen

I walk around his garage, taking it all in. He would probably blow a fuse if he came back to find me in here, but he's nowhere to be found. He left in the early hours of this morning and hasn't been seen since. I cried myself into a fit of exhaustion—apparently, repressing emotions will do that to a person.

I've called him, left voicemails, and sent texts. I know he'll come back when he's ready, but the funeral's tomorrow. Not knowing if he'll turn up or not is enough to give anyone anxiety, especially me. I pause when I see a frayed spine on a shelf staked with books, and lean closer. *Well, I'll be damned.*

Thirteen years ago.

I can't wait to see Nate's face when I give him his present. I saved all my pocket money so I could buy it for him all by myself. I look down to my feet for the bag, but I don't see it.

"Mum, did you put Nate's present in the boot?" I ask, looking around my feet.

"No honey, you wouldn't let me. You said you had it, remember?"

"Yes, I went to the bathroom… Oh no, Mum, we have to go back. I left it on the stairs!"

"Sorry, sweetie. We're over half way now. He'll understand."

I feel the tears brewing—my lip always wobbles right before I cry. Nate says it makes me look silly.

I shake my head, my braid whipping me in the eye. "But, Mum, he'll think I didn't get him anything." I look to Nana, pleading with my eyes.

She takes my hand in hers and squeezes it gently. "Don't get upset, honey," she says, leaning over and kissing the top of my head.

I can't help it. I was looking forward to giving it to him. I can't believe I left it behind. I'm so stupid. I look out of the window, and for the first time, the snow-covered surroundings do nothing to lift my mood.

Mum pulls into a petrol station and turns off the engine.

"Right, everybody out. We have shopping to do."

She opens my door and holds out her hand for me to take. I look up. Her smile calms my nervous belly.

"Here's what we are going to do… We are each going to pick out a present, then, sweetheart, you can call this Nate's novelty surprise present. The next time you see him, you can give him his real present, okay?"

I nod, sniffing as we head into the petrol station.

Nana claps her hands together in agreement as Papi comes round to take my other hand in his.

"Let's go have us some fun," he says in French.

Inside, the mat chimes as we all walk across it. I go back and walk over it again. Papi laughs and winks at me.

"Everyone split up. Let's get a quick gift for Nate, Lawry, and Evie." Mum says.

I look around. There's no way I'm going to find anything in here. Papi is studying something in his hand, his glasses on the tip of his nose.

"Here, look at this sweetheart," he says, holding it out in front of me.

I hear Mum from somewhere in another aisle say, "English please, Papa."

He rolls his eyes and hands me a small box.

"A puncture repair kit," I say with a smile.

He nods and takes it back.

Nana looks chuffed as punch when we find her down the next aisle.

"Look at this," she says, dangling a fluffy, pink dice in front of me.

I stroke it—all soft, velvety—and I nod in agreement.

"Right, so we have something for Lawry and Evie. So that just leaves Nate," Mum says, with the *Mum's can fix anything* expression, holding two boxes of Cadbury's milk tray.

"Chocolate's always a good back up, don't you think?"

"Yes. Are one of those boxes for me?" I ask.

She laughs, but I don't know why. I was being serious. *All because the lady loves milk tray*, I say to myself, the TV advert coming to mind.

I scan the shelves behind her. When I see a magazine with a big shiny car and a girl on the front, I point it out. She scans along the shelf until her fingers land on the one that caught my attention.

"There, that magazine right there. He'll love it."

"Oh, this one?" she says, her face beaming. "That's a lovely idea, sweet pea, but that is a little old for Nate."

Papi coughs and covers his mouth. I scrunch my nose at him, but Mum swats his arm, giggling, as she grabs a few bags of sweets hanging off some hooks.

I look around again and see a book with a map on the front. *AA Road Atlas*. I pick it up but have to use both hands—it's so big and heavy.

"Perfect," Mum says. "That's everything. Let's go pay and get going. I don't know about you, but I'm ready for my Christmas dinner."

I smile, my finger tracing the fragile spine. It's funny how a forgotten gift became a holiday tradition. An uncomfortable sinking sensation settles in my stomach. That's two years I've missed being here for Christmas.

My butt buzzes, and when I pull it free, it drops to the floor. Hastily, I answer, not even looking at the caller ID.

"Hello," I say, breathless.

"Hello… Felicity?"

I'd recognise that faint Australian accent anywhere. "Charlie?"

"The one and only. Listen, I wish I was calling under different circumstances—"

My stomach lurches, I don't give him the chance to finish before I interrupt him

"Is he okay?"

"Define…*okay.* I mean, if you can call his stupid drunk-self okay, then yeah he's fine."

"Oh, shit. Has he said anything to you?"

"He was wired when he turned up at mine this morning, and it was only after he followed me here and after a few drinks that his tongue loosened. I'm in a bit of a predicament. I didn't want to call Evie for obvious reasons, so I stole your number out of his phone. I hope that's all right?"

"Of course," I say, pacing the length of the garage.

"I'll cut to the chase. I can't get away—I'm already short-staffed. But I'm worried he'll drink himself into oblivion and with the funeral tomorrow… I could cut him off, but he'll just leave here and go somewhere else—even if I did get him in a cab. I know he's not your responsibility, but is there any chance you might be able to come get him?"

I fiddle with my wrist. "He was so pissed at me earlier. I'm not sure if he'll cooperate, but what have I got to lose?"

"He feels like a dick about that—believe me. When he sees you, I doubt he'll put up a fight."

"I wouldn't be too sure about that." I don't know him—not really. He switched so quickly, and right after I was feeling so close to him. I had reservations in the back of my mind and look where *that* got me.

"Felicity, I wouldn't ask you if I thought for one minute he would turn on you. And I'd like to think you still remember me enough to know I've got your back. Yes, the tool is my best mate, but I know what he needs—he needs you."

Charlie's words are so sincere, and I have no doubts he's got my back. But it's Nate needing me at all that I'm doubtful about.

"Okay, I'll need the address…"

"I'll text it to you—sorry, shit I've got to go. Call me when you get here." With that, he hangs up.

I'm not about to disturb Evie or worry her any more than she already is. Instead, I go to the key cabinet—which is unlocked, *thank God*—and grab the ones I'm looking for. I enter the address into the Sat-Nav, which takes me a good ten minutes to figure out.

Breathing deep, I count to ten before I head out—my hands shaking and stomach turning the entire drive.

I ring Charlie when I come to a stop. "I'm here," I say, looking across the street at the address of the bar he gave me.

"Okay, just go to the main door. My bouncer is expecting you."

What? Is he serious?

"I can't come in. I'm not dressed for a bar."

I hear him bark something to someone before he comes back on the line. "I'll bring you out back to my office," he says.

I shake my head and close my eyes as I squeeze the leather of the steering wheel.

"Felicity, are you still there?"

"Yeah…*right.* See you in a sec."

I switch off the engine, glad I parked close to a street lamp. I take the key between my knuckles, holding it like a lifeline and force my body in the direction of the entrance. A group of people are milling around outside—smoking, avoiding all eye contact. I focus on the giant of a man before me, and my breath gets caught in my throat.

"Felicity?" he asks.

I nod. With that, a smile spreads across his face, and all of a sudden, he's not quite so intimidating. I give him a small smile in return. He takes my elbow so lightly, I'd hardly notice if I didn't see him do it. He leads me through a very crowded bar. I weave between people, elbows, and feet, the keys still tight in my grip.

A tap on my shoulder causes me to jump. A squeal gets caught in my throat. I peer over my shoulder, let out a breath, and turn. A very handsome Charlie stands before me. He pulls me in for a hug, kissing me on each cheek before letting go—it's a natural reaction for him, and I don't have time to object…even if I wanted to.

"Follow me," he yells over the noise, waving his hand in the direction of his office.

I'm working my way through the crowd when a tug on my elbow jolts me out of step. Air rushes from my lungs as the blurred face of a stranger appears in my line of vision.

"Hey, gorgeous," he says, invading my space.

I try to move his hand from my arm, but it doesn't budge. My heart thumps wildly in my ears, my eyes dart left and right. When Charlie pries the stranger's hand away from me, he steps between us, and signals for the bouncer.

"Get him out of here."

No questions asked, the giant nods, looks down at the man who's holding his hands up and tilts his head in the direction of the exit.

Charlie spins back in my direction and leads me to a door that opens into a small hallway. He waves a toggle over a square box, and then a green light appears as he pushes the door open, waiting for me to enter first.

I wrap my arms around my middle.

"Sorry, that guy was already on his last warning. Hey, are you all right?"

I nod and then shake my head as I breathe in through my nose and out through my mouth. He holds his hand towards a small, two-seat leather sofa, and I sit. He crouches down in front of me, unscrewing the lid from a bottle of water, then passes it to me. I take a few sips and collect myself. I can feel him watching me. I squeeze the keys that are still securely tucked in my hand.

"Punters, who'd have them?" he says with a crooked smile. He always was good at easing tension.

"I'm sorry about that… Not the guy, I mean my reaction. I'm jumpy these days," I say with a shrug, fiddling with the bottle between my palms.

"Jumpy or not, no one puts their hands on you without your permission. I don't give a fuck who they are."

I learnt early on that you don't mess with Charlie. He's protective of those he cares about—always sticking up for the underdog. One thing he hates more than anything is a bully. I always thought he'd make a great boyfriend to some lucky girl someday.

I glance around the space that is his office—a desk on the back wall, computer, printer, and some monitors…which I presume to be CCTV. Cabinets align the wall opposite the sofa, and there's a fridge and glasses on a shelf above.

He claps his hands together once. "You all right to hold up in here for a sec? I'll go get Nate. Last time I saw him, he was visiting the little boys' room for the umpteenth time. The door can only be accessed by staff, so you don't need to worry about any unwanted visitors."

I smile—him reassuring me as he exits the door makes my chest tighten. A humming vibrates through the wall from the thrum of people's voices melding into one. I peel the label off the bottle as the door beeps. Charlie reappears—sans Nate.

"I just spoke to my guy, Olly, who's tending the bar. He saw Nate leave with a friend. I literally just missed them. I should've locked his sorry arse in here," he says, a mixture of guilt and annoyance crossing his face.

"Do you think he'll be all right?" I can't hide my concern.

"He will if he sleeps it off. He'll probably crash at Rachel's." His eyes widen, then he clamps his mouth shut, stuffing his hands in his pockets.

"Right." I don't know how else to respond to that.

"She can be quite persistent when she wants. I mean—" He puts his hand on his head and rakes his fingers through his hair, looking as awkward as I feel.

"It's none of my business. As long as he's safe, that's all that matters," I say, chewing on the inside of my mouth.

"It's not like that… She's likely just looking out for him. They're friends."

I raise my eyebrows. *Friends, my arse*. Why he feels the need to cover for him is beyond me. It's not like we're together. But that doesn't stop the stab of jealousy that tugs at my insides. It's like Déjà vu all over again.

A beep sounds as a guy enters. I look up and am met with striking, violet eyes and a pierced eyebrow. I scan his biceps—a tattoo escapes the sleeve of his t-shirt. He smiles and winks at me, causing heat to rise in my cheeks.

"Hey, sorry to interrupt, but it's picking up out there," he says, pointing his thumb over his shoulder.

"Two minutes, Olly."

"Cool." He smiles at me and wiggles his fingers before leaving.

"Ignore him, he's our resident playboy," Charlie says, shaking his head.

"It's fine," I say, taking another sip of water.

"I need to get back out there… I feel like a dick for making you come down here—"

"Don't be, it is what it is," I say as I stand.

"Come, I'll walk you out." He tilts his head to the door.

I follow as he leads me through the crowd of people, then signals to the giant.

"Jase, I'm going to walk her out. Don't let anyone else in."

He nods and crosses his arms.

Charlie places the palm of his hand on the small of my back, walking beside me until we reach the car. I click *unlock.*

He pulls me in for a hug. "Please, let me know you get home, okay? And I'm sorry," he says, looking around.

"Don't be. I'll see you tomorrow, right?"

"Of course." He kisses my cheek, opens my door, waiting for me to get in. He closes it behind me and watches as I pull away.

I drive in a daze. It's only when I pull onto the gravel that it registers I'm back. I shake my head—zoning out like that and driving do not mix. I switch off the engine and stare at the steering wheel. I feel a stabbing sensation in my chest again, but I'm not sure if it's jealousy or my hurt pride. Up until now, I would question if I still had any pride. But I do. And it hurts. He's angry, and I get that, but doing a typical Nate and hooking-up makes me sick to my stomach.

Am I naïve for thinking we had something? We crossed a line. He made me feel so secure one minute, and then trampled on it the next. It's all bullshit, and I'm a fool for even thinking there was a chance for us—for me to have a semi-normal relationship.

A buzz in the cup holder draws my attention.

Charlie: *I hope you got home safe? Try not to be too hard on him. Once he sleeps it off, he'll see what a dick he's been. If you need anything, you know where I am. I'm sorry we didn't get a chance to catch up properly, see you tomorrow xo*

Me: *I just got home. See you tomorrow x*

I wipe at the moisture on my face—crying isn't going to fix anything, least of all this shit-storm. I just hope for everyone else's sake, he turns up tomorrow. Trying to cover for him with the rest of his family today has been a mission and a half. My only saving grace is that they are all staying in the cottage, not the main house. But come tomorrow, if he's a no-show… No amount of words are going to cut it.

Chapter Nineteen

Tense sleep eludes me, and although my body is lethargic, I know the only thing that will help me right now is to run.

I don't manage to get very far. My legs feel like they are drowning in quicksand, and I didn't eat much yesterday. I need to have a protein shake or something. A cramp in my calf causes me to cease-up. I lift my leg and grab hold of my ankle. Balancing, I try to stretch it out. Once I think it's subsided, I head back towards the house.

I hear tyres crunch on the gravel. It's too early to be anyone for the funeral—it must be Nate.

I walk a little faster as I round the far side of the house, stopping when I hear the echo of voices. It's Nate. I smile as I see him leaning against the passenger door of a car I don't recognise. I also see a girl standing close—*too close*. She moves so she's practically between his legs, and I strain my ears, trying to ignore my heartbeat so I can listen to what's being said.

"You sure I can't do anything else? Do you want me to come in with you?" Her hand touches his arm.

"No thanks, and I don't think that's a good idea." He looks towards the house.

She moves her hand to his cheek. "What about a kiss?"

Oh my God.

She touches him with familiarity, making my blood boil.

My body begins to tremble, as I suck in short, sharp breaths, the air around me thick. The tips of my fingers go numb as I squeeze my fists tightly. My stomach clenches in anguish.

I watch on, frozen where I stand, unable to look away. She goes onto her tiptoes, angling her lips over his. His hand goes up to the back of her neck. An involuntary gasp escapes my lips. I cover my mouth, stepping back out of sight. Bile rises up my throat, and I scuttle back the way I came as I dry heave into the nearest bush.

The worst-case scenario—I thought he might hook up with her. But seeing *that?* I spent all day yesterday worried about him, feeling guilt over my omission, and *covering for him* just to be...*played.* I swipe away tears from my face angrily as I head in through the back door so they won't see me. I sprint through the kitchen and take the stairs two at a time.

I shut my door quietly as I kick off my trainers. I go straight into the bathroom and start the shower. Stripping off my clothes, I step straight in—not even bothering to check the temperature. I find the flannel and scrub every inch of my body vigorously. I want to rid my body of every touch, every kiss from the past twenty-four hours. My tears mix with the spray of water as it ricochets off my body until my legs give out, and I slump into a crouching position. Then I let myself cry in silence.

After I'm dressed and downstairs, getting everything together for today, my mum arrives. I rush to her as she envelopes me in her arms.

"Sweetie?" she asks, pulling back to look at my face. She studies me for a moment before taking me by the hand. We walk into the living room, and she closes the door behind us.

"Talk to me?"

I go to speak, but the words are trapped behind unshed tears. She pulls me into a hug and rubs my back. I concentrate on her breathing and inhale her scent—it helps to calm me, in a way only my mum has the power.

"Oh, Mum… I don't know what happened. One minute, Nate and I are getting on, you know? Like the last couple of years didn't happen. And then the next, he overhears me talking to Evie about Lawry, whom it turns out isn't—I mean, *wasn't* his biological grandfather. Did you know? I only found out right before we flew out here. He's so angry, he thinks I kept it from him on purpose, that I betrayed his trust."

"Oh, sweetie…I agree it wasn't your place to tell him. Whatever their reasons are between Nate and his grandparents," she says, wiping my hair out of my face.

"You knew?"

She nods. "Do you remember when Lawry was really ill? He was admitted into hospital?"

I nod as she continues.

"Evie was in a right state, and it slipped out, so Nana explained it to me." She takes hold of my hands in hers. "Listen to me, Nate is going through a lot right now, and finding out something like that on top of it would mess with anyone's head. When Nana told me how close you'd become over the past week, I was taken aback. You don't trust as easily, but you and he have always had a bond."

I let out an almost snort at her words. "What? No, I mean—" I put my hands behind my back.

"Listen, I know this is overwhelming. Just work on getting through today, okay?"

I nod. "I love you."

"Not as much as I love you. Now, come on."

We head back into the kitchen, where she leaves me to find Nana.

The hairs on the back of my neck rise. I know it's him before I turn to confirm it. He pauses mid-step. My eyes meet his. I want to look away, and the petulant child inside tells me to give him the middle finger, but instead, I hold his stare before I turn back to the kettle.

His footsteps echo as his dress shoes meet with the marble floor.

I feel his breath on my neck before I hear his words. "Did you pick up my suit?"

I nod but don't look at him.

"And the headache tablets…was that you, too?"

I nod again and glance at him.

He stuffs his hands in his trouser pockets.

"Thank you."

I shrug. "I did it for Evie." My words have a hint of anger, which isn't like me. But it's the truth.

Whatever rebuttal he might have dies on his lips. I turn as Evie enters, an audible gasp escaping her lips. She covers her mouth, eyes welling up. He shifts, and then in two strides, he wraps her frail frame in his arms.

I choke back the sensation in the back of my throat. My nose tingles while I busy myself, making them both a cup of tea. I almost laugh at the irony and at Sophie's words. *Why do us Brits think tea solves everything*? Out of the corner of my eye, I see him pull away. He's about to make some kind of speech or apology—I don't know—but I don't want to be here to witness it. I clear my throat.

"I made you some tea. Why don't you go to the living room for some privacy? The caterers will be delivering the food any minute. I'll take care of it."

"Felicity, you sure, sweetheart?" Evie asks behind a sniff.

"Yes. I'm here to help."

"You, my dear, are an angel," she answers, causing my embarrassment to rise.

Nate walks back over and picks up both cups off of the counter. I shift towards the sink and work on wiping over the kitchen counter as they leave the room.

"Knock-knock."

I turn around.

"Charlie." It's nice to see a friendly face. He pulls me into a hug, which I accept gratefully—I'm not tactile, but it's clear Charlie is a hugger, and I think I need the re-assurance or something.

"So, is he here?" he asks, fiddling with the lid of the kettle.

"Yep, he's in the living room talking to Evie. He sure as hell owes her an apology," I say, shaking my head.

"He does. You look tired. What time did he get his sorry arse home?"

"Early. I saw, who I can only presume is Rachel, with her tongue down his throat when she dropped him home."

He grabs the back of his neck. "Ah shit. I don't know what to say."

I put my palm on his chest. "There's nothing you can say. Don't fret about it."

He places his hand over mine, giving it a gentle squeeze. We're interrupted when the caterers arrive with many trays of nibbles. Evie has always been an exceptional host, and today is no different. Charlie helps me organise them as we take them into the dining room.

Everything set, Charlie approaches me. "Promise you won't be a stranger after today? I've missed you, and so has he," he says, tilting his head.

"Well, he sure has a funny way of showing it."

"That he does."

I feel myself begin to well up but swallow hard to keep it at bay. Charlie palms my cheek and I lean into it.

Someone clears their throat.

I step back, and he drops his hand. I know it's Nate, and I can't stop the unease and heat that floods my body.

"The cars are almost here," he says, monotone.

"Hey, man. How are you feeling?" Charlie asks, walking towards him.

"Like shit, obviously," he snaps.

Charlie holds up his hands, palms facing Nate.

"Shit I didn't mean—" Nate says, but Charlie cuts off his poor attempt of an apology.

"Whatever, mate. Water off a duck's back." He pulls Nate in for hug and a loud pat on the back.

"I'll see you outside," Charlie says, and then looks at me, his lips quirking awkwardly as he leaves.

I follow suit, beginning to leave, but Nate stops me with a hand on my arm. I push it away.

"Wait, Flick."

"What is it, Nate?" I don't want to be a bitch, but I need to keep my shit together and get through the funeral.

"We need to talk… What was that I just saw with you and Charlie?"

My head shoots in his direction. I give him a long, hard stare.

"Are you flipping *kidding me*?" I try to keep my temper in check, but my breathing accelerates as my nostrils flare.

"Shit… I don't know what the fuck I'm saying."

I see moisture in his eyes, and my anger dissipates, slightly.

"Let's just go wait for the cars, okay? Evie needs you right now."

"I know, and I need you," he says.

I want to kick him in the shin and run away, but instead, I take his hand in mine.

"Let's go then." I pull him with me to go join the rest of the family as the cars begin to arrive.

The funeral is bittersweet. I couldn't contain my tears when I saw Nate crying. The only time he let me leave his side was when he helped carry the casket, and when he gave his eulogy. I held on to one hand, and Evie held onto the other. It was a beautiful service, and an even better turn out—to know he impacted this many people is a testament to the kind of man he was.

Back at the house for the wake, it's full of people. Nate, Evie and the family speak to everyone who has taken time to pay their respects. Mum had to leave straight after the service—she has a shift tonight and couldn't get cover. I wanted to leave with her, but I can't. Not yet.

I've been looking everywhere for Nana. Worry begins to line my stomach—she's not in her room, or anywhere else I can think to look. *Where would she go?* I head to the library on a whim—it's the only other place in the house I haven't checked. Sure enough, when I push open the door, she's there, her back to me, staring out of the window. I approach. She's holding a small book close to her chest.

"Hey, I've been looking for you. Are you okay?" I ask, touching her shoulder.

"Sorry, I didn't mean to make you worry. Are you all right?"

I nod. "I'm fine." It's times like this I wish I had a poker face like Papi.

She tilts her head. “No, you’re not.”

I look out of the window. “It isn’t important. Besides, today isn’t about me.”

“It *is* about you, though. Don’t you see?”

Oh, no. Today has clearly gotten to her. “See what?” I ask, worried. It’s hit her harder than I realised.

“You and Nate.”

My mouth falls open as I turn to look at her. “What about us? There is no me and Nate,” I say with a frustrated sigh, crossing my arms.

“’Course there is.”

I shake my head.

“I can tell you’re trying to fight it, and you have reasons, but whether you want to accept it or not, I believe you’re destined to be together. Now is probably not the best time for this talk, so for now, can this old Nana of yours ask a favour?”

“Of course, but you’re not old,” I say, crossing my eyes.

“I’m old—let’s not drink champagne on beer money, dear,” she says, smiling. “Now about that favour, come and give me a squeeze.”

I smile and embrace her, breathing her in deep. Her warmth wraps around me like my favourite blanket as remnants of Coco Chanel tickle my nose.

“So, am I correct in presuming you’ll be leaving tonight?”

I stiffen a little. “Yes. With everything, I think it’s for the best, and I need some breathing space. How did you know?” I ask, curious.

“I noticed your case was by the door in your bedroom.”

I nod. I packed it as soon as I got out of the shower—whether Nate came back today or not, my mind was already made up.

"I'm sorry for letting you down. If you need me to stay, I will. I'll tell Simon not to bother picking me up."

"No, dear, I'll be fine with Evie. I understand...but what about Nathaniel?"

"He'll be fine. He has Charlie," I reply, and maybe even Rachel if she shows up. I feel the bile rising, so I cough, hoping it will subside. The last thing I want is to be sick.

"Charlie isn't *you,* though, is he?"

I shake my head. A few stray tears manage to escape.

"It's good to see," she says and wipes my face with her hankie. "As heartbreaking as it to see you hurting, it's better than you bottling it up. It's good for the soul—to cry."

It's easy for her to say. I've never felt more vulnerable.

Standing alone, I'm holding onto a plate of untouched food like a lifeline when Charlie approaches.

"You've been great today," he says, knocking his elbow into my shoulder.

I stare up at him. "It's what you do for family," I say, trying to shake off the compliment.

"It's not just that... I saw how you never once pushed Nate away—not even after what he's put you through. You, my friend, are a saint."

"Well, I'm not going to lie, I was *this* close to kicking him in the shin." I hold up my thumb and forefinger with the tiniest gap. "He had the audacity to insinuate something was going on with you and me," I say, waving my hand between us.

Charlie pauses with his glass at his lips. "He what?"

"*Exactly.* I know, right? And then to top it off, I see Rachel arrive with someone who—it turns out—is her *fiancé.* I don't know why I feel guilty, it's not like I'm the one cheating."

"Ah yeah...that is fucked up—I mean, *complicated.* I don't understand it, if I'm honest. Nate hasn't seen her for ages."

"Well, it's none of my business, and I don't really want to talk about it. I know I've been absent, but it wasn't an easy decision, and believe it or not, I *do* care about them." I don't want to go into detail, and if anyone would understand, it's him. Growing up, he was always more of an observer than a talker.

"It's called family, but that doesn't mean I won't be giving him an earful once today is out of the way," Charlie says.

I shake my head, beginning to collect plates. He falls in step beside me to help. It makes me smile when I see how many glasses he can collect—you can take the boy out of the bar, but you can't take the bar out of the boy.

A vibration alerts me to what I've been dreading. Simon is here.

"Charlie, you're going to think I'm a right heartless bitch, and the timing couldn't be worse, but I asked my friend to come pick me up. I need space. There's a lot to process. Can you promise me you'll look after Nate?"

"Of course. I don't think badly of you. Yes, he'll be crushed, but you have to do what's right for you. If anyone can understand that, it's me."

"I know I'm a coward, but I was hoping you could tell him once I'm gone. I'll ring him in a few days."

He looks torn but thankfully agrees. I go to find Evie and Nana.

"I'm really sorry that I'm leaving it's just with everything—"

Evie shushes me. "I understand, honey. He was hard on you, and I told him as much this morning. Just promise you won't leave for so long next time? You're like a granddaughter to me."

I nod, pulling her into a hug. "Of course, I won't," I whisper into her ear.

"Nathaniel might be by the tree house if you wanted to say goodbye," she says, hope in her voice.

I nod even though I have no intention of going to him. I don't know if I'll have the willpower to leave if I do. It's all too claustrophobic—being here at the moment.

Case in tow, I wait outside. Most of the guests have already left, so it's just the sound of Simon's car as it comes up the drive. He stops and climbs out, opening his arms. I go to him.

"Baby girl, sorry, but you look like shit."

"Thanks," I say into his chest.

He pulls back to look at me.

"Do you need to say goodbye? Or are you ready to go?"

"I'm ready." I smile as Sophie waves at me from the passenger seat. Simon throws my case into the boot while I climb into the back seat.

"Hey, you okay?" she asks, straining in her seat belt to look around.

"I've been better."

Simon gets in the car, about to pull away, but he pauses as I tap his shoulder.

"Seatbelt."

He rolls his eyes, staring at me from the rear-view mirror, but clips it into place.

"Satisfied?" he asks.

I hear my name being called and look out of the window to see Nate.

Shit.

"Go, Simon."

"Sweetness, I can't...he saw us looking."

I let out a frustrated sigh, unclip my belt, and get out of the car.

"Flick?" asks Nate, breathless as he jogs over to me. His tie is loose, the top button of his collar undone. I get the faint whiff of alcohol, causing my nose to twitch.

"Nate," I reply, crossing my arms.

"Charlie told me you're leaving."

I look over his shoulder. Charlie shrugs, hands in the air as if to say, *sorry*.

"Yeah, I'm going to Simon's for a few days."

He nods in Simon's direction. I look behind me. Apparently, he also got out of the car. His body language is guarded as he stands with his door open. Simon waves back to Nate—*not awkward at all.*

Nate leans closer. "Is this because of what happened yesterday?"

I lean away from the vapours of his drink-laced breath. "No, not really." I'm lying, I know I am, and so does he. I can't do this—not now.

"I'm sorry. The things I said were unjustified," he says, stuffing one hand in his pocket, pulling on his tie with the other.

"I understand. It wasn't the best way for you to find out," I say. My voice doesn't sound like my own.

"Please, Flick," he says, his look pleading.

But his words from yesterday haunt me—the way he turned so easily. And then seeing him with Rachel felt like a knife to the gut. I shake my head and hug him. Not giving him a chance to reciprocate, I pull back.

"I'll call you in a few days," I say as I try hard to keep the tremble from my voice.

"Can't you stay? So we can talk after everyone has gone?"

I shake my head. "Sorry, Nate, I can't."

I turn away from him, climb back in, and fasten my seatbelt.

Simon follows suit.

"Please, can we go now?" It's more of a plea than a request. My lips wobble. He looks at me in the mirror, eyebrows drawn in a V shape. He pulls the car away quicker than expected. Sophie looks quizzically at Simon and then strains to look at me. Her eyes go wide.

"Hell, to the no," she states, looking angry.

I look back out the window. Charlie's standing next to Nate, hand on his shoulder. Nate's head is hung low. I face forward as my sobs rattle through my body.

"Simon, stop the car *now*."

I flinch, ready to freak out. I don't want him to stop the car. I shake my head as she unclips her seatbelt. She turns in her seat, and unceremoniously, climbs over the centre console, landing in the back of the car at an odd angle. Then she tugs on her seatbelt.

"Go," she demands.

He does as he's told. The tyre wheels spin as he hits the accelerator.

She puts her arm over my shoulder, bringing my body as close to her as she can. Another onslaught of tears wreak havoc. Simon turns on the radio, and with the worst possible timing, the first line of *Against All Odds* by Phil Collins explodes through the speakers. He panics as he turns the volume up before switching it off, calling out *sorry* over his shoulder.

Chapter Twenty

Nathaniel

How did this just happen? Intimate moments we shared to a devastating revelation. I still can't quite digest that Gramps isn't my real Gramps, or that I keep thinking about him in present tense even though he's gone, but watching her *leave?* I felt like I lost a part of myself.

"I seriously thought she changed her mind when his car stopped earlier, man," I say to Charlie.

"Yeah, me too," he replies.

"Shit, what the fuck have I done?" I rake my hands through my hair—on the verge of pulling it out.

"I hate to be the one to point out the obvious, but you've fucked up, my friend. That girl came to pick you up last night. It didn't help that some prick grabbed her arm… I've never seen her look like that. I thought you were exaggerating about her anxiety, but you weren't."

I round on him, clenching my fists. "What the *fuck?* Did he hurt her?"

He shakes his head. "Of course not. I kicked him out. She waited in my office while I came back to get your sorry arse. But the fool that you are, you left with Rachel—oh and she saw her drop you off this morning, by the way."

He raises his eyebrows, waiting for my response.

"What the hell? Why didn't you *tell* me?" I ask, throwing my arms in the air.

"I didn't have the chance. Besides, I didn't think today was appropriate to start questioning your piss-poor judgement. Why you had your tongue down Rachel's throat is beyond me. Even more so when you have someone as special as Felicity bending over backward for you."

"It wasn't what it looked like. Nothing even happened with Rachel."

"And what did it look like? She saw her mouth on yours, dude," he says, clipping me around the ear hole.

I flinch. "I don't even know what happened… One minute, she was talking to me, and the next, her lips were on mine. I stopped it as soon as my brain registered. And *honest to God,* I didn't do anything with her last night, either. I was in no fit state, and even if I were, it wouldn't have happened. Flick is all I think about," I say, sitting down and unlacing my shoes. I pull off my socks and stuff them inside.

"Listen, it's not me you need to convince. I know you're hurting—it was a lot to handle, but for some dumb reason, she doesn't seem to believe you actually care about her."

"What? She said that?"

"Not those exact words, but the girl clearly has self-esteem issues, and whatever transpired between you two hasn't helped."

I pull at a handful of grass. "I was a complete *prick.* She tried to calm me down, but I only saw red. I completely went off on one about her and Simon, but what's worse, I used something bad that happened to her, *against her*." I feel sick to my stomach. Scrubbing my face with my hand, I jump up and rush to the bin by the garage—emptying the contents of my stomach.

"Shit, man. What the hell happened to her?"

I wipe my mouth with one of the hankies I think Flick loaded in my pocket. Fucking hell, even after the way I treated her, she still does shit like this.

"It's so bad—what I threw at her—honestly, if she never spoke to me again, I wouldn't blame her. It's not my story to tell, but the guilt is killing me, man." *I have to talk to someone.* "Promise me you won't mention this to her unless she does?"

"You don't even have to ask. I'll take it to my grave if I have to."

I nod—of course he would. "I know. Sorry, I think I need to take the edge off."

I go into the garage, grab the tequila, two glasses, and a bottle of water. I down half the water, then pour us a shot of tequila each. I pass him his, and he gives me a wide-eyed look.

"Believe me, you're going to need it."

He accepts it and knocks it back. I take a seat in one of the chairs by the open door of the garage, bottle in hand. Wiping my sweaty palms down my suit trousers, I take a deep breath and tell him what she told me.

He looks as sick as I feel, shaking his head. "And what happened to the arseholes? Were they prosecuted?" he asks, clenching his fists.

I shake my head. "No, that's the worst part. The place they woke up in was being used by squatters—no trace of who they were. There wasn't enough evidence or some bullshit like that."

"Fuck, and you used this *against* her?"

"Yeah," I croak out. Ashamed is an understatement. I crumble from the weight of what I did—feeling no better than those scum bags who violated her. I dig my palms into my eyes, not giving two shits what I look like. I hurt her, and then to top it off, she sees the whole fucked-up Rachel situation. I swallow the lump in my throat, unable to hold back my tears.

"You need to grovel. Tell her what a dick you were and *still are*. I'm not going to lie, I could totally kick your arse right now."

"And I'd deserve it."

"But it wouldn't change anything. You're a good guy, Nate. I know you'd never have said it if you were in your right mind. Let's put it down to grief."

"I don't know what to do. How the hell am I going to fix this?"

He shakes his head. "First off, we might as well finish *this—*" he grabs the bottle, "—and when you're hungover, and feeling your worse possible self, we'll begin Operation Get Felicity Back. You have a lot of work ahead of you."

"What if she never forgives me? She trusted me, and I threw it back in her face." Talk about a self-pity party.

"I don't know, but we'll think of something. You'll have to pull at those heartstrings of hers. Is your Nan still holding the Help for Heroes charity event?"

I nod, the tequila kicking in. "Yeah, she said Gramps wouldn't want it to be cancelled."

"Then, we'll start there."

I wake the next day like death warmed up, with the king of all hangovers. Like this isn't punishment enough, I have a day of chores ahead of me—no rest for the wicked. All day, I have been ignoring the letter that's been sitting on my desk. It's pathetic, but truth is I don't want to read it on my own…it means accepting he really is gone.

I grabbed the letter and jogged over to the tree house. I've been sitting here, with my legs dangling over the edge for the past hour, turning the envelope over in my hands.

It's not going to open itself.

I take a deep breath and rip it open. The paper I pull out holds his final words he'll ever leave me.

Nate,

Son, if you're reading this, it can only mean one thing. Believe me, I fought the disease, but when your times up, it's up. I can't complain. I've been truly blessed to have you all in my life.

I never talked to you about this, but it was hard for me growing up. My family didn't show affection, they never said I love you or told me everything was going to be all right. They just weren't wired that way.

I tried to be a good man. I never wanted any of you to feel unwanted, or worse— unloved like I did. All of you have always been the most precious parts of my life.

This is why what I'm about to say may cause you to doubt me, but I pray to God it doesn't. Truth is, I never found the courage to tell you while I was still here. I'd always find an excuse—your parents' death or my illness—I used it as an out.

I saw first-hand how these things affected you, and I didn't want to add to your pain.

My best friend growing up was Samuel. We named your father after him. He was like a brother to me. We did everything together. Even though we were from very different backgrounds, we never let anything come between us.

Like the young fools we were, we enlisted in the RAF, but he was killed during a training exercise. It was the first time in my life I experienced death and understood what it was like to lose someone I loved.

God, we were so naïve. We thought we were invincible, with the world at our feet. But the reality was and still is...life is fleeting.

Your Nan had been courting him, and already devastated with her grief, she found herself pregnant and alone. Her parents had no idea about their relationship, of course, but that was both a blessing and a curse.

He had been planning on asking her father for her hand in marriage. I was the one who broke the news to her, and if I thought she was distraught before, I was sadly mistaken.

Ana and I had been courting for over a year. In my mind, the two of us would marry and raise a family in a loving home where we could grow old together. She was my first love.

I spent so much time agonising over the situation. Eventually, I came up with what I thought was the only solution—a marriage of convenience to Evie.

Of course, she refused. She wouldn't do that, not to Ana and me. Even back then, she had the biggest heart of anyone I'd ever met. It was Ana who talked her into it in the end. She told her that if she couldn't do it for herself, then she had to think of the baby.

She knew her family would disown her if they found out the truth, so she agreed.

The day we married, I felt like it was happening to someone else. Ana supported us through it all, even though I knew it was breaking her heart while she stood by and watched.

But I had to believe it was the right thing to do, and if it was Samuel instead of me, and our roles were reversed, that he'd do the same.

It wasn't until Samuel Junior turned fourteen that he became curious and began asking questions. He didn't look anything like his brothers or me. He was the spitting image of Sami. Your father always was too intuitive for his own good. Evie and I discussed it long and hard before sitting him down. He took it better than we'd expected, of course he did, he was like Evie—empathetic to a fault.

I fell for her during that first year of our marriage. I didn't want to, I was still in love with Ana. I struggled with my conscience, my head and my heart telling me two different things. Being in love with both of them was like my heart had been ripped in two, but everything worked out how it was supposed to in the end.

I'm sorry I never told you. All I ever wanted was to be your protector. I hope that in time, you'll find a way to forgive an old, foolish man. Try not to harbour any ill feelings towards your Nan. God only knows she's suffered enough for one lifetime. And the thought alone cripples me—knowing I won't be there to ease her pain, to look after her. She'll need you now more than ever.

You are and always will be loved, and I'm proud of the man you've become. Don't be afraid to reach out to your Uncles or Aunt. Nothing has changed now I'm gone... Family is still everything.

Knowing I won't see you settle down and start a family of your own is a low blow, but you'll make a good husband and an even better father. The thought brings me joy.

You and Felicity may have drifted apart, but she has her reasons, and I have faith the two of you will find your way back to one another. And when the day comes for you to find the courage to ask her the most important question of your life... Your Nan and I would be honoured if you gave her Samuel's engagement ring...the one intended for your grandmother.

It's a daunting feeling—leaving—but I finally get to see my best friend again. I hope he isn't disappointed in how I raised Samuel Junior, and that I've made him proud.

Remember to always be true to yourself, to embrace life and love fiercely. Respect the life you've been given and remember it's a gift, not a given right.

Love always,

Your Gramps

I fold the letter carefully and place it back in the envelope. Then I wipe my face with my sleeve and look up to the sky.

"Hey, Gramps. I miss you so damn much, and I promise I'm going to do my best to make this right."

Chapter Twenty-One

Nate has been relentless since I bailed on the day of the funeral. Although I haven't spoken to him on the phone, he's been texting, and it wasn't long before I caved and began replying to him.

"What's up?" Sophie asks. The sofa dips as she plops down beside me, munching on an apple—she loves apples.

"Just my Nan being persistent about this fundraiser. It's not like it's just for the day, either, it's the whole weekend. There's only one way I'll be able to cope. I can't do it on my own, and that's why you're coming with me."

"What? No way, count me out," she says, shaking her head.

I turn to her and clasp my hands together. "Please? You used to go to those church shindigs all the time."

Her mouth gapes open, a chunk of uneaten apple in view. As soon as the words have left my mouth, I know I've put my foot in it.

"That's different." She chews the rest of her apple and swallows with a contorted look on her face.

"Exactly, so you'll come?"

She raises her eyebrows. "What the heck, you're serious? I don't want to… But I'll do it. But only on one condition."

I bounce up and down. “Anything.”

“If I have to go, then so does Simon,” she replies with a smirk.

“So does Simon what?” he asks, walking in, covered in sweat from his workout. He takes a huge gulp of water, perching on the arm of the sofa.

“A fundraiser at Nate’s for the whole weekend,” she replies, cutting her eyes at me.

He slaps his thigh. “Oh, *goodie*, count me in.”

Sophie looks at me, her eyes wide at his enthusiasm.

“Geez, gay much?” she says with a shake of her head.

He punches her in the arm. She’s quick as she shoves him, and he jumps up and grabs her in a headlock, sticking his sweaty armpit near her face.

“Simon, get your stink off me,” she says, trying to cover her nose.

He lets go, laughing to himself. “So, what are you going to wear?”

Sophie shakes her head. “No idea.”

I shrug.

“Excellent, I’m going to shower then we’ll go hit the shops. How about Bluewater?”

I don’t bother to answer, and neither does Soph. He’s already made his mind up.

“This is going to be so much fun,” he calls over his shoulder as we watch him swagger from the room.

“This is your fault,” she says, poking her tongue out at me.

She dislikes shopping even more than I do.

“Yeah, but he always treats us to the best lunch.”

She smirks. “That’s true.”

Friday has come around way too quickly. I've had text messages from Nate every day, but we are yet to talk. He hasn't brought up what happened, other than to say he wants to talk to me in person about it. My stomach is drowning in nervous knots. I want to pretend it never happened, that he didn't walk away when the going got tough. That he didn't make me *feel* and tear down my walls as the dam flooded my inner psyche.

I keep seeing him, standing there with *her.* The way she was so familiar with him, her hands unafraid to touch him as her lips found his.

I shake away the thoughts.

"Just a friendly warning. Nate's friend, Charlie, will be there...and let's just say he's hot. So, just be wary around him," I say, looking over my shoulder to Sophie, who's sitting in the backseat

"Don't worry, I'll keep my hands off. Besides, that would be forever awkward especially when you marry Nate," she replies, arching her eyebrows.

Simon lets out a snort of laughter.

"What the fuck? Why would you say that? I'm nervous as it is. Have you been drinking?" The words leave my lips before I have time to think about them.

Simon stretches his arm over and squeezes my thigh.

"No, of course I haven't, but by all means, feel free to insult me some more. After all, I am here doing *you* the favour," she says and flips me off. She turns her face away and stares out the window.

My insides churn in discomfort as my voice comes out unsteady. "Sophie, I'm sorry. It wasn't meant as an insult to you...let's just say he is a little promiscuous."

"Well, what makes you think it's her you need to worry about?" Simon says with a wink into the rear-view mirror, catching Sophie's eye.

"Unfortunately for you, he only likes beautiful women," I say, looking at Sophie.

"Well, do you know what I think? You're hormonal, and the sooner you and Nate get it on, the better," Simon says, holding out his fist over his shoulder.

Sophie sits forward as she snorts, and fist bumps him back, just as we pull into the driveway. The stones crunch relentlessly under rubber until we come to a stop.

"Okay, sweetness, you ready for this?" Simon asks as he swivels in my direction.

I shake my head, pulling my ponytail over my shoulder as I work my fingers through the ends.

Sophie unclips her belt and sits forward, her head between the headrests.

Simon rubs his hands together. "You've got this. You are one of the best people I know, current company included of course," he says, with a wink, Sophie nodding in acknowledgement. "If you want this thing with Nate to go somewhere, you need to stop thinking with this." He taps my temple. "And start acting with this," he finishes, pointing to my chest.

"Baby girl, please don't let the fears of the past dictate your future. You need to start believing in yourself again. There's only one of you—you're one of a kind."

I swallow hard. As cheesy as it sounds, he always knows how to hit a nerve with me. I swat his arm—what we like to call a love punch—playing off his compliment.

"Tell me again why we didn't work?"

"Easy, you're a girl," Sophie says, deadpan.

"Bingo. Under any other circumstance, you'd have been one hell of a lucky lady. But look on the bright side, you get the better option—my unconditional friendship—which will last a lifetime."

Sophie makes a fake gagging sound. Clearly, this is getting way too sentimental for her.

"Okay, girls, enough of this soppy shit. I don't know what self-help books you've been reading, Simon, but maybe knock them on the head for a bit. Flick, just try not to overthink things. And on that note, I'm out," she says and exits the car.

Simon and I both laugh. For all her rough edges, she really is as soft as a kitten.

"She said *shit*," Simon says, shaking his head.

I plant a kiss on his cheek and get out.

I feel as though I'm being watched. The hairs on the back of my neck stand on end. I turn around, and sure enough, I come face to face with Nate.

Swirls of light surround him like a halo. My throat tightens. Our eyes lock and I have to remind myself to breathe.

Sophie clears her throat to break the trance I find myself in.

"I'm Sophie, and you must be?" she asks, looking at him expectantly, knowing full well who he is.

"Nate. It's good to finally meet you," he replies. With a warm smile, he kisses her on each cheek—very smooth.

"Likewise," she says, returning his smile.

"I'm Simon." Sticking out his hand, he practically shoves Sophie off to the side.

Nate nods and shakes his hand once before letting go.

He steps towards me, closing the distance. I have yet to move, I don't think I could if I wanted to. He leans in and pulls me in for a hug, his warm breath tickling my neck—alighting my senses. Causing my pulse to race.

"Hey, is this a private party? Or can anyone join in?" Charlie says. He moves past Nate to take his place, picking me up and lifting me off my feet.

I let out a squeal.

Before he sets me back down, he whispers in my ear, "I'm glad you're here."

I glance over my shoulder. "These are my friends, Simon and Sophie."

"Nice to meet you," he says, taking Simon's hand first.

I watch as he moves to Sophie—it's almost predatory, his eyes scanning the length of her. He kisses her cheek.

Hold on, is she blushing? I try to hide my smirk.

"So, Sophie, tell me, are the rumours true?" he asks.

"What rumours?" she replies, cutting her eyes at him.

"All good, I assure you."

She tilts her head, a hand on hip. "I'll be the judge of that."

He taps his nose. "A secret squirrel tells me you make cupcakes to die for."

Her mouth gapes open before she licks her lips. I don't know what she thought he was going to say, but she looks relieved. He offers her his arm. She looks at it, then back to him before she takes it. As he pauses to take her bag, she glances over her shoulder, and mouths the word, *womaniser*.

I can't help but laugh as they walk away.

"Oh righty then," Simon says, looking bemused by their interaction.

"So, I hear you like cars?" Nate offers.

Is this what they call a male icebreaker?

"Did you, now?" He grins and winks at me.

Nate nods his head towards the garage. “Want to have a look before we head in?”

“Can do,” he says, falling into step with Nate.

I follow as they chat like they’re old friends. I need a time out. This is so surreal.

“I’ll leave you to it. I’m going to head in,” I tell them.

They both nod.

Nate’s eyes land on me before I turn and walk through the garage and into the back of the house. I stop as soon as I’m out of sight, but apparently, not out of hearing distance. I lean against the wall, the coolness of the bricks welcome.

“Okay, now we’re alone… I know you’ve got something to say, so let me have it,” Nate says. I don’t hear hostility in his voice…more a resigned fact.

“Fair enough,” Simon begins. “I don’t know you. I only know what she’s told me. But I couldn’t love that girl more than if she were my own flesh and blood, so you can’t even begin to imagine how I felt seeing her that upset. If it weren’t for the events of the day, I would have turned the car around and had it out with you, but I’d never want to add to her pain.”

I hear a sigh, which most likely comes from Nate. I can imagine what his hands are doing—sweeping through his hair, or wiping his palm over his face.

“I feel the same, and believe me, I never meant to hurt her. I swear that, too. I know I fucked up. My behaviour was diabolical, and I’ll do whatever I have to so I can make it up to her.”

“I don’t doubt your intentions, but seeing her cry like that was enough to bring me to my knees. She hasn’t been that upset since she found out what those scum bags—”

I can’t listen to any more of this. My chest becomes tight as it strangles my breath.

The smell of that room—the unfamiliar sheets, the yellow stained ceiling—comes flooding back like a tsunami. The memories threaten to consume me.

I stumble through the kitchen door and slam into something hard.

"What the hell… Are you all right?"

It's Charlie.

His voice is distorted as arms wrap around my middle. Panic settles over me. I struggle for air.

"Sit her down."

It's like I'm on a cloud—floating—removed from reality. I put my head between my knees, trying to regain deep, even breaths.

A hand rubs my back.

"Flick?" Nate—a blurry form kneeling in front of me.

I feel him, his familiar scent wrapping itself around me.

"What did you do?" Sophie asks, clearly annoyed.

I'm not sure whom she's speaking to until Simon pipes up.

"Nothing. She left us in the garage to come in here. I was just talking to Nate," he hisses back at her.

"About what?" She doesn't beat around the bush

"Just—"

I peer out of the corner of my eye as he raises his palms in the air. The room falls silent, apart from the low buzz that hums through my ears.

Nate lets out a sigh, his hand on my thigh. No one else says anything, but I feel eyes all over me.

"I just need a minute," I say as I get to my feet.

Nate stands. "I'll go with you."

I shake my head. "No, I just need a minute."

He stops as I walk away. I avoid everyone as I force my feet to move, concentrating on putting one foot in front of the other until I'm in the confines of my room.

I take a seat at the window, pulling my knees up to my chest, and stare out the window. A numb feeling settles over me as I shut everything out. I don't feel. I don't think. I just breathe.

A knock on the door brings me out of my trance, but I don't move to answer. The turn of the handle, the crack of the door, and squeak of the floorboard gives away someone has entered.

I know it's him.

I'd feel him anywhere.

I peer over the top of my knees. His eyes are focused with worry, and my fingers itch to smooth away the lines that have settled over his forehead.

"I needed to make sure you were okay." He reaches his hand towards me, but I move to my feet.

"Why wouldn't I be? Just another one of my episodes, nothing new there."

He puts his hands in his pockets, rocking on his heels. "I'm sorry. This was my fault."

"What? Don't be ridiculous. It's not like you were there. This was all because a couple of stupid, naive girls went to a party with strangers."

I scrunch my toes up in my pumps, and squeeze my fists closed, my nails digging into my palms.

"No, that wasn't your fault. But I'm talking about what happened downstairs. I fucked up. The way I spoke to you when I found out about my Gramps? Charlie told me you came to get me, and I know what you saw when *she* dropped me off, but it's not what you think—"

"Nate, I don't want to hear it. Look, I don't know what you want from me, but whatever it is, I can't give it to you."

I'm holding on, my emotions threadbare, ready to snap at any moment.

"I don't want anything from you except for you to be present...to at least hear me out."

I sit back down. He lets out a puff of air as he sits on the edge of the bed, facing me.

"It's important you know I never slept with her, and when she kissed me here at the house, I was stunned for a second, but I pushed her away when I registered what was happening. She knows I'm not interested in her—not like that. We had a thing for a while, but not anymore," he says, clasping his hands together between his knees.

"Well, good for you, and your restraint—not sleeping with her for old time's sake. Round of applause."

I don't know what's wrong with me, but I can't stop the poison from crossing my lips. He looks offended but continues, anyway.

"I left with her because I wasn't thinking... She suggested taking me to hers to sleep it off. I had no idea Charlie rang you. Otherwise, I wouldn't have gone."

If he thinks this is making me feel any better, he's sorely mistaken.

"I'm not an invalid, Nate. I can go to a damn bar and not lose my shit. Besides, it's irrelevant—you were already being taken care of."

The words taste as bitter as they sound, even to me, but the green-eyed monster has well and truly nestled between the cracks of my insecurities.

"I deserve that. We may not be together, but it's important you trust me enough to know it wasn't like that."

"You don't owe me an explanation. Like you said, we're not together, so it's really none of my business." I pinch the skin on the underneath of my arm, desperate to be alone, to find a release.

He stands, pacing. "But I *want* it to be your business. God, don't you see? You must know how much I care about you. Fucking hell, Flick, if I could be with anyone, it would be you. It's *always* been you."

He slumps down beside me. My whole body buzzes from his admission. The room fills with heat. What am I supposed to say?

"I don't think you know what you want. Grief has a peculiar way of blurring the lines."

I squeeze my eyes closed. What the fuck is wrong with me?

"You're wrong, I know what I want."

The way his eyes hold mine causes my heart to race. I swallow hard.

"I don't know what to say… I opened up to you more in a few days than I have with anyone in a long time. You hurt me, Nate. I don't know if I could trust you like that again. At best, maybe we could work on trying to salvage our friendship."

I went there—I pulled out the friendship card.

"You *can* trust me. I'll find a way to prove it to you. And after, if it's just friendship you want, I'd rather *that* than not having you in my life at all."

I nod, not trusting myself to answer.

A knock sounds, followed by Sophie as she steps into the room.

"Sorry to interrupt," she says.

"It's fine. I'll see you at dinner." He looks away before leaving without another word.

"Talk about bad vibes. There's only one thing for it, bunny, and that, my friend, is a cat nap—a close second to a cup of tea."

She flings herself on the bed, patting the space beside her. I force myself to join her. Together, we stare at the ceiling like it has all the answers.

"Want to talk about it?"

Where would I even begin? I turn to look at her, letting out a breath.

"I friend-zoned him, can you believe that? What a cliché. I want to be more, but it freaks me out."

"It'll be all right. Time will tell, you'll see." She squeezes my hand.

I feel a pang of guilt for making her come with me. I know why she stopped going to her church, to events like this, but she's here for me anyway. When other friends looked at us with silent pity in their eyes or fell off the grid because they didn't know what to say or do, she stayed. Her friendship never faltered. It didn't waver, not even once. Deep down, I hate what happened, but I'm also grateful that I didn't go through it alone. She is a force to be reckoned with, and the embodiment of loyalty and friendship.

Chapter Twenty-Two

The bed dips when Simon scoots in between us, wriggling around, complete space invader.

"Hey, bitches."

Sophie's fist connects with his shoulder. "Do you have to say '*bitches*'?"

He sure knows how to push her buttons. I can't help but smile—such a wind-up merchant.

"No, I just love to watch your pretty little nose scrunch up like that," he says, tapping her on the nose.

She looks at me, eyebrows raised, leaning up on her elbows.

"Get him," she announces as she dives and begins to tickle him. I join in—solidarity in numbers, besides, girls rule and boys drool.

He makes a noise between a squeal and a groan as he grabs for a pillow. Holding it like a shield, he stands, and the whole mattress sinks in the middle as he raises it above his head.

"Don't you dare," I say, grabbing for the nearest cushion within my reach.

Sophie is already armed.

Pillows collide with faces, butts, arms—it's full-on war. As we scream and swing like our very dignity depends on it.

The door bursts open, bringing us all to a standstill, our breathing heavy, appearances dishevelled. Nate stands, looking perplexed, taking in each and every one of us before speaking.

"I heard screaming… I thought—" he shakes his head, "—never mind sorry." He turns his back to leave.

I scramble off the bed and race to the door, following him out. Still hanging onto the pillow, I swing it and hit him on the arm.

"Nate, wait."

His pupils dilate as he stops to look at me.

"I didn't mean to barge in like that, I heard you scream—"

I can't stop the laugh that escapes my mouth.

"It's not funny, Felicity, I thought something was wrong."

My laugh dies on my lips. "We were messing about. Big kids, what can I say?" I shrug.

He looks over my face.

"Do you think we could talk again later?" I ask, squeezing hold of the pillow.

I made Simon and Sophie come with me in the hopes that I could use them as some sort of barrier between Nate and me, but who am I kidding? His words from earlier have settled in my memory like a brand.

"Yes, okay." He smiles, and I swear it's the one he reserves only for me—the one that says, *you are worthy*. My insides tighten as I chew on my lip.

"That look suits you by the way," he says.

"What look?"

I glance down at myself, and then back up to him. He reaches out his hand to tilt my chin towards him.

"Happiness. I saw it on your face when I walked in. It's still there—like an afterglow."

My body hums with heat. "I'm just really lucky to have friends like them."

I glance back toward the door. We may be a little messed up, but they are my surrogate family, and I wouldn't change them for the world.

"No, see that's where I disagree… They're the lucky ones to have you."

I go to shake my head, but when his palm cups my cheek, my body leans into it like the needle of a compass—finding north. I close my eyes and relish the contact. It's so light, I think I might be imagining it. His breath tickles my lips, followed by a feather-light kiss. A small gasp escapes me as he pulls back, just a fraction. I open my eyes.

His voice is low. "I'm sorry, Flick, but I can't just be friends with you."

I want to say the same to him, but the words are locked in my throat. He takes a step back and drops his hand from my face.

Simon comes bowling out of my room, Sophie glued to his heels.

"We're going to go get ready for dinner, see you guys in a bit. Oh, and don't do anything I wouldn't do," he says over his shoulder as they walk away.

I choke on my embarrassment. I'd bet my favourite book they were eavesdropping at the door.

Nate looks as if he's about to follow them, but I grab hold of his hand and tug him inside my room, clicking the door shut behind us. I take a deep breath before I turn around. He's so close, we're toe to toe.

"Nate—"

How do I say what I want to say when I can't even form the words? The look he gives me is one full of reverence, all the while my insides fight an internal battle with my will. I do what I've wanted to do since I got here.

I go onto my tiptoes and cover his lips with mine. His hand goes to the back of my neck, tipping it enough to deepen the kiss.

He is the light of hope and everything in between. I'd been living in my own shadow for so long, I'd forgotten that colour was a feeling, too, and here he was—about to reignite my soul.

The backs of my knees connect with the bed. I didn't realise we'd moved. He slowly lays me down, and leans over me, supporting his weight on his elbows.

"Always so beautiful, Felicity."

My stomach aches, a deep want settling low between my legs. I reach up. My hand trembles as I stroke his jaw. Our lips gravitate towards each other, my pelvis shifting of its own accord.

He leans more weight on me, so I'm flush with the bed. Then raises slightly, the light trace of warm fingers trailing a path over my body…down to my stomach, to my thighs, finally brushing between my legs.

Every touch has my body sparking to life. My breathing accelerates. His eyes flutter to mine, a luminous smile gracing his face. I lick my lips and swallow hard as desire sweeps through me.

He pushes his hand up and under my dress.

My legs part—a silent invitation.

He strokes me before he moves my knickers to the side, slipping his finger inside with slow, deliberate ease, closely followed by another. My walls tighten around them as I push off the bed.

Every experience with him makes another brick come loose from the wall I've erected. I open myself to him. I move my head, intending a nod, and open my eyes. Looking down, he's obscured from my view, his head between my legs. Hot breath washes over my thighs, followed by a peppering of kisses, sweeping his tongue out.

Whoa.

"Nate," I say, reaching out to pull his head towards me and away from the place I want him so badly—uncertainty making a cameo.

His palm covers my belly in a protective gesture. "You know if you want me to stop, I will."

The sincerity of his words is clouded by the mist of lust in his eyes. This boy would never do anything I wasn't ready for, and I love him for it.

I love him.

"It's okay," I say. My body heats from the intensity of it all.

"I need you to be more specific, Felicity. If you want me to continue, I need you to say the words."

"Yes, I want you to," I say with sudden bravado.

He lifts my thighs, my buttocks rising off the bed. My legs tremble as he slides my knickers down my legs and over my ankles.

He's back before I have a chance to miss him, his tongue flicking over me in one, sure movement. I buck at the contact. I close my eyes as firm hands spread my legs open. Maybe I should feel shy or something, but he has a way of making me feel wanted, cherished. He dips his tongue inside me. All coherent thoughts evaporate. *Holy shit.*

"Jesus!"

It feels so good, I push my body into his tongue. My brain and body are disconnected as a craving comes to the surface.

His thumbs join the assault as his tongue and lips work me with an expertise to be in awe of. This is overwhelming. I'm not sure if I want him to stop or to go faster, but I'm afraid to let go—to give myself to him entirely.

The build-up is so intense, any control I might have had has now dissipated. He's the navigator—not me.

"Nate, I think I'm going to, ah—"

The relentless torture of his tongue is my undoing. All my reservations melt into oblivion as I buck into him mercilessly. His hand is firm over my stomach, holding me in place.

My eyes roll into the back of my head as I feel the release to the tips of my toes.

I've never experienced anything quite like this. Yes, I've heard of earth-shattering climaxes, and I thought my last one with him was pretty good, but it doesn't even compare to how exceptional this is.

My hands grip the sheets as an explosion of euphoria alights my body. I surrender myself completely.

Heavy breaths pass my lips as he trails kisses back up and over my stomach until he reaches my face. I'm not sure I want them on mine after they've been down south, but he doesn't give me a choice, and maybe I don't want him to. I taste myself on him—sweet—and lose myself to his tongue as it nips and teases.

Out of breath, he rolls onto his back, pulling me to his chest. I bury my face just under his chin, starting to come back down to earth.

Tendrils of embarrassment latch onto my subconscious.

"Please don't do that—"

"Do what?"

He tilts my face up towards his. "Overthink what just happened. It was beautiful, seeing you let go of your inhibitions like that."

All my instincts tell me to shy away from his words, to pick apart every touch, every feeling. I shake my head, willing the thoughts away.

I cling to his shirt and concentrate on the rhythm of his heart. Thoughts weigh heavy on my mind. I need to clear the air. "I owe you an apology, too, Nate."

He adjusts us so his back's against the headboard and pulls me with him.

"Why would you think that?" He cocks his head, frowning.

I chew on my bottom lip. "For not telling you…about Lawry."

He shakes his head. "Flick, it wasn't your story to tell. I'm a hot head, nothing new there. I'm the one who's sorry." He rubs his index finger over my top lip, tracing the scar he put there. "I never meant to hurt you, not then…and sure as hell not now. Maybe we can draw a line under it, start looking to the future instead of the past."

Smiling, I nod. "I'd like that."

He leans down, his eyes darting between my eyes and lips. I part them, desperate to feel his on mine again, but instead, it's the faintest tickle of his breath.

"I should go and get ready, but I have to ask you one more thing before I do," he says.

"Okay," I manage, swallowing my voice.

"Are we good?" He points between us.

I smile and nod.

"Promise?"

How can one word be my undoing? I feel something well up inside me, but I push it away and clear my throat. "Yes, Nate, I promise." And it's the truth.

Finding my hand, he brings it to his lips and turns it over to kiss the inside of my wrist. It's possibly the most intimate thing he's ever done.

I follow him to the door. When he comes to an abrupt stop, I collide with his back.

I let out a giggle as he turns back towards me and takes either side of my face in his hands. Leaning down, he kisses me. Each time it feels new—different—and yet…it feels like home. He kisses the tip of my nose before taking a step back. Hands raised, I laugh as I watch his retreating back. The smile which engulfs my face a welcome ache.

I worry that everyone can see right through me, like they know what transpired between Nate and me earlier. It's stupid, I know. It's my own insecurities causing me to feel this way. But seeing both Nate and Simon interacting like they're old friends is surreal, and if I'm honest with myself, it causes my pulse to race. Two worlds I'd kept separate for so long have now crossed paths, whether it was intentional or not.

Glad to be alone and back in my room, I try to read, but it's impossible. My thoughts are hijacked by every touch, every caress, and every kiss Nate placed over my body. *Restless*. I want to run, but it's too early in the morning for that, so instead, I find myself in the kitchen. I clutch my chest as I switch on the light.

"Shit—"

"Sorry," Nate says, as he stifles a laugh.

I look around. "Why the heck are you sitting in the dark?"

He shrugs. "Couldn't sleep. The milk's still hot if you want some hot chocolate."

"Sounds good," I reply, heading towards the hob, but I'm intercepted.

He touches my shoulder. "I've got this. You sit down."

Warmth tickles my skin. I trace the pattern of the oak table when he places the mug on the coaster in front of me.

"Thank you."

"That's your welcome."

I smile—he used to always say that to his parents.

"Do you mind if I switch off the light?"

"Sure."

I blink away the brief darkness as my sight adjusts to the brilliant silver of the moon filling the room.

"Cheers." Gently, he taps his mug against mine.

I blow on the hot liquid before taking a sip. We sit in a comfortable silence, his leg so very close to mine. My body tingles with anticipation.

"Do you remember when we used to sneak down here?" he asks in a whisper.

A chuckle escapes my lips. "Of course, we'd always end up getting in trouble for the mess we'd make. My favourite memories are the ones here with you…"

"Mine, too." He rubs his thumb over my arm.

"I was thinking about you the other night."

The corner of his mouth turns up. "Oh yeah?"

I smack him on the arm. "Mind—gutter."

"What? I'm a guy."

I laugh before continuing. "It was the first year we started the Christmas novelty gifts."

"You got me my AA Road Atlas… I still have it. One of the best presents I've ever had."

"You're just saying that."

"No, a tradition started from it."

"I missed not seeing you these last two Christmases. It didn't feel the same."

He nods in agreement. "I hope this year will be different… Flick, I want to ask you something—" He clears his throat and turns his body to face me. Raising his hand, he tucks the hair behind my ear, my body on tender-hooks. "I want you to consider staying here with me. After the fundraiser."

I shake my head. Worry takes root as all-consuming tentacles creep up my spine. I can't stop the shiver that rolls over my body. "I don't know…" And it's the truth.

"Please, let me show you how sorry I am."

I look into my mug like it holds all the answers.

"What is it you're so afraid of?" he asks.

I release a sigh. "Pretty much everything. Anxiety is a battle I face daily. It's never truly gone away…sometimes even getting out of bed is a struggle."

He shakes his head and looks away from me. "That's not what I meant."

Something squeezes in my chest as I clear my throat. "I'm afraid of how you make me feel."

"Why?" he asks, gazing back at me.

I fidget in my seat and clear my throat. "Because I already feel too much. Before I came back, I was able to compartmentalise everything. But seeing you, being around you…something shifted."

The world I'd become accustomed to no longer full of sepia hues. There's now colour—light and warmth I never knew I was missing…not until he sparked life back into me.

He pushes his mug away and takes my hands in his.

"Something shifted in me, too. The moment I saw you at the airport. I knew—I had an epiphany—it's only ever been you. I can't imagine my life where there isn't a me and you."

"I don't know what to say. I care about you, you know I do. But I'm not good enough for you." I look away.

"What do you mean?" He pulls my chin so I'm eye level with him. "Flick, listen to me. I could spend a lifetime showing you how much you mean to me, and still, I'd be the one not good enough for you."

I shake my head. "Nate, you say that, but I remember all the whispering. The way people would stare when they thought I wasn't looking. Friends who treated me like a leper—as if they'd catch something by even talking to me. It takes something like that to show peoples' true colours. There's a stigma that follows me now, and I don't know how to rid myself of it."

"I can't pretend to understand what you've been through. I know none of it was your fault, and it doesn't define you. It pains me to know I wasn't there for you to lean on or confide in. Let me show you I can be that man." He strokes the pad of his thumb over my lips. "At least say you'll think about it?"

I nod. "Yes, I'll think about it," I say in barely a whisper.

He leans towards me, leaving a feather-light kiss on my nose before pulling me into his side. I rest my head on his shoulder and close my eyes.

Chapter Twenty-Three

"Nate!"

Her scream wakes me, sending my heart racing. I pull her closer, shushing her. "I've got you, it's okay. I'm right here." I rub her back, smoothing the hair off her face as her eyes flutter open.

"Shit… I had a bad dream," she says, exhaling.

I feel her body shiver and pull her closer.

"Do you want to talk about it?"

She wipes her face with the sleeve of her cardigan. "We were in the tree house, and you fell, but I couldn't catch you…you slipped right through my fingers." She holds her hands up in front her, turning her palms over.

"It was just a bad dream. I'm right here."

She places her palm on my chest—as if to make sure I'm real. Seeing her this vulnerable makes me want to never let her go.

"Come on, let's get you to bed." I pull her to her feet, keeping my arm around her shoulder.

"Can I ask you something?" she whispers as we make our way through the house and walk past the grandfather clock.

"Anything."

"Can I stay with you tonight? I don't want to be alone."

I smile, squeezing her. "Flick, I had no intention of leaving you." And I mean it. I will make it my life's mission to show her how much I care about her.

Closing my bedroom door behind us, I walk her over to the bed and pull the cover back.

"In you get."

She climbs in, and I fold the cover back over her before stepping away.

"Where are you going?" she asks, sitting up and clutching the edge of the cover.

"To switch off the light."

I reach my hand over the back of my head, pull my t-shirt off and toss it on the floor. I step out of my joggers and adjust myself in my shorts before I climb in next to her, the bed sinking from my weight. She scoots backward. I've never been a spooning kind of a guy, but with her, I can't think of anything better than being the big spoon. One arm under her head, the other around her waist, she settles in, linking her hand with mine.

"Sweet dreams," I whisper.

Our breathing syncs, evens out, as we begin drifting off. I'm on the cusp of being dragged under when I hear her.

"It's only ever been you, too, Nate."

I tighten my hold on her but say nothing in return as sleep takes hold, my heart full.

Our children play in the tree house whilst their mother and I watch from below. She repeats my words back to me. "I can't imagine a world where there isn't a me and you either, Nate."

I pull my wife in for a kiss at the exact moment the kids come bounding down the ladder. I look heavenward. Typical.

"Why don't you two go inside see if your lunch is ready?" I say, holding their mum in my arms, refusing to let her escape.

They clap their hands together before running off into the house—no questions asked. Well, that was easy. I tug her, pulling her towards the tree house.

"After you," I say, and take a bow as I wave my hand in front of me, signalling for her to go first. What can I say, it's the gent in me...plus I get to watch her as she climbs the ladder.

I bite my lip, still in awe she chose me. I slap her on the butt as soon as we're out of sight and guide her back towards the giant beanbag. I kiss her neck before I nibble her earlobe—it always makes her crazy. She turns, slowly pushing her backside into me. I might lose it just from that contact alone. She takes my hand and places it over her breast. A moan escapes me as my other hand works up and down her thigh. I slide my hand from her breast and down her stomach as I inch lower...

I've stirred awake to the biggest hard-on ever, and it's dawning on me that it wasn't only the dream that has me aroused. Flick is rubbing herself into my hard length, my hand over her stomach—heading down south of its own accord.

I stop, ready to pull my hand away, when a soft moan escapes her in protest. I freeze, my palm flush against her stomach.

"Please, don't stop."

Her voice is groggy from sleep. I don't know what to do.

"Flick, I don't think you're awake," I say, my throat hoarse and deep.

"I'm awake enough to know I want you to touch me."

I suck in a deep breath, my hand trembling as I slide it down and over her shorts. Even through the material, I can tell she's wet.

She fidgets and wriggles out of them, moving them to her knees. I help slide them the rest of the way off.

I place my hand back over her bare skin, stroking her before dipping my middle finger inside her, all the while my hard length continues to push hard into her lower back. She pushes into me, and I let out a strained grunt. As I kiss her neck, she angles her head to the side, so I have better access. I nip and suck on her earlobe like in my dream and am rewarded with a soft whimper.

It's almost dreamlike—the power she has over me, the way she makes me feel. I want to reward her with the same want, the same need.

I move my thumb over her centre while my finger makes slow circles. I slip in another finger, working her as much as I can from this position, her breathing ragged. As if she reads my mind, she adjusts her hip, giving us more freedom to move. I kiss her shoulder. Her breathing grows heavier, her walls beginning to tighten around my fingers. I increase the pace, not easing off until she comes hard and fast, twisting her face into the pillow to stifle her moans. I feel pre-cum on the tip of my hard length, desperate to join her.

Her body comes down as she begins to relax. She twists to face me, and I lean in, kissing her softly. She moves her hand, stroking my length. When her grip tightens around my girth, a moan vibrates through my chest, willing her to pump her hand harder, *faster*. Her other hand cups my balls. *Fuck me.*

"Nate?" she breathes into my mouth.

"Yes?"

"I want you inside me."

My eyes pop open. I want that too…so damn bad.

Her eyes pierce mine, the green deep and alive with want.

"I can wait, Flick. There's no rush…not with us, not with you."

"I don't want to wait," she says with certainty, her hand tightening around me, moving faster.

If she carries on like this, I'll lose it. I take hold of her hand and pull it up to my lips, planting a kiss on the inside of her wrist. Her eyes flutter closed.

"Are you sure this is what you want?"

"Yes, I need this. I want you."

I can't hold back.

I kiss her into a frenzy—teeth-knocking clumsy, haphazard. I pull away to catch my breath, and roll her, pushing her back, flush against the mattress. Taking the hem of her t-shirt, she lifts her upper-body so I can tease it off and over her head.

I take in her silhouette.

"You are so beautiful, Felicity." I kiss her neck and work my way down to her breast where I take a nipple in my mouth and suck on it while playing with the other one between my finger and thumb. She pushes into my touch.

"Oh, sweet Jesus," she hisses.

Hearing her voice—how I make her feel—turns me on even more.

Her fingers work their way over my chest. I can feel the nervousness from her touch. I slip my fingers inside her again, and she bucks up, grabbing hold of my dick. I circle my fingers as deep as they'll go.

She tightens her hand, matching me touch for touch. She pulls me closer to her entrance, to where I want to be so badly.

Her hand moves up and down me, expertly. My fingers continue to penetrate her—deep and fast.

"I need you, please," she begs in a whisper.

I slowly pull my fingers out. She lets go of me when I lean over, pulling the drawer of the bedside table open. I rifle around until my fingers connect with a condom. I watch her before ripping open the foil packet. Taking myself in my hand, I slide it down my shaft, watching her watching me. Now my hands are the ones trembling. I stroke the length of myself, getting lost in the want that emanates from her.

"You can tell me stop," I say, wanting to reassure her.

She grabs hold of my arse and pulls me closer.

All my resolve melts away like hot butter. I enter her, slowly. Tipping my head back, I moan. Nothing has ever felt this good.

I take my time as I fill her, pausing as she lets out a gasp.

"Are you okay?"

"Yeah, just need to get used to it. You're huge."

I laugh. Isn't that what every guy wants to hear?

She wiggles a little, causing me to harden even more, then surprises me, pulling me into her—deeper. *Fuck.*

I don't know how long I can last. This right here was worth waiting for. I kiss her—long, deep, hard—sucking her bottom lip before nipping it with my teeth.

I pull almost all the way out in a slow, deliberate move, but then with one quick movement, I'm deep inside her.

Each time I pull almost all the way out to tease her, I go in harder and faster. Her nails begin to dig into me.

"Faster," she pants.

I never thought one word could be so damn sexy. I don't want to hurt her, but I can't get enough as I thrust myself inside her, her warm centre engulfing me as she tightens around me. She bites down on my shoulder, and it's the beginning of the end—I can't hold off much longer.

"I'm sorry, Flick, this is too good. I think I'm going to come," I say

"Me too," she says, pulling me even deeper, my thrusts causing her whole body to move up towards the headboard.

Her legs spread wide, only gripping my thighs as her body succumbs to the orgasm.

I grunt with my own release as I climax. She lets out a muffled groan as I fill the condom.

After I let my body relax on top of her for a moment, I move to the side, holding onto her while I'm still inside, not ready to remove myself while her clenching channel twitches from the aftermath of the orgasm. Once it's all but passed, I pull out, tie the condom, and wrap it in a tissue before tossing it in the bin.

"Did I hurt you? I got a little carried away, I'm sorry."

"No, you didn't… I was right there with you," she replies, her eyes sated and satisfied.

"Flick, you mesmerise me." I kiss her forehead, too tired to move or even clean up. Her eyes flutter shut, and a contented sigh passes her lips as I pull her closer to me.

I wake to find her wrapped around me. Her leg is slung over my thigh, head nestled under my chin, hair fanned across my chest, her arm around my waist. I smile to myself. I made love to the girl of my dreams. Thinking back to how she tightened around me as she came in pure ecstasy, is giving me morning wood.

If I could freeze one moment in time, this would be it. This would be my perfect moment. I'd die a happy man if I got to wake to her every morning, wrapped in my arms. She's my little piece of heaven—the sexiest angel if ever there was one.

She begins to stir.

"Well, if you're not a sight for sore eyes—post coitus—I don't know what is," I say, my voice still gravely.

She peers up at me through her long eyelashes, then rolls onto her back, pulling some of the cover up over her. Her face glows crimson. I lean onto my elbow to look down at her.

"Did you sleep well?" she asks, stretching with a shy smile

I laugh. "No, your snoring is terrible."

"Liar." She pokes her tongue out.

I gently push the loose hair from her cheek, tucking it behind her ear. I need to move away before I lose all self-restraint. I want her again so badly.

"I'm going to go shower, long day ahead of us," I say, reluctantly walking away.

"I think I'll join you."

I let out a choked sound—surely, I misheard her. "What?"

She shuffles around and leans over to grab her shorts and t-shirt, pulling them on under the sheets before joining me in the middle of the room. Slowly, she begins to walk backward towards the bathroom. Raising her index finger, she signals for me to follow.

Mouth agape, I comply like a loyal puppy.

We make slow work of washing one another and exploring each other's bodies. I have no idea what time it is when we finally remove ourselves from the shower, our skin pruned from the duration.

Just as I cover her in a towel, a knock at my door causes us to freeze. I put my finger to her mouth.

"Yeah?" I call out.

"It's me, mate, you up?" Charlie calls from the other side of my door.

We both look down at my towel, where I am pitching a tent. She stifles a laugh.

"'Course, just got out of the shower."

"Cool, but get a move on. Your Nan is already ordering us around. Oh, and they can't find Flick."

She covers her face with her hands.

"She probably went for a run."

"Whatever, mate, just hurry up."

I hear his footsteps as he walks away.

"Here." I pull out a t-shirt. "You better head back to your room before they send out a search party."

She nods as she pulls it over her head. She kisses me once on the lips before spying out of the door, then turns back to me and pulls me in for another kiss. Then she disappears down the hall.

Chapter Twenty-Four

I can't wipe the smile off my face. Being with Nate last night triggered something in me. He's like a fix I can't get enough of. I can still feel him when I move, and every time I think of his lips on me, or the way his fingers caressed me, my body fills with want and longing.

I inhale the summer heat as I look over the fundraiser that's now in full swing. A calm engulfs me—one that is so unfamiliar, I'm trying to fathom if it's short-term bliss or a taste of what is yet to come.

I agreed to take some photos, so I've been busy in the background, taking pictures when no one's looking. There is something spectacular about an unprepared shot. When you catch the light, the pose, at just the right moment, it's naturally beautiful.

I zoom in on Nate. My smile dissipates when I see Rachel walk up to him and give him a chaste kiss…right on the lips. A surge of jealousy floods my reprieve—my body now tense, my heart pounding in my ears.

"You know he doesn't have feelings for her, right?" A soft Australian accent hums next to my ear.

I flinch and turn to look at Charlie.

He laughs, putting an arm over my shoulder.

"I hope not," I reply honestly.

He looks to Nate. “Of course, not. Come on, you know you’re gorgeous, right? So…where were you this morning?”

I try to school my features at his comment. He wriggles his eyebrows.

“Running.”

“Hmm, I think not. I sure as hell didn’t see that fine derrière of yours while *I* was out running.”

Shit, busted. My ears heat, and it spreads to my face and neck as I struggle to think of a response. He shakes his head with a warm smile and winks.

“Be still, my beating heart. Are you actually flirting with me, Charlie?” I say in mock horror.

“Who, me? No never…and don’t worry, your secret’s safe with me.” He zips his lips and throws away an imaginary key. He kisses my cheek and places a protective hand on the small of my back.

I watch him as his gaze drifts away, eyes locked on someone. *Sophie.*

“Like what you see?” I elbow him in the ribs. Now whose turn is it to blush?

“Of course, not…I mean, she’s feisty and gorgeous, but what I mean is…any friend of yours is a friend of mine.”

“Which is *exactly* what I’m worried about,” I say, raising my eyebrows.

He shakes his head. “I know she’s off limits. Besides, I’m sure there’s a saying…something about not shitting on your own doorstep?”

I slap his arm, but he laughs it off and pulls me into his side. Nate looks over with a frown on his face. I smile. He returns it.

Charlie takes me by the elbow over to the auction stall. I survey the prizes, watching him as he writes a price on a piece of paper. Maybe I should have looked away, but it's too late now. I let out a slow whistle.

"Don't be like that, it's only money. Besides, it's for a good cause."

He tries to shake it off like he didn't just bid on afternoon tea for two at the Ritz for two thousand pounds. He tears off the bottom of the slip and stuffs it into his pocket. I can't help but marvel at his kindness. I put my arm around his waist and look up at him.

"Charlie, hidden under your womanising, wayward ways, is a really decent guy. Your Mum would be proud of you."

I feel him tense.

"I hope so," he says, his voice laced with melancholy.

"You're one of the good guys. Come on, let's go get us some cake."

He shakes his head with a laugh, dispelling the moment of sadness.

I find a clear patch of grass and sit down with my glass of Pimms and Lemonade. Looking through the viewfinder of my camera, I find Sophie smiling as she talks to Charlie. He's animated as he regales her with goodness knows what.

It's nice to see her so at ease with herself. She can come across to people who don't know her as standoffish—snobbish, even. She's anything but—it's all a front. She builds barriers just like I do. We handle things differently, but truth is, she doesn't want to hurt any more than I do.

Simon sits down beside me as I snap a couple more shots. He gently elbows me, and I lower my camera.

"She's doing better, you know? Getting her away from her sorry excuse for parents has done her good. Can you see how she breathes a little deeper now? Like she isn't having the life sucked right out of her?" he says.

I let out a sigh—it infuriates me. "I just don't understand how they could turn their backs on her so easily, especially being *church people*. I mean, who does that to their own daughter? Why go through all that trouble to adopt, then treat her like this? What kind of people are they?"

Simon pulls at the grass. "I wish I knew, but she'll always have us." He winks.

Her ears must have been burning because she's heading our way. Smiling, she flops down beside us. Both Simon and I gawk at her carefree smile. It's a good look on her.

"What?" she asks.

"So…where did Charlie go?"

She raises an eyebrow before answering. "No idea. I'm not his mum. He probably went off to find the girl who was eyeing him up when he was talking to me."

I choke on my drink.

"Just cough," she says.

My eyes fill with tears, and my nose runs. How very fetching. Simon hands me a serviette, which I take, gratefully, as people stop to stare.

"Seriously, that's all you had? To save my life, you tell me to cough," I say, hoarsely.

"Yeah, that's what I was taught in that first-aid course." She shrugs.

Simon lets out a belly laugh.

"Wow, thanks. Oh, and about Charlie and the mum note, I know you were only joking, but she passed away when he was younger."

I watch as sadness clouds her features as I take a sip of water. "Not the best analogy then, but noted for future reference."

Simon turns to her. "So, you like him?"

He goes straight for the jugular; I hold back a laugh—mainly through fear of choking again, but he could be right. There's…something there.

"Who, Charlie? He seems nice enough. What's not to like?"

I roll my eyes.

"Come on, don't be all coy. He means, *do you fancy him*?"

I don't know why we suddenly feel the need to interrogate her. Maybe it's from seeing how she looked all flustered just a moment ago.

"What? No." She snorts. "Besides, he's way too much of a womaniser…even *I* know better than to go there."

"Aside from that?" Simon asks, not willing to let it go.

She chews the inside of her cheek. "He's nice to be around, and yes, he's a little easy on the eye… I see what you're both getting at. Do not even *think* about trying to set me up."

"Who said anything about setting you up?" Simon replies, wiggling his eyebrows.

"Setting whom up?" Charlie asks, appearing from nowhere.

"Nothing, no one is setting anyone up," Sophie says, her eyes widening with a frustrated look—directed at me.

I laugh as she shakes her head, her cheeks growing a shade darker. Charlie takes a seat next to us.

"So, where's Nate?" she asks.

"Last I saw he was over there." Charlie points outward. We all look over at the exact moment Rachel plants a kiss on his cheek.

She really needs to keep her damn lips to herself and off him. I can see her rambling away—does she ever shut up? I watch as she takes hold of his hand. *What the fuck?* Unease settles in my stomach, I try to calm my racing heart.

"You okay?" Sophie asks, sending evil daggers in Nate's direction.

Why would he want someone as messed up as me, when he can have someone like her? I look down at myself in silent resignation

"I'm fine," I stutter, which is complete and utter bullshit.

Charlie elbows me gently to gain my attention. "Hey, come and get a refill with me?"

I nod, feeling grateful for the distraction. He stands, holding his hand out, pulling me swiftly to my feet.

"You guys want a drink?" he asks.

"No thanks, I'm good," Soph replies.

"You sure you don't want anything stronger than water?"

"No, honestly, I'm on a detox, but thank you."

Simon holds up his practically full cup and shakes his head.

Charlie turns and leads me away, his palm on the small of my back. A few weeks ago, this alone would have caused me to freak out, but I'm getting there. Slowly.

"Honestly, you know, whatever that was, there's absolutely nothing for you to worry about, right?"

I shake my head, doubt filling me. "I didn't like seeing it. I've already seen them kiss, remember? And knowing they've been together…it just doesn't sit right with me. I hate to admit it, but I'm jealous, and I know it's an ugly trait if ever there was one. But then I feel guilty—it makes me question if I could ever be good enough for him."

He turns his head to look at me.

"You *are* good enough. God, Flick, you know that boy *loves* you?"

"Of course, we're like family."

"I didn't mean it like that, and you know it."

I chew on my lip. "What if he only thinks he does? After losing Lawry…maybe it's the nostalgia of it all. This—whatever it is—is too fast…"

"Fast, my arse. My boy, Nate, has been in love with you for years. The loss of Lawry just made him realise how short life is."

"Like I said, we're practically family. That's the kind of love he feels."

He shakes his head in frustration. It would actually be amusing to watch if my stomach wasn't turning over as we speak. He grabs the back of his neck just like Nate does when he's anxious.

"To hell with it… I'm just going to tell you something, and this is going to do absolutely nothing for my male ego, so try to be gentle with my feelings when you hear it, okay?"

"Okay," I say, feeling slightly dubious. Do I even want to know?

"Don't let on to Nate—I don't fancy fighting with my best mate—not again."

My eyes go wide. "What do you mean by again?

"Because we had a fight over you… Do you remember that time when I had a busted lip and a messed up eye a few years back?"

"Yeah you and Nate were both a little beaten up, you said some guys got in your faces."

"Yeah, that's the thing. There were no other guys involved, it was only Nate and me."

I shake my head. "Why were you even fighting over me?" I put my hand over my mouth, trying to stifle a giggle.

Is he blushing?

"I said, no mocking." He raises his eyebrows.

I cough, correcting my face as I wait for him to continue.

"I had a bit of a crush on you, so I decided to make a move, and of course I told Nate. Not only because he's my best mate, but also, I thought it was the right thing to do. I mean, he always acted like he was an over-protective big brother. Up until that moment, he'd never let on his feelings for you. He freaked out. I didn't even see the first punch coming. I was so shocked, and before I knew what was happening, we were full-on fighting."

"Oh my God." I don't know how to digest this revelation. The thought of either of them hurting, especially over me, makes me feel like shit.

"Yep," he says, popping the p. "We didn't talk for two days. I was so angry with him. But then I was pissed at myself for not seeing it sooner—all the signs were there. We cleared the air, however, I was told to leave you alone. You were too special to just be another notch on my bedpost. He admitted he'd had a crush on you for a while, but was waiting for the right time to tell you. And that's when I knew he didn't just have a *thing* for you. He was in love with you."

"I don't even know what to say." I can't hide my smile.

He looks me straight in the eye, causing my breath to hitch. "I'm not going to lie, if it was anyone else but Nate, I would have made a move on you. But he's a brother to me, and I wouldn't trade that for anything. Not that you wouldn't have been worth it. You're special, Flick. Hell, you're like family. Well…more like a hot second cousin." He winks, elbowing me.

I smile sheepishly—there's the Charlie I know and love. I shake my head. He looks over my shoulder, his face smug. Before I have a chance to question him, he leans down, planting a chaste kiss on my lips. My adrenaline spikes, confused…until I hear him.

"What the actual *fuck*, Charlie?"

I turn to see him charging towards us. I back into Charlie, who's holding his hands up. *Shit bag.*

"Whoa, there, easy tiger…calm down," I say, trying to play it off.

Nate's hands are fisted at his sides.

"Hey, mate, behave yourself. It wasn't like that." Charlie holds up his hands as he begins to back away.

Tosspot knew exactly what he was doing. I'd slap him myself if I didn't think Nate wouldn't push me out of the way to throttle him first.

"Really? Because I'm pretty sure I just saw you with your lips on hers."

He shakes his head. "Just a friendly peck, I promise, scouts honour," he says with a salute.

Nate still looks like a predator protecting his prey. I'd be lying if I said I didn't like it deep down. He takes another step closer. I turn to Charlie and pat him hard on the chest. He responds with a fake flinch.

"Way too much testosterone. I'm standing right here, enough already."

"But—"

I turn back to Nate. "No, Nate, did you see me striding over to you like a full-on bunny boiler when Rachel was pawing all over you?"

"Well, no, but it wasn't like that…"

I cross my arms. "No, really? And it's not like it's the first time she's done it, either. Charlie was winding you up, for heaven sake. So stop acting like a dog who needs to piss all over me, and *grow up.*"

Charlie begins to laugh. I give him an incredulous look.

"You're not helping yourself right now and to be clear. You're lucky I didn't knee you in the baby makers."

He cringes and takes another step back. Nate chuckles from behind me. *I'll deal with him later.*

I look over Charlie's shoulder. "Are you all in heat or something? Is that guy seriously trying it on with Sophie? She doesn't even look interested. Take the hint, bucko!"

Charlie's head spins round so fast, I wouldn't be surprised if he has given himself whiplash. I think he was hoping I was joking.

"What the hell, is Marcus for real? What a prick."

"Well, if he's a prick, I'd prefer it if he wasn't sniffing around my best friend. Here's an idea: maybe you should go and make yourself useful and interrupt them or something. What hurts her, most definitely hurts your *hot second cousin*," I say with a wink.

"Dude, she's most definitely a keeper," he says, holding his fist out to Nate who bumps it with his before heading in their direction.

Nate puts his arms around me from behind. "Are you going to tell me what all that was about?"

"Just had a little heart to heart is all," I say, wrapping my arms around his.

"Hmm…anything I should be worried about?" he asks, placing a soft kiss to my temple.

"Should I ask you the same thing about Rachel?"

"Touché." He pulls his arms away and turns me to face him. Cupping my cheek, he leans down and kisses me. I forget about everything.

Chapter Twenty-Five

After eating my weight in cake and a few too many Pimms, I make my way to the ladies'.

I've never seen toilets like these in my life. It has sinks and everything—the posh version of port-a-loo. I enter and hear someone inside one of the stalls throwing up. That's not good.

I tap on the door. "Is everything okay in there?"

"Yes, sorry, two seconds."

I don't know why she's apologising, there's another cubicle I can use. The door opens, and out walks Rachel. I take a step back, surprised to see her, but it's my kind of shit luck.

"Sorry…morning sickness clearly doesn't just mean *mornings*."

I feel like I might throw up, myself. Bile begins to rise in my throat. *She's pregnant*. I lean back on the sink for support. My body teeters.

"You're not pregnant, too, are you? You look a little peaky."

I shake my head. "No, must just be the heat and all this nice weather we're having." I swallow, trying to calm my thoughts. If you can't think of anything good to say, you talk about the weather, right? Truth is, I'm trying not to freak out. The girl he used to sleep with is pregnant, for fuck's sake.

She finishes washing her hands and grabs a hand towel from the basket.

"Tell me about it. I'm lucky it's only my first trimester, otherwise this heat would be worse—oh where are my manners? I'm Rachel," she says, holding her hand towards me.

"Felicity," I reply, and take her hand.

She cocks her head, eyeing me. "Oh my…you're *Nate's* Felicity, aren't you?"

"I wouldn't say that, but yes, I'm her," I say with a shrug.

"I'm such an idiot," she replies. "I have a confession."

Right, so we're actually *doing this*—talking in the ladies' toilet. "Oh…" I have no idea what's going on. I don't even know that I *want to,* either. I take a deep breath and wrap my arms around myself, pinching the skin on my elbow.

"I answered the phone to you once. I didn't tell him…he found out a few weeks ago and freaked out. I want to apologise."

I blink in surprise. "No need, it was ages ago."

She shakes her head. "Yeah, but still, I know this may sound stupid coming from a complete stranger, but I've had time to think about how I've acted in the past. I was looking for love in all the wrong places. It's why I decided to own up to myself and split from my fiancé."

"Oh, I'm sorry." This is so weird. Is she suffering from heat stroke or something?

"We weren't right for each other… I have a baby to consider, now, and that's my priority." She looks at her reflection and fixes her hair.

"What about the father?" I ask her.

"He wants in, which surprised me. Should be interesting, but I think we'll be better at co-parenting than being engaged. I don't want a baby born into a loveless relationship."

"That's brave of you."

I try to control my racing heart—it's *not* Nate's—and now I feel like the biggest bitch that a part of me thought it was a possibility.

"Like I said, love in all the wrong places. Which brings me to Nate…"

I don't want to hear any more. "Listen—"

She cuts me off, and she puts her hand on my arm.

"I don't know if he ever mentioned me, *talked* about me...anyway that's neither here nor there. He got wasted the night before his Gramps' funeral, and not once did he stop talking about *you.*"

"We had a falling out…"

She shakes her head. "I was jealous even before that. I mean, who wouldn't be? He is one of the good ones. Anyway, I want to be a good Mum, and that means being less of a bitch, you know?"

I nod—but it's a moot point. I don't know her. "I'm sure you'll make a wonderful mum."

"Thank you, I don't have many female friends…probably from being such a *cow*, but I can see why he's smitten with you. Anyway, the last thing I want is to cause animosity if we happen to bump into each other…having friends in the same circles."

"Of course."

She goes to leave but pauses. "I really hope you and him work things out. He's been in love with you since I've known him." She winks, letting the door close behind her.

It takes me a moment to remember why I'm here. *I need to pee.* Relief and apprehension flood my consciousness as I do. How can I move forward with Nate when I have so many issues of my own to still deal with?

I'm washing my hands when the door opens.

"Oh," I say.

Nate locks the main door behind him. "I wanted to speak to you."

I nod, looking around the room. "Everything all right?" I ask, not sure why he has collared me in the toilets of all places. I dry my hands for something to do.

"It's been easier having you here. I miss him, though. This is the first time he's not been here—" He looks at the floor. "I miss him."

I take hold of his hand "I know you do."

It's quiet. The only noise comes from the humming of the distant music and my heart beating in my ears. The air grows thick.

"How do you feel about me? Do you want me, Flick?"

I look at him. "Well…I…what do you mean?" I stutter.

"Do you want to *be* with me?"

I smile. "You want to put a label on it?"

He shakes his head with a frown. "Not when you put it like that, no. But I want you to want *me* the way I want *you.*"

I bite my lip, swallowing what feels like grit.

"I do. I gave myself to you. I let go of my insecurities to be with you, Nate."

I don't think he understands how hard this is. Sometimes I can hardly catch my own breath—it's like the oxygen has been sucked out of the room.

"Physically, you did, Flick, but not *all* of you. Emotionally, you're holding back."

I move back and put some distance between us. "What is it you want from me, Nate?"

He takes a step towards me. "I don't want anything from you, except for you to be present. I want you to be as invested in me, as I am in you."

"It's too much too soon. I don't deserve you… God, Nate, Rachel told me she was pregnant, and the first thing that came to mind was that it was yours."

I keep waiting for the worst. Like anything good will evaporate through my fingers, and whatever this is with Nate, will vanish into thin air and I'll be left to drown in quicksand.

He clenches his jaw. "I'm by no means a perfect man, and trust is something you earn, and I *will,* Flick. I'll show you *every day* that you're worthy, that we deserve to be together— flaws and all."

The door rattles, interrupting us, causing me to flinch. He puts his hand on my shoulder and holds his finger up to his mouth. Silence. Whoever it was appears to have left.

Giggles bubble from my chest, the seriousness of the conversation now passed.

He rolls his eyes. "I didn't mean to accost you in the ladies'," he says. But the smirk he's wearing is anything but apologetic.

"What would your Nan think of your unruly behaviour?"

He smiles, bringing his hand to my cheek again. "Promise me you'll try not to overthink this—*us*?"

I take his hand. "I'll try."

He leans in close, stopping a fraction from my lips.

I make up the distance.

My lips meet his, my insides tightening low in my belly. A want develops between my legs as his tongue tangles with mine. I pull him closer, feeling his hard length through his jeans.

He ends the kiss and rests his forehead against mine.

"What are you doing to me?" I ask.

"No more than what you're doing to me."

I breathe him in deep.

"Come on, if we stay in here any longer, I won't be able to hold back."

Is it all kinds of wrong that the thought excites me? Even though we are in the toilet, and there is a hoard of people only meters away…

Sophie grabs me by the elbow. "Where were you?" she asks, looking between Nate and me.

"Toilet," we both say in unison.

My face is on fire as I turn into Nate's chest to hide my mortification. Sophie laughs her head off, and when it subsides to a snort, I peek up to see Charlie strutting in our direction. Did he go to some kind of male finishing school to master that walk, or is it natural?

"What's so funny?" he asks, smiling towards Sophie.

She fans her face as she catches her breath. "Nothing, just these two lovebirds crack me up—" Her voice catches, and her face pales, her body going rigid.

I step forward, as does Charlie. He takes hold of her elbow, worry crossing his face.

"Soph, what's wrong?" I ask, but she's somewhere else.

I follow her line of sight and let out a frustrated groan. This cannot be happening, for fuck's sake.

"What the hell is *he* doing here?" I mumble under my breath

Nate takes hold of my hand. "What's wrong, who's here?" he asks, pulling me into his body.

Adrenaline pulses through my body, the sight of him pissing me off. "No one important...just someone we used to know," I say through gritted teeth.

Charlie looks to see whom we are staring daggers into.

"Put it like this, if I ever saw him again it would be too soon—" Her voice hitches, her lips quiver, all her emotions coming to the surface.

I rack my brain, *what do I do?*

Charlie clears his throat. "I came to find you guys because Evie needs volunteers to get the cupcakes ready for the raffle draw. There's a lot of numbers involved, and seeing as cakes are your forte, I thought you could help me?" he says looking at Sophie.

A wobbly smile crosses her face as she rolls her eyes. "Well let's have at it," she replies.

With an exaggerated move, he offers her his arm. She waits a beat, then takes hold of it before they walk away.

"Remind me to thank him later. The man deserves a hug for that."

Nate pulls me into his body. "No way. He's already had his lips on you, he can keep his hands to himself."

I smack him playfully.

His smile fades. "Jokes aside, she looked like she saw a ghost, is she all right?"

I shake my head. "She might as well have…but it's not my story to tell."

He tightens his hold on me and keeps me anchored as I try to keep my nerves at bay.

"Felicity, is that you?"

I let out a sigh—louder than intended. My heart picks up speed, my pulse racing in my ears so loud, I wouldn't be surprised if they can both hear it. I want to pretend I didn't hear James ask my name, but as his hand touches my shoulder, I know I can't avoid him.

A shiver rolls over my body. I twist to look at him, removing myself from his touch.

"James," I say, unable to keep the contempt from my voice.

I plaster on a fake smile. My wide eyes flit to Nate. His fingers gently squeeze my waist, giving me the strength to hold it together. The last thing I want is to have a meltdown in front of all these people, but with Nate by my side, I feel like I could tackle a mountain.

"I thought it was you. Did I just see Soph walking away? How is she?"

I grind my teeth. Is this idiot *kidding* me? I nod as an involuntary shudder escapes me. Nate's hand moves to the small of my back, rubbing small circles to steady me.

"Hmm, you mean after you walked away from her? Or do you mean figuratively speaking? Don't answer that, you have no right even asking. So, let's cut the crap. What brings you here?" I say, my breathing accelerated. I clench my fists, my nails digging into my palms with no mercy.

He shakes his head. "It-it wasn't like that…but if you must know, I was just picking up—"

"His fiancé," says a nasally voice, as she clutches his arm, staking her claim.

My senses are assaulted by the overpowering whiff of her perfume. I cough, trying to dispel the taste. Her hand is limp, flashing the most ghastly engagement ring I've ever seen.

"Dawn," she says, in way of introduction.

As if I should know who she is. I couldn't give a shit, not while she's looking at Nate like she is ready to eat him up. She looks him over before licking her lips and pushing out her chest.

"Come along, darling, we really must go. I need to get to the hall…there is still so much to organise for tomorrow."

He nods, his obedience evident.

She turns away not so elegantly; he trails behind her. What a pretentious bitch. I look at James' retreating back. *You reap what you sow—karma is a bitch.*

Nate whispers into my ear, the hairs on the back of my neck rising. "Awkward, much?"

"No shit, Sherlock," I reply, unable to keep the agitation from my voice. "Sorry, I didn't mean to snap…it's just I never expected to see him. I need to check on Sophie."

He kisses me on my temple softly and pulls me closer.

"No apology necessary, come on." He leads me away.

As we approach, I see her laughing at something Charlie is saying, and it softens my heart. He has such a gentle approach with her. I've never seen it before, other than with me.

"Hey, how you doing?" I ask.

Her eyes dart between Nate and Charlie. She shrugs and her bottom lip quivers.

"I don't know about you guys, but I'm thirsty, anyone else want a drink?" asks Charlie—to the rescue once again.

"I could. I'll come with," Nate replies.

I've never been more grateful in my life. Who says all men were born in the stupid factory? I try not to laugh at my own thoughts, or the memory of a pencil case Nate bought me with *boys were made in the stupid factory* written all over it…after he accidently sat on my pencil set and broke my favourite pencils.

Sophie and me both shake our heads as they leave us alone.

"Shit, Sophie… right after you left, that fucker walked right over to me."

She purses her lips. "Don't swear. I thought he saw us, but I was grateful for Charlie's piss poor excuse to get me away from there, so I didn't have to find out." She rings her hands in her lap.

"There's more to Charlie than maybe even *I* gave him credit for. You knew about the engagement, didn't you?" I ask. It's all beginning to add up now—the accidental overdose.

She nods and looks away. "I heard a rumour, but I wasn't sure, so I scouted Facebook and sure enough…" She looks up at me, guilt crossing her face.

"This is why you were so upset, wasn't it? When you ended up in hospital…"

Shame fills her face, her eyes filling with tears. A whimper escapes her, and I step forward, pulling her into my arms. Her body shakes through the tears.

"I know what happened to us was bad enough, but when he ended it with me afterward, a piece of me shattered. It's as though all that hope and self-belief I had disappeared with his love. I don't think I'll ever be the same again—I'll always be broken."

I hug her tighter, knowing how she feels. Not exactly, but more than most. It's why I'm so frightened to open up to Nate and risk it not working out—when he leaves me, there'll be no coming back from it.

"You're the strongest person I know. Every day, you get up, and you *fight*—no matter what. I understand, though, it's one of my fears with Nate. He could break my heart just as easily."

She pulls back that stiff upper lip of hers, and stands, squaring her shoulders. "He is nothing like James." She sniffs back her tears, gaining control of her emotions.

"No, of course not, but I'm only human—I can't help but have reservations. I mean, not to drag it up, but you were so close with James before—"

She shakes her head. "Listen, I know what I had with him was one-sided on my part. And do you know what? It's all right. I would want someone who loves me the way I love them. I don't want to talk about him. Not anymore, he doesn't deserve the satisfaction. Look how you've started to open up to Nate. He hasn't done a runner. He's still here, holding fast. For that alone, the man deserves the benefit of the doubt."

"I worry I'm just not ready."

An all-knowing grin appears. "I don't buy it, and if I didn't know better, I'd even say you've slept with him."

I look away. "Is it that obvious?"

She slaps my arm. "I wasn't sure, but something about you was different. How was it?"

"It was more than I could have imagined. When it's just the two of us, he makes me almost forget about everything else but him."

"Baby got back. I'm glad you finally got laid again. I didn't want you to shrivel up."

It's my turn to slap her arm. "For someone who detests swearing, you have a potty mouth. You sure as hell don't have any problems talking about sex..."

She winks. "It's all part of the circle of life. So, did he...you know...make you come?"

I shake my head. My face radiates my embarrassment as we break out into a fit of giggles until our eyes water and my sides hurt.

Chapter Twenty-Six

I begged Flick to come to my room once everyone else was in bed. She was so reluctant, I thought she wasn't going to.

My door opening tells me I was wrong. I release a sigh as the uncertainty escapes me.

She locks it behind her, the soft scent of apples floating across my face. I don't give her a chance to say anything as I rush to her and take her face in my hands. Her eyes are glassy from the alcohol.

I push her against the door, leaning into her body until my mouth claims hers. She parts her lips. The kiss is slow and sweet. I could kiss her for an eternity and still want more. I pull back enough for us to catch our breath, my temple against hers. Her sweet breath caresses my lips.

"Wow." She lets out in a small huff of a whisper.

I move back and kiss the tip of her nose.

"Sometimes when I'm around you, it's like I can't breathe."

Worry settles in the pit of my stomach. "I never want you to feel like I'm suffocating you." I move away, only keeping my hands on her shoulders.

"I don't mean it in a bad way. You knock me off my axis, and then, in one swift move, you breathe life back into me. And it's like I'm aligned again. It scares me—how you make me feel without even trying."

I take her hand to lead her over to my bed and pull her into my lap.

I stroke my thumb over her velvety pink lips. "I know how strong I'm coming across, how this may seem sudden. But deep down, I always had hope. You found your way back to me. Since the moment you told me you wanted to marry me in our tree house, it's only ever been you. It will *always* be you."

Her body hums with warmth. She takes my hand in hers, linking our fingers. "I tried to pluck up the courage so many times to come back, but the longer I stayed away, the harder it became. I never thought it possible to feel this connection with you—not after everything…"

I pinch myself to make sure she's real, and not a figment of my imagination.

"We can take it slow… I want to show you how we can be. Let me take you to dinner, the movies. In the words of my Gramps…let me woo you." I squeeze her waist.

Her shy smile melts the very heart of me.

"But what if whatever this is between us is just a fluke?"

I look at her face. What I feel is no passing fluke, and there's no denying the sexual chemistry.

"Not possible. I don't want to scare you, but you are it for me. I'm not the most patient man, but for you, I can wait. I'll give you time if that's what you need."

Her vulnerability hurts my insides. She bites her lip, the worry evident.

"I mean it. I'd wait a thousand lifetimes if I had to, but tonight, will you stay? I just want to hold you."

She smiles, her dimple prominent. "I'd like that," she whispers.

I scoot her off my lap and pull the covers back. We both snuggle down, and she rolls to her side, facing me, tracing the lines of my face with feather-light fingertips. I harden beneath her touch but keep my lower body away from her.

"Sophie told me today how she felt broken—like a piece of her would always feel that way. She gave James all her firsts, and when the going got tough, he left her in the worse way possible."

"Charlie and I gathered as much. What a fool. Did you notice how protective Charlie was over her?"

"I did. He's the kind of man I want her to end up with. Don't you think they'd make a nice couple?"

I let out a chuckle. "No comment. I have enough to worry about with you. Though I'd pay good money to see Charlie smitten."

I sit up, I almost forgot. "I have something for you," I say, as I run over to my wardrobe and pull out the gift bag.

"Really?" She sits up legs crossed, suspicion clouding her features.

"Yes, really," I say, sitting in front of her and placing the bag between us.

She looks to the bag, then back to me.

"It won't bite—they're presents I got you, in the hopes you'd come back over Christmas."

She tucks her chin in, hair falling over her face. I tuck it behind her ear and cup her cheek.

"Don't go all shy on me, just open it."

She dips her hand in, her tongue poking out the corner of her mouth as she retrieves one wrapped in newspaper.

"Novelty present," she says, smiling.

I send her a wink. "You got it."

Delicate fingers rip at the edges of the paper to reveal a PG tip monkey and a box of tea bags. She bursts out into a fit of giggles—this girl loves her tea.

"I love you, monkey," she says in small, northern accent, hugging it.

I pull out the next one. She doesn't mess about this time when she takes it from me and rips off the paper, scrunching up her nose.

"A troll doll?" She pulls at the pink Mohawk, holding back her laughter.

"I know, right? It was in the garage when I was getting fuel—there was no way I wasn't getting it for you. You used to collect them, remember?"

She smiles, and that's when I see her—the Flick I used to know. She's about to say something, but I hold up my finger.

"There's one more," I say, and reach back into the bag.

She looks heavenward, as if annoyed, but I see the sparkle in her eyes.

I hold out the blue bag, her expression priceless.

"This is your real present."

Her throat bobs up and down as she gingerly takes the bag hanging off my fingers. Hands shaking, she dips inside the small bag and pulls out a little blue box tied with ice-white ribbon. She pulls the bow loose and opens the box, to reveal a small, drawstring bag. She pulls at the strings and peers inside, turning the bag upside down on her palm.

Silver sparkles back at us.

I take it from her hand and hold each end. Opening the clasp, I signal to her wrist. She holds it up, and I fasten it before spinning it round.

She's silent as she looks at it. Her eyes spring to mine then back to the bracelet. It's an infinity charm. She rolls her finger over it before moving to her knees and throwing her arms around my neck. She pulls back, giving me a chaste kiss on the lips.

"It's beautiful, Nate, but it's too much. You shouldn't have, but I love it, thank you."

I watch her smile as she lies back down, admiring the bracelet on her wrist. Relief floods me. I'm glad she loves it.

I wake to the first orange-hued rays of sunrise as it floods the room, casting a warm glow over Flick. I run my fingers over her hair, then stroke down the arch of her nose, then down over her soft, supple lips. Her mouth curves into a smile.

Eyes closed, she asks, "are you watching me sleep?"

"Maybe," I say and run my fingers over her collarbone.

"That's not creepy," she replies, as she opens her eyes and stretches her arms.

Her hand brushes over my morning glory. Her eyes flutter to my face she swallows and licks her lips.

She springs out of bed. "I'll be right back," she calls, jogging to the bathroom.

When she returns, she climbs back in next to me like it's the most natural thing in the world, smelling all minty.

I tap her on the nose. "Did you brush your teeth?" I ask

"Maybe," she whispers.

I hop out of bed and run off to brush mine, too, adjusting myself, so I don't piss all over the ceiling.

When I return, her eyes are closed as if she's sleeping. "Flick?"

She doesn't say anything as I climb up the bed and slowly pull the cover down. Her chest rises—her breaths growing heavier.

I give one quick lick of my tongue up her thigh.

"Whoa," she says, her eyes springing open.

"Oh sorry, did I wake you?" I say, in no way apologetic as I trail kisses all over each thigh. She wriggles at the contact.

"Did you want me to stop?"

I push up on my hands, ready to sit up, but her hand finds my head, stilling me. My lips return to her skin as I pepper her with even more kisses, licking as I move to her inner thigh. Her legs fall open, while she laces her fingers through my hair.

"Anytime you want me to stop, just say the word, you know the drill," I whisper as I push up her nightshirt and pull down her shorts. Returning to her centre, I blow on her clit.

She lets out a cross between a whimper and a moan. Before I lose the will to live, I take one, long lick and insert a finger. My mouth moves over her clit. Her response to me is captivating as she stiffens, her hand tightening in my hair.

My name rolls off her tongue as she comes.

I hover over her and capture her lips with mine. I insert another finger, hitting the spot she seems to like so much. She pulls away from my lips, panting.

"Ahh, again." Her eyes roll into the back of her head. "Stop," she says. I pull my fingers almost all the way out.

Her eyes spring open.

"Nate, don't fucking *stop.*"

I laugh and thrust them back inside her, hard and fast.

"I want you," she says, hands now gripping my arse.

"You've got me," I reply, with a grunt.

"No, I *want* you."

She cups my balls and squeezes, almost disarming me. She moves her hand up and under the waistband of my shorts to pull them down. I roll onto my back and push them the rest of the way down and past my ankles. She moves to her side and takes my length in her hand. I raise my head to watch as she slides her hand up and down my shaft. It's too much. I slam my head back against the pillow.

I open my eyes as she straddles me. She dips her head and licks just the tip.

"Flick, no, you don't have to—"

Her lips close around my tip before she takes me in her mouth. My whole body shudders.

She does this thing with her tongue and teases my balls. I feel like I am about to lose it. I take her by the shoulders and push her back. She releases me.

"I need to be inside you," I say.

She sits up and leans over to kiss me on my lips. I hold her face between my hands. I feel her take me in her hand, and releasing her lips from mine, she gently lowers herself onto me. A unified sigh escapes us as she places her hands on my shoulders. I hold onto her hips as she slowly, and torturously begins to ride me. She sinks further onto me—all the way to the hilt. It feels so damn good. My eyes spring open.

"Fuck, condom," I croak out.

She stills on top of me. "I've been tested, I promise I'm clean." A look of utter mortification engulfs her face as she blinks back tears.

"Hey," I say, sitting up which only makes the feeling of being inside her more intense. I suck in a breath and lift her chin until her eyes meet mine. "That wasn't what I meant. This feeling right here," I say, as I move upwards inside her. "Is like heaven. You're my heaven."

She shakes her head, trying to hold back tears. "I just thought because of you know… I'm sorry."

I pull her face down and kiss her cheekbones, her nose, and her lips.

"Never apologise. Having no barrier between us is bliss, but not at the risk of getting you pregnant."

"I'm on the pill," she says, hopeful.

I grow harder. "Well, in that case, I'm still good if you are?"

She begins to move, letting me know she is.

I forget about everything, worshiping every inch of her sweet body. I have never felt a connection like this, not with anyone. She's the only girl I would ever allow myself to not use protection with, and I want to keep it that way. Everything about her is exactly as it should be—insecurities and all. I inhale her scent, and look at her face, committing it to memory. She's the girl I want to grow old with. Now all I have to do is wait until she accepts that, too.

Chapter Twenty-Seven

Nathaniel

A distant noise rumbles away in the background. I let out a groan and stretch, my arm connecting with soft tissue. I squint my eyes open just as Flick lets out a yawn. I smile. Damn, she looks good.

"Nathaniel, are you awake?" Nan calls through the door.

Flick clutches the cover and brings it up to her face.

I laugh, shaking my head. "The door's locked," I whisper in her ear.

"Yes, I'm just going to grab a shower, and I'll be down."

"And what about you, Felicity?"

She pulls the cover off her face and squeezes her eyes shut.

"I won't be long either," she croaks out.

When we hear the floorboards creak, and the sound disappear, Flick looks at me. "How did she know I was in here?" she whisper-shouts.

I roll on top of her and pin her hands gently above her head. "Why? Does it bother you?" I reach down and tickle her.

"Nate, stop it," she squeals, trying to wriggle away.

I shake my head. "Not until you answer my question."

"Yes, Nate, it does, now please." She kicks her legs.

I kiss her on the forehead. "Nope, not until you give in and admit that you're my girl."

"I mean it, Nate, I'll wet myself…"

I smile. “Oh, I love it when you talk dirty.” My words only make her laugh harder. I continue to tickle her as she wriggles around like a snake.

“Stop it,” she tries to say it with more conviction.

“I’m sorry, did you say you were my girl?”

“Yes, Nate, I’m *yours,* now please, stop.”

“Finally,” I say, scooping her up into my lap, “Just as I’m all yours.”

I kiss her on the nose—she likes it when I do that—there’s something about the look she gets in her eyes.

I try to hold back my desire when he does things like this, but it’s hard to hide how he makes me feel. I lean my face towards him and kiss him until we’re both breathless.

I pull back. “I need to go get ready.”

He stands and pulls me to my feet.

“Here, put this on.” He tosses me a hoodie.

I slip it over my head, breathing in the all-familiar scent of Nate. “Thanks,” I say before turning away.

He swats my backside just before I leave.

Back in my room, I stare at my reflection, looking well and truly sated—my hair a tangled mess. I shower in a trance, thinking back over the last two days. I’m just finishing getting dressed when a sound comes from the door between Nana’s room and mine.

“You look radiant this morning,” Nana says when she enters, giving me the once-over and a kiss on the cheek.

I know I’m blushing.

“Morning.” I tie my hair in a plait and pull it over my shoulder.

“So, is it official? Are the two of you together now?”

I half shrug. “Kind of, but I want to take things slow. This is all still kind of overwhelming…”

She sits on the ottoman. “That’s understandable, but you deserve to be happy, Felicity.” She pats the space beside her.

She takes my hand in hers as I sit to join her.

“We had hoped you’d find your way back to one another. Sometimes life has other ideas and gets in the way. I know, now—the real reason Lawry and me weren’t meant to be together—” She looks away, caught in a distant memory, one only she knows. “It was so you and Nathaniel would find your own happily ever after.” She plays with my plait. “Are you sure you don’t want to come back to France with Evie and me…finish the rest of your holiday which was cut short?”

I shake my head. “No, but thank you. Besides, I think it will do you both good to get away.” I lean forward as she pulls me for a hug.

I see the fragility in her so much more, now, and it worries me. It’s as if she’s getting ready to say goodbye, as morbid as that may sound. It’s a worry I carry. She’s always been a light force, no matter what. Even with Sophie and Simon, she treats them like her own. I try to bury the thought of losing her, I know it’s inevitable, but I’m not ready, and neither is she.

Simon is leaning against the kitchen counter when I walk in, coffee in hand, looking right at home.

"Hey, sugar lips."

"Morning," I say with a warm smile.

I lift the kettle, giving it a shake, and empty it before refilling and putting it over the hob and igniting the ring.

"Wow," he exclaims.

I squint my eyes at him. "Wow...*what*?"

He waves his hand up and down my body. "You're glowing."

I find the cup I want and dig down for a tea bag, before shaking it three times and dropping it in the mug. "Don't start."

He leans against the worktop. "I'm not starting anything, but it's about time, honey." He places his mug on the counter and pulls me in for a bear hug.

I let out a breath as he lets go, and then I go back to preparing my tea.

"So, will you be staying on for a couple of days now, then?"

I know Nate asked me, but I put it to the back of my mind. I have the new term starting in a few weeks, so it's not like it would interfere with my work.

"I haven't had time to think about it."

He takes the teaspoon from me and taps my nose. "Well there's really nothing to think about, is there?"

Sophie and Charlie enter. "Morning," they both say in unison, glancing at each other and shaking their heads like they're privy to an inside joke. I look at Simon who just shrugs.

"Guys, I've got to split. I have shit loads of orders to put in before I miss the deadline." Charlie swoops me up into a hug that takes my breath away, whispering in my ear. "Look after my boy." He places me back on my feet and kisses my cheek.

"Come to the bar anytime, that goes without saying. You guys, too." He steps towards Simon and shakes his hand, pulling him in for that half-hug thingy.

I watch him as he steps in front of Sophie. After a kiss on each cheek, he scans the length of her body so quickly. I would have missed it if I weren't already watching. He turns to me with a wink before walking away.

"So, all things considered, I think the weekend turned out all right," I say as I go to grab a cup for Soph.

"Speak for yourself," she says with a snort.

I instantly feel like a shit friend. "Sorry."

"Don't be daft. Besides, I realised last night, even though James hurt me, he doesn't have the power to hurt me *anymore*. Granted, I'd rather drink my own urine than ever having to speak to him again, but from what you told me, he's made his bed now."

Simon raises his coffee in a toast and takes a sip.

I take the kettle off the hob and pour the water over the tea bags, watching as the colour changes from clear to a burnt gold. "Hey, do you fancy doing something? Just the three of us?" I ask, squeezing the tea bag and dropping it onto the dish. I stir, the clinking of the metal against china soothing me, and add a dash of milk.

"Sorry, kitten, I have a date," Simon says with a smug look on his face.

I hand Soph her tea. "I have work," she says with an eye roll.

I twist the bracelet on my wrist. "I might stick around here for a few more days then…"

"Sounds like a plan," Nate says from behind me.

He wraps his arms around my waist and rests his chin on my shoulder. I turn my head to look at him, and he kisses the tip of my nose.

"Morning, beautiful," he whispers in my ear.

My whole body strums to life.

"On that note, are you ready to bust a groove, Simon?" Sophie asks.

He nods, polishing off his coffee.

"You fancy coming to take the old folk to the airport later?" Nate asks.

"Nathaniel, less of the *old folk,* if you please," Evie says as she walks over and swats him on the arm.

After Nan and Evie have successfully loaded Sophie and Simon with an abundance of leftover cake, they finally let them leave. I sit at the kitchen table and eye the cheesecake.

"Go on, you know you want to."

I laugh and grab a fork, my eyes fluttering shut as the flavours assault my palette.

"You like that, huh?"

I open my eyes. Nate is transfixed on watching me. I push his arm, but he grabs my hand and pulls me towards him, my bum rising from the seat to reach him. He leans, kissing me on the edge of my mouth before a quick flick of his tongue. I flop back on my chair.

"Fucking *delicious*."

My knickers feel wet—what the hell is he doing to me? I swallow hard. He raises an eyebrow, knowing the effect he has on me, and now I'm not too sure spending time alone is such a great idea.

"I'm going to go help Nana pack."

He stands in front of me and rubs my upper arms. "I'll see you a bit later then, I have some work to do in the garage." He winks and turns away.

At the airport, I give my Nana a long hug goodbye.

"I'll be home before your birthday," she whispers.

I tense, unable to speak. She pulls back, the apology clear across her face. I shake my head in silent warning—I don't want to make a scene. I concentrate on my breathing. I hadn't even thought about it with everything that's been going on—I was too pre-occupied.

Dread consumes me as soon as they are safely through check-in. I excuse myself from Nate to use the ladies'. I can't control the urge to throw up, my thoughts playing havoc with my subconscious.

I reach for my hairband, and ping it, but realise too late it was my bracelet. It snaps, and I can't stop the onslaught of frustrated tears. I pick it up and put it in my purse, hoping like hell I can get it fixed.

I gather myself together and leave the confines of the toilets before Nate comes looking for me. His face drops when he sees me, and he's by my side before I can blink, taking hold of my elbow.

"Shit, you don't look so good."

"I don't feel so good. I think I've eaten something that hasn't agreed with me."

He pulls me into his side, not picking up on my excuse. He knows full well we all ate the same food.

"Let's get you home, then."

He pays for the parking and spots the vending machine where he buys a bottle of water and hands it to me. It's stupid, but that tiny act has me wanting to cry. I think I preferred it when I didn't cry over every little thing.

"Thank you," I say, barely above a whisper.

On the drive home, I begin to relax, closing my eyes to concentrate on my breathing. But when Nate reaches out to touch my leg, I flinch. I turn to look at him and see the hurt on his face. I hate that I was the one to put it there.

"Flick, are you okay?" His eyes dart from the road and back to me.

"No, not really. I think I need to go lay down when we get back."

As soon as we're back, I waste no time getting out of the car and make a beeline for my room. I would put money on it that Nate isn't far behind.

I go straight to my bathroom and slide down the wall, placing my head between my legs, trying to fight the nausea.

"Flick, are you sick?"

I shake my head. "I'll be fine."

"Then let me in."

His words have more meaning than opening the bathroom door.

"I just want to be left alone."

"Hell no, if you're ill, I want to be here for you."

He frustrates me sometimes. I stand, too quickly, my head fuzzy. I inhale a deep breath and pull the door open with more force than necessary. Nate stumbles forward.

"Damn, you look awful."

"Well, thanks very much," I say, too harshly.

"I didn't mean it like that, but I'm worried…just talk to me. Please?"

I sit on my bed and look down, my chin towards my chest, the tension palpable. I hear his heavy footsteps as he walks towards me and sits down.

We sit in silence, our breaths mingling until mine is the same rhythm as his. He takes my hand and interlaces our fingers. My body reacts to him. I rest my head upon his shoulder, and his other hand strokes my hair in a soothing motion. I feel him shift.

"What?" I blurt out.

"Shush, you fell asleep. I was just laying us down."

I cling to his shirt and rest my face on his chest. His arm tightens around me, and that's when the silent tears begin to fall. He holds me and lets me know I'm not alone, but when all is said and done, we *are* alone—in our heads—no one really knowing what Fucked-up-ness goes on up there.

Chapter Twenty-Eight

I feel her shoulders begin to shake, my shirt getting wet from her silent tears. What the fuck happened since leaving the airport? She withdrew into herself—like she's a completely different person from the girl I just spent the weekend with.

I don't want to push, but as I feel her cry into my chest, it damn well breaks my heart, and I don't know what the hell to do.

"Flick, baby, what's wrong?" I can't hide the crack in my voice, and the last thing she needs is for me to lose my shit.

I hold her a little tighter because I can feel her pulling away from me emotionally. But I won't give up on us—on her.

I release her once her breathing evens out, tears all dried up. I move away to peer down at her face when a small whimper escapes her lips. I look at my watch—it's late. When did minutes turn to hours? A vibration in my pocket distracts me. As carefully as I can, I retrieve my phone. It's a text from Nan—they've arrived safe, and I'm to keep an eye on Felicity.

I also have one from Charlie that makes my eyebrows rise. Something about Sophie turning up at his bar a little worse for wear but not to worry, he'll look after her, but to not tell Flick. Great, let's start an already rocky relationship hiding secrets.

Hold on. Sophie is half-cut, and Flick is having a meltdown? I pull up the calendar on my phone, putting two and two together. It's Flicks birthday soon, which means…

"Fuck," I whisper-shout to myself.

I'm such a self-absorbed arsehole. I thought I heard Ana whisper something about a birthday. I feel sick, my whole body tensing as I grind the hell out of my back teeth.

Flick is restless. Whatever she's dreaming about, it's not good. She fidgets, and I try to whisper words to comfort her, to let her know she's safe, that I'm right here. I'll always be here.

Tears escape from under her closed lids, and that's all it takes for me to shed a few of my own. If I could change one thing in the world, it would be that she never had to endure what she did. I've never felt so helpless. I need my Gramps now more than ever.

I wake feeling groggy. I have a hangover from hell, and reality floods me. I feel around for Flick, but she isn't there. The bed is cold without her. Light breaks underneath the bathroom door. I get up and walk over, tapping on it.

"Flick?" I say in almost a whisper.

"Nate," she responds.

I try the handle and push.

She's sitting in the empty bathtub, her knees up to her chest, arms wrapped around her. Her hair is wet, and it's freezing in here. I grab for the nearest towel.

"Fuck, Flick, how long have you been in here?"

She doesn't answer. As I wrap her in the towel, I see her skin—it looks sore from scrubbing with the loofah by her feet. Her teeth chatter without mercy.

I pick her up underneath her legs, heaving her out, careful as I set her on the toilet seat. Shivers roll off her.

Goddamn it.

I grab one of the hand towels and rub the ends of her dripping hair. I want to take her in my arms—hold her or shake some sense into her—but what good will that do? I can't bear the distance between us. I help her up and sit so I can pull her into my lap and wrap her in my arms. Her skin is glacial. I rub her back, hoping to generate heat.

"Sorry," she finally whispers.

I say nothing as I stand, keeping her cradled in my arms while I walk back into the bedroom.

I sit her on the ottoman and pick up the hairbrush. Slipping in behind her, so she's between my legs, I brush her hair as gently as I can. I remember watching Ana doing this to her as a kid. Her hair always reminded me of a lion's mane.

The hairdryer is plugged in on the dresser, so I reach for it and slide the button. The hum is soothing. She closes her eyes. Ana would have put it in one of those plait-thingies, but that so isn't going to happen. I pull the hair tie from the handle of the brush and manage to pull it into a shit poor ponytail.

I pull my t-shirt off. "Up," I say, tapping her arms, pulling her arms through the sleeves of the shirt and slipping it over her head.

I guide her to the bed and sit her down. She pulls herself into the foetal position. I switch off the lamp, but when an audible gasp escapes her, I turn it back on.

"You want me to leave it on?" I ask.

She nods.

I climb into bed next to her and pull her back against my chest, wrapping her in my arms. She grips hold of my hand like a vice.

"Sleep, I've got you," I whisper, and kiss the back of her head.

Flick

I had a full-on meltdown when we arrived back from the airport. I kept pushing Nate away, but even when he found me in the bathroom, an utter mess, he stayed. The nightmare I woke up to was so vivid. I couldn't expel the smell from my nose or the residue left on my skin. It was all too real. No matter how hard I scrubbed, how hot I had the water, I still felt dirty.

He was so patient and tentative as he dried my hair. All the while, I sat there—an echo of the girl he spent the weekend with—hollow, emptiness engulfing me. I wondered what he would be like if we ever had a daughter. Would he leave us like my father did? Replace us with new, better versions?

The dream I woke up to just now was even worse—all my fears played out like a nightmarish symphony. In it, Nate told me how he could never love me, not really. I saw pity in his eyes, disgust as he pushed me away.

It would be so easy to let him in, only to ruin me completely. I'm a coward, though, and the truth is, the one I trust the *least* is myself. He would hold the power, the ability to shatter my heart into a kaleidoscope of fragmented pieces that I could never repair. James did it to Sophie. Her parents did it to her. My father did it to my Mum and me.

You can't help how you feel, and love isn't a choice. If it's not reciprocated, are they the ones in the wrong? Probably not.

I don't have a day that I don't think about what happened that night we went to the club. Whether the thoughts are brief or all-consuming, they're always there, hiding in the dark shadows—the silhouettes of the faceless monsters who took something that didn't belong to them, an innocence that once it's gone, you can never get back.

I spiralled into a state of self-hate once before. It was a grief I thought I'd never be able to break away from, but I did. Sophie always says we are a work in progress—broken but not decimated. We both carry internal scars…ones others cannot see, or will ever understand the weight of the burden that drowns us.

I left Nate sleeping. If my dreams disturbed him as much as they did me, he must be knackered. I've been in the tree house long enough to see the sunrise, its rays as it kissed the lake and the trees, lined with burnt oranges and reds, casting light in every direction.

Sunrise signifies a new day, a new dawn. But for me, the inner turmoil is attaching itself to my subconscious like a tick with a mouthful of hooks, and I am helpless to stop it.

It's going to get a whole lot worse before it gets better, and I don't want to burden Nate. I don't want him to suffer at the hands of my inner demons. He deserves better. And I know for me to get past this, I can't be here. As much as I want to, it's not fair to him. So, I'll do what I do best—I'll run, and go stay with Simon and Sophie. I know they won't ask questions.

I trudge my heavy body back to my room and creep in. I grab my travel case and call myself a cab once I'm in the kitchen. I'm a coward. I should at least wake him, tell him bye…leave a note, even. But he will dig his heels in, I know him. He wants to protect me, but he *can't*—not from myself.

Outside, the gravel crunches mercilessly beneath my trainers. Every noise has me jittery. I let out the biggest breath when I see my cab approach. My heart doesn't stop racing until we're a good twenty minutes away, the thought of Nate catching me leaving would have been too much.

I call Sophie.

"Hey, bunny."

"Hi," she replies. The *click, click, click* that sounds like an indicator in the background throws me off.

"Are you driving?"

"No, just getting a lift back to Simon's."

I pick at the skin around my nails. "Will you ever call it home?"

"Probably not."

"I'm on my way, I'll see you in a bit."

"But I thought you were staying with Nate."

I sniff back the tears. "It's complicated."

"Isn't it always… Left here." I hear a muffled response in the background. "I have to go, I'll see you when you get here."

"Okay," I say as I hang up. Wonder where she's been?

I see a text from Nate. Cursing myself with shaky hands, I can't not read it.

Are you okay? I woke up, and you were gone!

I don't know how to respond. *Ignore it.* When my palm vibrates, I look down. He's calling. I divert it to my voicemail.

A buzz alerts me of another text.

Flick, pick up your phone. I'm worried

How can I ignore him? Shit. Hands trembling, I type a reply.

Sorry, I just need some space. Don't worry.

Seconds later, another buzz.

How could I not? I woke up, and you were fucking gone.

Damn it!

I try to think of a suitable reply. But he's already sending another text. I bite my lip hard.

Sorry, it's just you were so upset yesterday and I wake up and you've vanished.

I squeeze my eyes shut, and count when it starts to vibrate again. I contemplate ignoring it, but he deserves better than that…after all, this is my fault.

"Hello," I say hoarsely.

"Flick, just come back…so we can talk."

I clear my throat. "I can't, sorry."

"Would you stop saying you're sorry already? Just come home, Flick."

"Nate, I can't…it's too complicated." I rub my face.

"What is?"

"This...me and you." I don't even know what the heck I'm saying.

He goes silent. I have to look at my screen to see if he's still there.

"Nate," I whisper.

"Flick, I fucking love you. I want to be with you."

Tears I can no longer hold back are free falling. I wipe at them angrily and glance up to see the driver looking in his rear-view mirror. He looks back to the road.

"I just can't."

He lets out a frustrated sound. "What do you mean? Can't? Or do you mean, you *won't?* I know you love me, too. You're just scared... Fuck, I don't want to be having this conversation over the goddamn phone. Just come home, *please*."

"I can't. It's too hard."

I hear the clatter of metal and what sounds like a door slamming.

"I know why you're pulling away, but you don't have to. Let me help you."

I take a deep inhale of air. "Nate, you don't understand what it was like. Sophie and Simon have been through it before. It's not something I want you to see." I pick at the skin underneath my elbow.

"That's *bollocks.* When you love someone, you stick together through the bullshit, the good, the bad and the damn right ugly."

"I need time, Nate. You need to understand that I can't be fixed. I am not one of your fucking cars." I need to get through to him. He has to know what I'm saying makes sense. How can I expect us to work, when the shit has already hit the proverbial fan?

"I'll give you space if that's what you want. But I'm not happy about it. This isn't my choice. I'm respecting your decision, but it doesn't mean I agree with it."

"Sorry…" I whisper.

He lets out a groan. "Stop saying you're fucking *sorry*. You say it like you're saying goodbye." The anger drips from his voice like fat off a griddle.

"That's not what I meant." I ping my band so hard, it breaks. The sting does nothing to ease my nerves.

"I know…it's me being an arsehole."

"I have to go."

"Call me later, or at least text, let me know you're all right."

"Okay."

"Be safe. I love you." His voice cracks.

"I know you do." I end the call. Saying it back would have made it harder. I want to sleep, to not have to deal with life. These suffocating emotions… I'm fed up with treading water. I'm exhausted. It's like my body is shutting down. I just want to forget the world.

Chapter Twenty-Nine

It's been four fucking days.

Apart from the text to say she arrived at Simon's, I haven't heard from her. I've sent her texts, but still…*nada*. I've nearly trashed my phone at least twenty times just to stop myself from ringing her. I drowned my sorrows into a bottle of whiskey, but it didn't numb me like I wanted. If anything, it made me ache for her more.

I just want her to want me, to let me be there for her. Words can only do so much, but I need to *show* her that out of the darkness, there is light.

Am I hurt she pushed me away? Of course, I am. I'm jealous of the relationship she has with Simon and Sophie. Angry they get to be there for her, and I don't. But I know that's my ego talking. All she'd be doing if she gave in is stroking it, and that's not what I want. I want her to *want* me.

I'm taking all my frustration out on this damn engine, but at this rate, I'm more likely to fuck it up beyond repair. I throw my spanner at my toolbox, knocking the contents on top all over the place.

"Easy, mate, don't blame the tools," Charlie says.

"Whatever."

He holds his palms up. "Whoa, who took the jam out of your donut?"

I sit down and drop my head into my hands.

"Sorry, man," I say, scrubbing my face.

"No offence, but you look like shit. What's happened?"

I look up, letting out a frustrated sigh. "It's Flick."

"What about her? You both looked fine the other day."

I grind my jaw. "We were…until she left."

He sits down, eyebrows raised. "What do you mean? She left?"

"I woke up the other morning, and she was gone."

"What?"

Fucking hell, do I need to spell it out to him? What part of this does he not get?

"She was a wreck after we came back from the airport. It was the night you texted about Sophie. It's her birthday soon…dredges up bad memories."

"Might explain why Sophie was a mess after her friends bailed on her. She ended up back at mine—"

I shoot to my feet, glaring at him, my fists clenched.

"Fucking hell, not like that. I'm not an arsehole. It was a lift, that's all, but she passed out. I had no idea where she lived."

"She lives with Simon," I say, and lean back against one of the cars, too wired to keep still.

"She does?" He looks perplexed

I nod. "Yeah, it's a recent development. Apparently, her parents are jerks."

He shrugs. "I ended up taking her to mine to sleep it off. It was all above board. I even drove her home the next morning, but don't say anything…she was adamant Flick would be disappointed if she found out."

"Thanks for taking care of her."

"It's fine. It makes sense now why her behaviour was a little erratic. She never once took her eyes off me when I served her a drink. It's not surprising after what they've been through..."

I throw my hands up. "It's the reason Flick is pushing me away."

"Then give her time."

"I'm trying, but it's already been four fucking days."

He grabs the back of his neck. "I don't think there's a time limit on something like this..."

"Whatever, man. Do you really have to make sense all the time?" I may not have my Gramps, but I've at least got Charlie.

"I can't help it, what can I say? I'm special."

I cock my head. "You keep telling yourself that."

"Someone has to," he says, smoothing his eyebrows.

"I'm sure there are plenty of women who'd happily tell you how special you are."

He shakes his head, the smirk gone. "What? And end up like you over a girl? No thanks."

I smile for the first time in days. "She's not just any girl, though. She's *my* girl."

"And she loves you, she always has, it's as clear as day. Just try to be patient with her."

I grind my jaw. At this rate, I'll need dentures. "Don't you think I'm trying?"

I grab hold of my hair and push off from the car.

I hear a crunching sound, followed by the screaming of metal.

I spin around just as the car slides down the ramps. It's like everything slows down as the car comes straight for me.

I fall backward.

The air is knocked out of me.

My head bounces off the floor and jars my mouth. My teeth smash against one another.

My ears ring so loudly, it's as if a firework has been set off in front of my face. Bright light flickers in and out before I'm pulled into complete and utter darkness.

Chapter Thirty

I have a tendency to clam up, but this time, it's different. It isn't just about me—I need to consider Nate's feelings in all of this, too.

With my Nana being back in France with Evie, and Mum smitten with Luke, I don't want to be a burden. I've been trying to keep busy, running and taking photos, but everything I do brings me back to Nate. I've been waking in cold sweats from the nightmares to the point I thought I'd wet myself. The only thing that made them bearable was waking up in Nate's arms.

Simon said nothing when I arrived on his doorstep, my face tear-streaked. He opened his arms and held me as I cried for all the things I want, and all the things I've lost.

Sophie throws a cushion at my head. "I can't tell you what to do but you and I both know you're just putting off the inevitable. If you ask me, you and Nate belong together. Whether that time was yesterday, today or tomorrow…you are meant to be."

I hug the cushion, running my palm over the soft material. "I love him, but I keep hurting him every time I push him away. He could have pulled back after the airport, but he didn't. He's so attentive, sweet and kind…and that's what frightens me."

She looks at me like I'm bat-shit crazy. "What? That he's sweet and kind?"

I shake my head. "No, giving him the power to break me."

"Flick, if you can trust anyone, I think it's him. Come on, think about it, how good was he and Charlie, for that matter—when that idiot showed up at the fundraiser? Besides, there are worse things than letting someone love you."

You would think after the way she's been treated, she'd be *anti-love*—not pro. She never ceases to amaze me. I'm going to try to take some strength from her and make things right with Nate before I push him away for good.

I dig around in my bag for my lip balm, but as I move my phone, I notice a missed call. I swipe at the screen to see who it's from.

"That's weird."

"What is?" Soph asks me with a concerned look on her face.

"I have a missed call from Charlie."

Her lips form a straight line as she watches while I listen to the voicemail.

I sit forward, an overwhelming urge to throw up.

"Shit," I get to my feet and begin pacing. "There's been some sort of accident… Nate's been taken to hospital." My voice wobbles as panic sets in.

Sophie stands, coming into my line of sight and takes my hand in hers. "Which hospital? I'll drive."

I reel off the hospital as she makes quick work of rounding up her bag and keys. She ushers me out of the door—apparently, my legs seem to have forgotten how to work.

She guides me by the elbow towards the car and coaxes me to get in before fastening my seatbelt.

"I think you may be in shock," she says, leaning over to the glove box and pulling out a pack of tissues before handing them to me. "Everything is going to be fine." She types the hospital into the sat nav.

I nod and wipe my eyes. With shaking fingers, I pull up Charlie's number. When he answers, my throat closes up, and instead of speaking, a choked sob escapes. I can hear him but can't make out what he's saying.

Sophie has already pulled away. She glances over to me. "Flick, hang up. I can call him on hands-free. Type the number into my phone."

I manage to do what she asks. After one ring, his voice echoes through the speaker.

"Hello?"

"It's Sophie, you're on speaker phone. Can you tell us what happened?"

"There was an accident. A car fell off the ramp, and he was trapped underneath."

I squeeze my eyes shut.

"How bad is it?" she asks, her voice eerily calm.

"I don't know. When the paramedics arrived, he was unconscious. Flick, are you all right?"

I cannot believe he is asking after me, of all people.

"She'll feel better once we're there."

"Understandable, how far away are you?"

She glances to the sat nav. "About half an hour, forty minutes at most."

"Drive safe. If anything changes, I'll call you."

The remainder of the drive is silent, apart from the sat nav.

Time seems to slow down.

Every second feels like a minute.

Every minute feels like an hour.

Charlie is outside of accident and emergency when Sophie drops me to go park. He jogs over, pulling me into a hug. I feel numb.

When Sophie finds us, he already has me sipping on a cup of tea. He stands when he sees her approaching. She walks straight into his open arms before she sits down beside me.

"Any news yet?" she asks.

"Not a word. This is fucking ridiculous." Charlie slumps down in the seat opposite.

"How did it happen?" I stare at his knees—covered in dirt and blood—and take a deep breath.

His hands hang between his legs. "I don't know. One minute we were talking, then the next thing I know, the car has come off the ramps, headed straight for him. I called an ambulance and managed to get the jack under the car, but I didn't want to risk moving him—" He grabs hold of the back of his neck. "What if I fucked up? What if I made it worse when I took the weight off him?"

Sophie goes to kneel in front of him. "Charlie, you did the right thing. He was lucky you were there." Taking his hand, she gives it a squeeze. "Waiting is the hardest part. We need to let them do their jobs. I'll go see if I can get an update."

She stands, looking around him. "Did you not get yourself a tea?" she asks.

He shakes his head.

"You need sugar, too. I'll be back."

Charlie sits next to me. "She's really something, isn't she?" he says.

I nod and sip my tea, hoping like hell I can keep it down. The thought of Nate being trapped under a car conjures ghastly images in my head that I'd rather not see.

Charlie bounces his knee up and down. "I'm so sorry, Flick."

"What? God, Charlie, it's not your fault. You were *the*re. I hate to think what would have happened if you hadn't been…"

He nods and stands when Sophie walks back over with his tea. "That was quick," he says.

She shrugs. "I'll be right back. Look after her," she says, pointing.

"Sitting right here," I say.

She smiles. "Glad to hear it. I'll see what I can find out." She turns and heads in the direction of the main reception. I watch in awe at her ability to be so in control of a really fucked-up situation.

A nurse comes out to see her, and she points in our direction after an animated conversation and hand movements. Together, they walk over. The nurse ushers us to a private room and slides the tab to occupied before we enter. Then she softly closes the door behind us.

"Due to the impact of Nathaniel hitting his head, it would appear he's suffered possible head trauma. As you may know, he was unconscious and unresponsive upon arrival. Necessary steps were taken by putting him into an induced coma."

Air clogs in the back of my throat. *A coma.*

I put my hand over my mouth, shaking my head in disbelief.

She continues.

"Apart from a few minor lacerations to his upper body, we're concerned there may be internal bleeding and possible damage to his spleen, however, we are hopeful these are superficial."

Charlie pulls me into his side before my legs give out.

The nurse gestures towards the chairs, but we don't move. She's not finished yet.

"He is being taken for an MRI, so we should be able to ascertain the full extent of his injuries. Depending on the results, we will determine whether surgery is required. Until then, he will be monitored closely in our intensive care unit."

"What happens when you have the results?" I ask. My voice catches.

She looks at me sombrely. "Like I said, that will all depend, but as soon as we know more, we'll update you. And hopefully we can get you in to see him, but I warn you, it may only be brief. In the meantime, you are fine to remain here, in the family room."

"Thank you," Sophie says gratefully as the nurse leaves us alone.

I sob. The reality of what's happening is too much. Sophie wraps me in her arms, and Charlie takes my hand in his as we try to comprehend the situation.

"How did you get them to speak to us?" Charlie asks.

"I lied…told her he was my brother," she answers, looking sheepish. One thing she is not, is a liar. "I'm sorry, I didn't know what else to say. I just had to try to help. I'll probably go to hell for lying."

"Thank you, and so not going to hell," Charlie replies.

It's not long before he's pacing the size of the room. It's the first signs I've seen of his discomfort being here. He watched his mum's condition deteriorate in a hospital.

Sophie associates hospitals with the trauma of what happened to us—that she'd likely never be able to bear children.

So, right now is more reason than ever for me to fight off my demons and try to keep my shit in line.

"I need to let Evie know," I say to no one in particular.

Charlie shakes his head. "I already did. I wasn't sure if I should, but she is his next of kin. Besides, she's the last person I want to get on the bad side of," he says with a warm, affectionate smile. "I said I'd keep her posted."

It wouldn't surprise me if she and Nana were on the next flight home.

"So, she knows about the...coma?" My voice catches.

He avoids my gaze. "No, I rang her before you arrived. But I'd rather wait until we know more from the MRI scan. Do you agree?"

"Yes, but he's in a coma, for fuck's sake," I say, panic beginning to strangle me from the inside out.

Sophie grips my shoulders. "Sweetness, I know it sounds bad, but it was induced, which, believe it or not, is a good thing. They can monitor him better this way, and most importantly, make sure he gets enough oxygen to the brain."

I think my mouth gapes open.

She rolls her eyes. "Oh, don't look at me like that. You hear things when you're stuck in hospitals, that's all."

I pull her in for a hug. She doesn't pull away immediately like she wants to. She's not tactile at the best of times, but deep down, there are times when she needs human contact just as much as the rest of us.

After what feels like forever and a day, we're informed that Nate has been moved and that we can go see him, but only two at a time.

"You two go. I'll check on the parking. Charlie, what's your reg number? I can check on yours, too, if you want?"

Once he exchanges the information and passes her his keys, we both take off to see Nate.

They warn us about the ventilator and tubes, but to not be alarmed when we walk in. Charlie steps in first, closely followed by me. I gasp aloud, feeling light-headed, like I might pass out. Charlie takes me by the waist, keeping me rooted, as I look at the mess that is Nate.

Chapter Thirty-One

I approach the bed, the machines beeping like mad as the whirring noise of the ventilator hums a sombre tune. The sight of the tubes attached to him is all too much. His face is peppered with bruises, and he looks lost in that bed, surrounded by all the equipment. I want to lie down beside him and hold him until he wakes up.

Charlie reaches for a chair and begins pulling it towards the bed. It screams in protest—the legs attacking the floor. I cringe, the sound harsher than nails being scraped down a chalkboard.

He ushers me to sit. I stare, unblinking, until my vision blurs and place my head between my legs. *One, two, three*. The smell of disinfectant assaults the back of my throat as I swallow, making me gag.

Charlie squeezes my shoulder. "I know they told us… But shit, I would have lost it if you and Soph hadn't got here when you did."

I place my hand over his as I sit up. "She went straight into fight mode. While I was a complete mess, she took control. She was the same when her parents practically disowned her—she kept going."

He rubs my back in small, circular motions. “She is pretty incredible. Something about her that reminds me of my mum.” His voice catches.

It doesn’t matter if you lose someone you loved yesterday, or ten years ago, the grief is always there. You learn to carry it like an unspoken whisper. You know you were the lucky one for having known them, and you smile at their memory. At least, it’s the way I feel when I think of my Papi. Every time I smell cinnamon, I think of him.

I lean forward and take hold of Nate’s hand. What I wouldn’t give for him to squeeze it. “Please, you need to be okay. I only just got you back.” I wipe my face angrily. “I can’t lose you, not now.” I stroke his face. His skin is cold; he’s naturally warm by nature.

I don’t know why, but I need to keep talking. “You know that saying, absence makes the heart grow fonder? It’s the truth. I knew the first moment I saw you—well, heard your voice at the airport—it hit me like a tropical storm. It was alien, that sensation. I was used to going through the motions. God, Nate, you made me feel full again. You gave me space when I pushed you away, but I was coming back to you, Nate—”

There’s a noise followed by a commotion as people come rushing in, saying things I don’t understand. I stand. The room is a flurry of activity. We’re told we need to leave, but I can’t move, I won’t.

I pull against Charlie as he twists my body towards the door and pushes me forward. I dig my heels in until he lifts me off my feet. Grunting, I try mercilessly to get away from him, but he’s too strong.

I can’t breathe—it’s like the air has been vacuumed out of the corridor.

The wash-white walls… the flickering fluorescent light…

A deep pulse clouds my ears as everything around me blurs. Disappears.

Nathaniel

Summers like this are always my favourite. I swing my legs back and forth over the ledge of the tree house. In the distance, I see my parents walking together—hand in hand. My heart beats faster, my stomach churning with a new-found anticipation. I blink to clear my vision, but they're still there…heading this way.

Carefully, I rise, all the while keeping my eyes fixed on them. My heart thunders in my ears as I look down. My mum raises her head and hand, shielding her eyes from the midday sun.

"Well?" she calls up. "Are you going to come down and give me a hug, baby boy?"

My throat constricts. Sweat trails from my temple and down my cheek. I force myself to move, the weight of my body like nothing I've ever felt before. As I descend the ladder, every rung I meet is with moist palms. Afraid to slip, I grip each one tighter until I reach the bottom.

I round the base of the tree, expecting them to have been a mirage. Standing, waiting for me, are indeed my parents. Each step is slow and precise as I move closer, my breath locked inside, afraid of them vanishing before my very eyes.

My mum is the first one to move towards me. She opens her arms and wraps me into an embrace I've craved so very much. I breathe her in deep, the sweet smell of flowers tickling my nose.

As she whispers into my ear, her breath fans my cheek. “My handsome boy, you’ve grown so much.”

I grip her tighter, afraid to let go. Someone clears their throat. Peering over my mum’s shoulder, I see my Dad wearing a proud smile. He envelops us both in his big, strong arms.

I choke back my tears—I’ve missed them so much. I started to forget what they looked like, how they smelt. A sob escapes me. I’m afraid I no longer know what’s real.

My mum pulls back and takes my face in her hands she looks me straight in the eye—oceans of blue staring back at me. It warms me from the inside out. The moment of fear no longer holds me hostage. Tears dry, replaced with unwavering love that only a mother can give.

“Sweetheart, we are both so very proud of the man you’ve become.”

I protest. “I wish that were true.”

My dad steps in. “It is. Your grandparents raised you well. It broke our hearts that we had to leave you behind, but it wasn’t your time, son.”

I pull away. “I let Gramps down… I was selfish. He was sick, and I let him down. And when I found out he wasn’t your Dad, I lost it.”

He smiles, his crooked front tooth on display. “You were hurt, no one thinks any less of you.”

I rub at my chest, a shooting pain making every breath sting.

“Come on, let’s take a walk.” My mother links her arm with mine, and my Dad places his arm over my shoulder as we walk towards the water.

It’s so calm and peaceful. I can see the reflection of the surrounding trees and overhead skyline—eerily tranquil.

I have so many questions. Where have they been? Why did they have to go? Can I stay with them?

Mum signals to Dad. "Sami."

My whole body convulses.

"It's okay, sweetheart, someone else wants to speak to you."

I turn to the side as two men walk towards us. Squinting, I try to make out their faces. It's him, but he looks so different—vibrant, full of life and colour. I don't remember him at that age, but I know it's him. It's how he looked in the photo with Nan on their wedding day.

"Why does he look so young?"

Dad lets out a chuckle. "It's when he was at his happiest." He says it like it's something everyone should know.

The man beside him has his hands in his pockets—so carefree and unassuming. *No*—it can't be…can it?

"Nate, meet Samuel."

"Samuel, meet Nate," my father says with a pride I've never heard before.

He holds his hand out to me. I take it, and he places his other one over the top.

"It's good to meet you. I helped create your father, so in turn, I feel as though I had a hand in creating you."

I look between all three men. This is so surreal.

Gramps clamps his hand on my father's shoulder. "It's time."

My father nods in understanding. "Nate, we have to go, but your Gramps wants to talk to you."

I leap towards him. "Please don't."

"Nate, we have to, dear, but we're always with you." My mother kisses my forehead and pulls me into her chest. I breathe her in, not wanting to let go.

I feel the emptiness before I even open my eyes. Everyone has gone all except my Gramps.

A horrible shooting sensation pulsates through my head.

He pulls me in for a hug. I hold on tight, still feeling his loss the most. He releases me and sits. I join him, my arms hanging limply between my legs—mirroring him. I can't stop staring. He looks so different, and yet, the same all at once.

"Gramps, am I dead?" I ask the question I'm most afraid of.

He lets out a throaty laugh. "No, son, you're not dead."

"So, am I dreaming?"

He picks a small blade of lavender, brings it to his nose, and inhales. "I guess you could say that."

"Gramps, I am so sorry," I say.

"You have nothing to apologise for."

I shake my head. "But I do. I disrespected you. After I found out about my Dad and you, I was hurt—betrayed."

"It was never my intention. It doesn't change my feelings for you or your father. I was blessed to have the life I did, and I never once took it for granted." He spins his wedding ring. "I embraced it the best way I knew how."

I touch his arm. "I grew up knowing I was loved. You're the best man I've ever known."

His laugh rattles from his chest. "I don't know about that. I never felt deserving of the life I had. Evie understood me, though. Better than I understood myself. She never resented me for loving Ana, and I never stopped. She was my first love—the kind that imprints on your subconscious. But with your Nan, it was all-consuming. I'll love her forever."

He wipes at his face. "I miss her, but I'm in no hurry for her to join me. Love has a surprising way of being patient. You tell her when her time comes, I'll be under our tree—waiting. It was the first time I told her I loved her and meant it."

"She misses you," I say as I pull at the grass, the texture foreign between my fingertips, like pins and needles.

"I know. And I also know you have a lot of people worried about you. It's time for you to go back."

I shake my head. "But I don't want to leave you." *I'm not ready to say goodbye.*

"I know, but it's not your time. We live inside you, son. As long as you remember us, you keep our memories alive."

Chapter Thirty-Two

It's been three days. That's seventy-two hours, four thousand three hundred and twenty minutes.

How do I know? Because I counted. Just like how I know there are forty-eight ceiling tiles in Nate's room. It's what keeps me grounded and awake.

Nana and Evie arrived yesterday. I haven't cried since before I fainted. I watched as they both cried and held one another when they came out from visiting Nate. I had to remove myself from that part of my reality.

I have been whispering to Nate constantly. Mostly insignificant babble.

We had a small reprieve when his results came back. He has swelling on the brain, but it's decreased considerably since his first scan. They say the possibility of some memory loss is likely, but we won't know for sure until after he's awake.

It's the bruising to his spine they are still trying to ascertain, but again, they won't know more *until he wakes up*.

Every time they say that, I want to shake them. They're the ones keeping him asleep. *They're* the ones who put him in the coma, but they are going to bring him out of it later today.

It's been a hive of activity. Charlie, Simon, and Sophie—they've all rallied round—airport run, hospital runs, and yet here I am, refusing to budge. Like I have some claim over Nate. As if my feelings matter more than everyone else's. It's my fault. I left him. We could have been in his room, watching a DVD, or cuddling on the sofa, but instead, he's wired to machines.

My head lulls and I force myself upright. The cheap hospital chair protests my movements as I try to get comfortable.

"That's enough, Flick," Charlie says, "I'm taking you home for a few—"

I shake my head. "No."

"Yes. For a few hours. You want to be semi-alert when he's awake, don't you?"

"I don't want to leave him." My body rattles with nervous tension. I turn to see Nana and Evie, just outside the door.

"Come on, he'd kill me. This isn't good for you. I'll bring you back after you've had some rest, I promise."

"He's right, Felicity. You need to go home, take a bath." Evie has a determined look on her face.

I resign, no use fighting them both.

Charlie puts the palm of his hand on the small of my back as he walks me away from the ward, out of the hospital, in the direction of his car. He drives in silence back to Nate's.

I sit on the edge of my bed but think better of it, and head to his room instead.

It's like he got ready this morning and popped out. His bed is unmade, a towel hanging on the chair. I feel him in every inch of his surroundings.

I enter the bathroom, turn on the shower and strip. I hover under the showerhead before reaching for his body wash and lather myself, inhaling the familiar essence. I don't bother with my hair. I don't have the strength.

Wrapped in his dressing gown, I hunt through his drawers and pull out a t-shirt and swap it for the robe.

I climb up his bed and wrap my arms around one of his pillows. My eyelids are heavy, my eyes so dry, I let them close, just for a moment.

"Well, are you coming, or what?" Nate asks.

He's awake and standing in front of me, holding out his hand. I nod and take his hand in mine. I see my reflection in a mirror. I'm wearing a beautiful, white lace dress, and Nate is dressed to the nines in a suit and cravat, his top button undone.

He has never looked at me with so much love.

"Dance with me, Mrs. Davenport."

Tears spring to my eyes as I repeat his words. "Mrs. Davenport?"

He nods and pulls me into his arms. This is right where I want to be. He pulls back to look at me.

"Flick, you look beautiful. I can't wait to start my life with you."

We float around the dance floor, surrounded by a million fairy lights. He pulls me close, his breath spreading like wildfire over my skin.

The song fades out, and the lights begin to dim.

His form slowly turns to shadow as he slips further away from me. I scream, but no sound comes out, no matter how hard I try.

I blink rapidly as a face comes into focus.

Sophie strokes my arm. "Hey, Bunny, you were having a bad dream," she says, wiping my face. "I came by to check on you. Charlie thought you might be here…"

"How long have I been asleep?"

"Most of the afternoon. I came because he's awake."

I sit up and swing my legs over the edge of the mattress. "What the fuck, Soph?"

She flinches.

I grab her hand.

"Come on, let's get you back to the hospital."

I pull her in for a hug. "I'm sorry."

"Don't worry about it." She stands, holding out her hand for me.

I hop from one foot to the other, working the band around my wrist over and over again, when Nana steps out of the room.

"How is he?" I ask, breathless.

She looks at me, worry in her eyes. "He hasn't really said much."

Squeezing my eyes closed, I count to five before opening them again and letting out a breath.

"Why don't you go on in and see him now," she suggests.

I look over to Charlie and hold my hand out. He takes it.

Relief floods me when I walk in. The ventilator is now gone. His eyes are open, and I rush to his side.

"Nate, it's me."

His eyes lock with mine—a spark of recognition before he glances towards Charlie. His eyelids droop heavily and close again. I sit down and squeeze his arm. Charlie places his hand on my shoulder, neither of us moves until a nurse comes in.

"If you can please wait outside. I'll call you back in when I'm finished."

I feel like all we've done is wait, and quite frankly, it's taking a toll. I sit down in the seating along the corridor. Placing my face in my hands, I let out a groan of frustration.

"Come on, it won't be long," Evie says, rubbing my back.

Why didn't he say anything when he saw us? Is he still mad I left him? What if he doesn't remember me? What if he can't forgive me?

I get up and make my way to the toilet and lock myself in a cubicle. I bite the inside of my cheek until I taste iron. Silent tears fall. I clench my fists until red crescent moons appear. I hold my breath for as long as I can before I release it. I struggle to get my breathing under control before finally opening the cubicle door.

I've been in and out of a hazy sleep.

A nurse stands beside me. "Hi, You're in hospital. Can you tell me your full name and date of birth, please?"

"Nathaniel Lawrence Davenport. Twenty-second of March, nineteen eighty-four." My throat feels raw, I cough, but it scratches, making it worse.

"Excellent, are you thirsty?" she asks with a wonky smile.

I nod. She brings a plastic cup towards me and holds the straw to my mouth. I lean forward and sip, releasing a sigh when I sit back.

"How are you feeling?"

"Confused, what happened?" I ask, my throat still uncomfortable.

"Don't you remember?" she asks, writing on my chart.

I try to think, but it's foggy. "Not really, no."

"What is the last thing you remember?" she asks, pen poised.

"I'm not sure…" Why the fuck can't I remember? My head pounds. I raise my hand and feel a bandage.

"That's normal. You're probably feeling disorientated. It's to be expected."

"Expected… What happened?" My fists clench the sheet beneath me.

"You had an accident in your workshop. Does that ring any bells?"

I shake my head, but stop—that isn't helping with the pain. I close my eyes and think. I don't have any recollection of having an accident.

"Okay, let's try something a little easier. What is the last clear memory you have?"

I think for a moment. My gut tightens—Gramps is gone. My heart breaks again as I try to breathe through it.

"I remember the fundraiser, but after that, it's foggy."

"That's good. I'm going to send for the doctor. She can come and talk to you. Would you like me to send your family back in?"

I wince and carefully touch my head.

"Are you in pain?" she asks.

"My head, and my ribs when I breathe."

She pats my leg, but it's as though I'm having an out of body experience—I saw her do it, but it's like she was touching someone else's leg.

"I will see about getting you a little more pain relief. Does anywhere else hurt more than the other?" she asks, scribbling on the chart.

"Well, it's weird… Maybe it's just me, but did something happen to my legs?"

She looks at the chart and back to my face. "Are they hurting?"

"That's the thing. I can't seem to feel them," I croak out.

She looks to my legs, and then to my face. A blanket of calm washes over her face, but in her eyes, I see it—the uncertainty and concern.

As soon as she leaves, I try desperately to move my legs. I reach my hand down to my thigh and slap it hard.

I hear the vibration but feel nothing.

Nan and Charlie enter.

“Hi, Nan,” I say hoarsely.

“Nathaniel. I can’t leave you for one minute,” she says in mock annoyance.

I bite my lip. “Where did you go?” I know it’s a daft question to ask at a time like this, but to be honest, the whole thing has me completely discombobulated.

“I went to France with Ana, don’t you remember?”

I nod, but truth is, I don’t remember. I shake my head once.

“I’ll fill you in later, it’s not worth getting worked up about. We’re just pleased you’re awake,” Charlie says.

I’m not even sure how to respond. It’s a lot to take in all at once. It’s like when you go upstairs to your bedroom to get something, but when you get there, for the life of you, you just can’t remember what it was. And the thought terrifies me.

“Are you okay?”

I don’t want to lie to her, but I’ve seen her heartbroken over Gramps. I can’t tell her that the last time I felt this scared was when my parents died. I swallow back the lump in my throat. “I’ve been better, but don’t worry about me, I’ll be fine.”

She pulls out her hankie to conceal her sniffle. Charlie rubs her back.

“I’m sorry I made you all worry.”

“Sorry doesn’t quite cut it. If you ever scare me like that again, I’ll kill you myself,” Charlie replies, earning himself a swat on the arm from my Nan.

“Oh, that’s awful.”

He gives her a sheepish look and kisses her temple. She shoos him away as she breaks out a small smile.

"I think a certain someone is desperate to see you," he says, angling his head toward the door.

Nan kisses my head. "We'll be back in soon."

I hold up my fist to Charlie and he gives me a quick fist bump in return. I flinch when I get a pain in my ribs. If only I could feel pain in my legs.

I feel her before I see her.

When she walks in, I scan her face. She looks as tired as I feel. I can tell she's nervous. And I feel almost frustrated with her, but I'm not sure why… It's like when you dream of arguing with someone, and you're still annoyed with them when you wake up.

But when her eyes meet mine, all ill thoughts and feelings disintegrate.

"Sorry, do you work here?" I ask.

She lets out an audible gasp. Her eyes go wide as she searches my face.

I smile wide.

"You arsehole," she says. She sucks in her bottom lip between her teeth right before she bursts into tears. My chest tightens.

"Shit, Flick, please don't cry," I say and reach for her hand.

I pull it to my lips and kiss her palm. They look sore, but I don't say anything as I kiss the inside of her wrist.

"Nate, I thought you might never wake up… I thought I'd lost you." The sombreness of her words makes my heart skip a beat.

"I'm awake, it's okay. Come here," I say, needing her close.

She holds still. "I don't want to hurt you," she says, stifling a sob.

I close my eyes before opening them again. "You'll only hurt me by not letting me hold you…now, come here already."

I pull on her arm until she lowers her head. Reaching up, I place my hand on the nape of her neck, pulling her close. I kiss the tip of her nose and wipe away her tears. If there is one thing I haven't forgotten, it's how much I love this girl and always will.

"I have so much to say to you, Nate."

"I know, but not now. I hate that you're this upset because of me."

She shakes her head, her hair falling over her shoulders. "I'm not upset. These are happy tears. I'm just so glad you're awake. It petrified me—seeing you attached to that ventilator. I love you, Nate. Don't scare me like that again."

I suck in a breath. My ribs react in protest. "Did you just say you love me?"

She raises her eyebrows, her entire face flushing a delicious shade of red. "Yes."

"God, I love that you love me too. I never meant to make you all worry."

She strokes my face. "We're just glad you're all right." She sits and rests her chin on my arm.

I want to tell her I'm not all right, about not having any feeling in my legs, but I'm afraid if I say it out loud, it will make it real—too real.

Chapter Thirty-Three

Nathaniel

It's been a couple of days since I woke up. They've advised me to give my body time, that it's a waiting game until the swelling on my spine goes down. They have me in traction and on bed rest.

I'm pissed off. Where do they think I'm going to go? I can't move my legs, for fuck's sake. I'm also pissed with this goddamn catheter—I feel useless and frustrated. It's humiliating having complete strangers giving you a sponge bath.

Flick has been a rock, a real trooper, but I'm finding even she's rubbing me up the wrong way. I can't give her what she deserves. I know I'm an insensitive bastard with what I am about to do, but I have no choice. I love her too damn much to keep dragging her down with me. She'll be better off without me.

Mid-conversation, I just blurt it out.

"Felicity," I say sharply.

She stops talking, her jaw slack.

"I want to talk about us."

I can see it in her eyes—she knows it isn't going to be pleasant.

I clear my throat. "There's no easy way for me to say this, so I'm just going to come out with it. This thing between you and me isn't going to work," I say, pointing my finger back and forth.

"What the hell are you talking about?" she says crossing her arms.

"I can't see us working. I thought I was ready to be in a relationship, but after having this accident, it's made me realise that I'm not. I'm sorry."

"Nate, I don't believe you."

"Believe me, the last thing I want to do is hurt you. It's why I'm telling you now."

She shakes her head stubbornly. "No, you don't mean it."

"We're over. God, Flick, we never even started," I say, my eyes burning straight into hers.

"*No*," she says, raising her voice. She drops her hand and hovers over me. This is a side of her I haven't seen in a long time. I'd smile if the situation weren't so serious.

"I want you to leave. I really am sorry, I never meant to hurt you."

Her face is a picture, all her features tense. "Nate, you're scared, I get that, but don't be a fucking idiot."

I think I might laugh when a nurse enters.

"Everything okay in here?" she asks, glancing between us both.

"It's fine," Flick snaps, which is so unlike her.

I take that as my cue. "No, it's not. I want her to leave," I say, looking straight at the nurse. I keep all my focus on her and off Flick.

"Nate, don't do this," Flick says, her tone pleading. It's nearly my undoing, but she deserves better after everything she's already been through.

It's why what I am about to say next is even harder.

"What's wrong with you? Are you fucking deaf? Go!" I lift myself up in frustration. I let out a groan, pain shooting through me.

The nurse rushes over to my bedside

"Nathaniel, I need you to please try and stay calm." She gently pushes me back towards the pillows.

"I will as soon as she takes the hint and leaves." My voice doesn't even sound like mine—I've never felt more ashamed than I do at this moment.

"Sorry, love, but he needs to stay calm, and this isn't helping, I'm afraid I'll have to ask you to leave." The nurse looks uncomfortable. I can tell from the way she's looking at Flick, that she feels sorry for her, but patients do come first and all that.

Flick strides over to the opposite side of the bed, she takes in a few deep breaths I see rise and fall of her chest. What if she has a panic attack, *fuck!*

I'm about to reach out to her but stop myself, biting the inside of my cheek.

"Fine, Nate, I'll go. I don't think it's what you really want, but I won't be your emotional punching bag either. If you need to talk, I'm here, but if you don't want to talk to me, do yourself a favour and talk to a professional. Don't bottle it up."

She storms to the door. "Oh, and Nate, for the record… I'll be the one to say when we're over."

I blink away the sting in my eyes. She deserves better than a cripple.

Two days ago, I let Flick leave, thinking I didn't want to be with her. Since Charlie smuggled my phone in, I've been tempted to message. To avoid that, I decided the best thing was to keep it switched off. Besides, I keep telling myself the last thing I want to do is fuck up some poor bastard's heart monitor.

I feel so alone, even with the steady flow of visitors. Charlie openly told me he thought I was being a prick where she's concerned. Then he left it at that. Why any of them are putting up with my bullshit is beyond me. I've considered asking how she is, but then I play the martyr instead, and suffer in silence.

During another zombie-induced snooze, stuck in my sterile prison, the door swings open. The hairs on my arms stand up. Her scent floats over me.

I look up, and she's staring straight at me. I look away as my stomach lurches.

"So, I take it you're still wallowing in self-pity?" She places a bag down on the tray over my bed. "I'll take your silence as a yes."

I say nothing and avoid making eye contact. I watch her every move as she pulls a laptop from the bag.

"Oh, and so we both understand one another, I've spoken to the ward sister who agrees this—" she waves her hand over me, "—is not doing you any good. We're going to be left alone. They'll only come in to do their checks, so don't try pressing the call button. If something is wrong, I'll let them know."

I forgot how tenacious she could be.

I reach for the call button and press it, wanting to poke out my tongue.

She crosses her arms, with an, *I told you so look.* I don't want to be caught in her snare, so I lower my eyes and close them. Her breasts look good in that vest top. I roll my head to the side.

"Like I told you, Nate, no one's coming to save you."

Has she always been this annoying, or is this a new development? I want to say something so badly, but I keep my mouth shut.

I hear her shuffling around and the rustle of plastic. My curiosity gets the better of me. I turn to see her pulling out popcorn and bags of sweets amongst other things. She struggles to pull the over-sized chair closer to the bed—it makes a god-awful noise as the legs scrape against the floor—until she's satisfied with where she has it positioned.

I'm mostly lying down in the bed, but it's low to the ground, so when she finally sits down, the cushioned seat sucking her in, we are the same head height.

Leaning forward, she grabs the bag of popcorn, opens it and places it next to my elbow. She loads a DVD in the laptop and presses play. I want to roll my eyes when I see what film it is—she's pulling my own moves on me.

I see her smile out of the corner of my eye as she rests her feet on the bed rail and grabs a handful of popcorn to settle in to watch the film.

I close my eyes with the intention of acting like she isn't here, attempting not to watch the film. But it doesn't last. I get caught up watching it and smiling at our favourite bits. I even sneak a few handfuls of popcorn. *Whipped, totally whipped.*

The film finishes, and she leans forward, rubbing her hands together. The creaking of the fake leather armchair makes itself known. "Right, are you ready to talk yet? Or shall we move on to film number two?"

I ignore her question. She shrugs and ejects the disc, replacing it with a new one. "Film number two it is then."

My eyes dart between her and the film. I find myself desperate to sing along to *Rocking Robin* at the opening credits of Stand By Me. She's really pulled out the big guns.

I wiggle my toes.

I hold my breath. *Shit, did I just wiggle my toes?*

I calm my nerves and continue to watch the film. Surely, that was just my imagination, *right?*

Stand By Me by Ben E King plays, letting us know the film's finished.

"I have nowhere else to be. I have enough DVD's for a movie marathon and then some."

I keep my mouth shut but find myself beginning to relax for the first time since I woke up here. I act like I'm indifferent by it all. But it's nice—her being here. She brings me peace. I could have had this the whole time if I hadn't kicked her out.

A nurse enters, checking the catheter and my obs before she hands over my pain relief in a small, plastic cup. I watch Flick on her phone when she hops to her feet.

"It's about time," she says, walking toward the door. "I'll be right back, don't go anywhere."

I let out a snort as I glare at her retreating back.

And then it happens.

I feel more sensations, similar to pins and needles. I look in the direction of the end of the bed where my feet are securely hidden under the blanket. I wriggle my toes again, and I swear, this time, I'm pretty certain they moved.

Voices outside, followed by a cackle of giggles, gains my attention. If I didn't know better, I'd say Charlie's here.

He struts in, carrying a chair in one arm and what looks like a takeaway bag in the other. I'm assaulted by the most succulent and mouth-watering smell. My stomach grumbles.

"Sounds like someone's pleased to see me," he says with a wink. "Hey, mate, Flick asked me to bring some food—so here I am," he continues, like this is all perfectly normal. "What movie are you up to? Number three?"

"You know about that, then?" I ask.

Flick pauses when she walks back in and glances between Charlie and me, the flicker of hurt palpable. She takes the bag from Charlie and starts unpacking the take-out boxes onto a small trolley. It hits home then—I haven't said one word to her since she got here.

"Chinese and all your favourites, courtesy of the beautiful Felicity," he says.

Flick looks at Charlie with a blush, and just like that, a pang of jealousy ignites deep in my belly. I give him a cold, hard stare. He holds his hands up, palms facing me.

"Whoa, man, if looks could kill…"

Flick finishes loading the plates and hands one to Charlie and places mine on my tray, pushing it closer to me.

"Thanks," I say. It's strained, but it's a start.

She fiddles with her chicken chow mein, twirling it around her fork like you might do with spaghetti before bringing it to her mouth. Her eyes connect with mine. I look back to my food and get a forkful and shove it into my mouth. Once she's satisfied I'm eating, she tucks into hers.

We eat in silence, apart from the occasional groan or sound from Charlie. Flick stacks all the containers and plates as her and Charlie make small talk.

Charlie passes out the fortune cookies. She cracks hers open. She reads it, her face turns a lovely shade of red. She nibbles on the cookie, waiting for Charlie to open his.

"Yeah, no, I don't think so," he mumbles.

I crack mine open. *Time heals all wounds; remember patience is a virtue.*

I scoff at that. Charlie opens the door, and I slip it under my pillow. She wheels out the trolley, the door clicking shut behind her.

He stands at the end of the bed. "Mate, seriously, you giving her the cold shoulder is killing her, you know that right?"

"What?" I reply irritated. What does he know about it?

He crosses his arms, looking full on protective mode. *What the fuck?*

"She broke down, Nate. I thought she was going to have a full-on panic attack. I've never seen her like that. I was checking on Ana, same as her, and she crumbled."

"You don't know anything about it," I say on the defensive. He doesn't fucking get it.

"Yeah, I do… I was there when the car fell on you. I thought you were dead. I *know* she doesn't deserve to be treated like this."

I let out a frustrated sigh. My stomach drops and my chest aches. "No, what she doesn't deserve, is to be stuck with a god damn cripple," I all but yell.

He flinches. "What the fuck? Who said anything about a cripple? I know for a fact you would never call anyone else that, not ever."

"No, I wouldn't, but this is *my* body and the thought of being stuck in a wheelchair… I can't do that to her… I won't, she deserves better."

"You are a prick. We have friends who've had life-changing injuries. It hasn't stopped them from living. And don't you think she deserves to make the choice for herself?"

"It's not her choice to make, it's mine."

"No, Nate, it's as much her choice as it is yours. It takes two to build a relationship, and you need to stop being such a stubborn bastard. Rehabilitation isn't a one-man band; it's a team of people. It's friends and family supporting you. You know that first hand, isn't that why we support Help for Heroes?"

"So, if our roles were reversed, and it was, let's say… I don't know, you and Sophie in this predicament, what would you do?"

He pulls his eyebrows together. "I don't know, but I'm not the one throwing away the girl he's loved since forever, am I?"

"No, but if it was you?"

"Okay, hypothetically speaking, because obviously I am not with Sophie… Besides, that girl is way too good for me. But if it were my dream girl, I would try my fucking *hardest* to make it work, no matter the situation. I saw how my dad loved my mum right up until she took her last breath. That right there is love. It's not rainbows and unicorns, it's all the shit in between, too." He comes round to my side of the bed. "You two have had your own fair share of shit. Don't let this bump in the road ruin something that has the potential to be epic. You need to keep fighting."

I'm stunned and a little in awe by his words. "I might never walk again, and that I can deal with. It's life-changing, but what if I can't give her a family?" I say.

"I know you must be freaking the fuck out right now, but you know as much as the doctors do. You were told to wait until the swelling went down. If they really thought you wouldn't walk again, do you think they would have given you false hope?"

I rub my hand over my face. My chin is scratchy, I need a shave.

"Fuck, man, you're right… What the heck is wrong with me? I'm sorry."

He lightly punches my shoulder. "I get it, mate, I really do. But I'm not the one who you need to apologise to."

I don't have a chance to respond as Flick enters the room. There is a moment of awkward silence. At her interruption, Charlie clears his throat.

"Wow is that the time? I've got to shoot, I'll drop by tomorrow, though."

I nod.

"Thanks again." I hold out my fist, and he bumps it with his before walking toward Flick. He pulls her in for a hug and whispers something in her ear. She nods then he kisses her cheek before leaving us alone.

She walks over, sliding the tray back into position before resuming her place in the chair. She presses play on The Green Mile. I stare at her. She glances back, a timid smile crossing her face before she looks back to the screen.

Chapter Thirty-Four

Nathaniel

I blink my eyes open as a nurse enters. I look to my left, a panic hitting me like ice to the chest. But she's still here, and it looks like I wasn't the only who fell asleep.

The nurse glides over to my side.

"I need to change your catheter. Do you want me to wake her?"

I look to Flick. A loud part in the film booms through the speakers, startling her awake. She holds her chest for a moment, looking to the nurse, then to me. Without a word, she gets up and heads for the door.

"Flick," I call, my voice rough.

She twists her neck to look at me.

"You're coming back?"

She nods and leaves the room.

I take a deep breath and work up the courage to ask her about my legs.

"So, I don't know if this means anything, but I have noticed a kind of pins and needles sensation in my legs, and I am pretty sure I wiggled my toes more than once today."

Nurse Lynn glances at me with a smile. "Well between you and me, I think that's a very good thing. The neurologist is going to be here early in the morning. You be sure to tell him. I'll also make a note of it on your records, and be sure to let us know if you get anymore feeling."

I nod, and for the first time in what feels like forever, I actually feel an excited kind of nervous.

Flick comes back in looking tired. I can see the uneasiness she must be feeling coming to the surface. I know that's probably my fault, too, and it doesn't do anything good for her anxiety. I keep my eyes trained on her as she walks over and sits. She reaches her hand out to press play, but I stop her, covering her hand with mine.

"Don't," I tell her. It comes out a little more aggressive than I intended.

She closes her eyes and takes a breath. "Listen, Nate, I know me being here isn't what you wanted, but I had to at least try. If you want me to go, I will. I'll give you whatever it is you need, but all I really want is for you to talk to me."

"You," I say. "I just want you."

Her eyes spring to mine. "What?"

"I shut you out, and for that, I don't think an apology will cut it. I don't know what I was thinking pushing you away… Actually, that's a lie. I thought I was protecting you from this," I say, lifting my arm and waving my hand in the direction of my legs.

"I don't need protecting, not from you. I believe things happen for a reason. Even the shitty stuff."

"I think you could be right. I've been an insufferable twat, and the one thing I'd never want to ever do is intentionally set out to hurt you. I know my memory is a little sketchy from just before the accident, but I do remember telling you I love you, that I wanted to be with you. And contrary to my last bout of verbal diarrhoea, I meant it."

She nods as she chews on her bottom lip. "Can I ask you something?"

"Yes, anything."

"What is the last thing you remember?"

I pause. "It's kind of hard to explain, but honestly, my most vivid memory is us being together…me worshipping your body."

Her neck and ears change colour. "I hate that you don't remember, and this makes it even harder."

"What does?"

"Because this doesn't carry the same weight for you as it does for me, but I still need to apologise."

I take hold of her hand. "Apologise for what?"

"For being a coward. I was so afraid to let you love me, to give you the power to hurt me, so I left. But I'd already given you my heart…it just took longer for my head to catch up. I'm sorry for being too afraid to give us a chance."

I'm stunned. Is she saying that we weren't together? "I'm confused. Flick, are you saying we broke up?"

She quickly shakes her head. "No. We hadn't put a status on what we had. I guess you could say we were at a crossroads, but the thought of you breaking my heart literally took my breath away. I thought what I experienced when we were younger was heartbreak, but knowing what I know now… I was naïve. Truth be told, I was breaking my own heart by holding back from you, from what I really wanted."

I smile and pull her toward me. "Flick, I know what I can be like, and no doubt you obviously felt pressurised by me. Look at what happened, the reservations you had were plausible. I know I will fuck up a lot, but I also know that no one else will ever love you as much as I do. And although I handled this whole thing in the worst possible way, I only had the best intentions at heart."

She wipes at her face. "Nate, I'm pretty much scared majority of the time. I pop anxiety pills like they're skittles, for fuck's sake. I still get anxious over the stupidest things, but being around you has helped me more than I ever thought possible."

I pat the space next to me. "Come closer, please."

She slips off her pumps and gets on the bed with me.

I raise my hand to her face, rubbing my thumb over her plump bottom lip, which is the most natural, perfect kind of pink I have ever seen. I move my thumb under her chin. She licks her lips and smiles.

I move towards her but wince when she scoots closer, gently pushing my chest. She tilts her face up towards mine. Our lips find each other. I let out a soft, contented groan. The kiss deepens, intensifying the feeling coursing through my body. I pull back from her lips with a gasp, the sensation sending me off-kilter. I let my head fall back on the pillow.

"Are you okay?" Concern laces her voice.

I can't contain the smile that spreads across my face. I nod towards the direction of my waist. She follows my gaze and lets out an *oh* sound.

Her eyes hold me captive.

"I fucking love you, Flick," I say, kissing the tip of her nose.

She touches my cheek. "I love you too."

Chapter Thirty-Five

Felicity

It's been three long months since the accident.

Nate has undergone surgery to relieve the blood that was pressing on his spine, causing the loss of feeling. With intense physical therapy, he's been recuperating well.

He's been like a bear with a sore head at times, but I wouldn't change him for anything. Most of our arguments have been about sex. I refused to take the risk until we were certain it wouldn't affect his recovery. Besides, it's not like he's gone without. I've learnt that heavy petting and foreplay is something he really enjoys, too.

Evie and Nana are at a spa retreat for the weekend. They asked me to go, but he asked me on our first official date. I surprised myself more than I would ever have imagined. Coming back was the best thing I've ever done.

The anxiety has its cameos more than I would like. It's hard to pinpoint what my triggers are. I'm still mortified over my state of panic before I drove him home from the hospital. He talked me down, but I kept imaging having to brake too hard and the implications of hurting him further.

I know it's my own insecurities at the forefront of my mind that are messing with my confidence. I even suggested we call Charlie to drive, but he was adamant it would be okay, and with his support, I managed to get him back home—alive and in one piece.

I finish getting ready for our date and head to his room, twisting my bracelet, so grateful they were able to fix it.

He comes out of the bathroom as I walk in. I see in his eyes what's reflected in mine—a mixture of love and lust, heat and desire. It tingles over my entire body like popping candy.

"Fuck it," he says and struts toward me. His eyes roam over the full length of me.

My stomach clenches low and deep. I step back and meet the wall.

He stops right in front of me. "You look beautiful," he says nipping my chin, sending goosebumps up my neck.

"There is no way I can sit across you at dinner and think of eating anything else but you."

My mouth drops open. He sucks my bottom lip, and I pulse between my legs. Hand on the back of my neck, he pulls me closer and plunges his tongue in my mouth.

I exhale a heavy breath, moving my head to the side. His lips work their way to the crook of my neck. He runs his fingers over my collarbone. A hiss escapes my lips. His hand cups my breast, the other slides down my thigh. He raises my leg up to his hip, lets go of my breast and wraps his hands underneath my butt.

"Lift your legs, Flick." He says it like a command.

I push my hands down on his shoulders and lift up, wrapping my legs around his waist. He walks us over to the bed, lowers me to the mattress, and kneels over me. I dig my heels into his backside to pull him closer.

"I'm going to make love to you," he says.

I bite my bottom lip and nod.

He sits back and pulls his t-shirt over his head. I'm quick to follow as I shuffle out of mine, only leaving on my underwear.

My heart hammers as I watch him stand and drop his trousers. Then he takes his hard length in his hands.

"See what you do to me?" he says as he strokes it.

I let out a whimper and move forward. I reach for his wrist, so he releases himself, then I lean down and take him in my mouth. A hiss escapes his lips.

"If you keep doing that, this will be over before its even begun." His last word is said with an exhale of breath as I take him deeper.

He stiffens. Reaching for my shoulders, he pushes me away. I release him from my mouth with a popping sound.

"Are you sure about this? You'll be careful?" I ask as I move back up the bed.

"Yes, I need to be inside you. It's been way too long."

He slides the thong down my legs and over my feet. I remove my bra, slinging it on top of the mounting pile of clothes. His eyes rake me up and down, his body casting a shadow over mine.

"Wait," I say in a whisper, sitting up on my elbows. "Come lie down."

I stroke his chest as I straddle him. His mouth makes an O shape. Leaning down, I trail a line of kisses all the way down to his belly button, sucking gently.

I'm nervous but in a good way. Being on top of him like this makes me feel in control, brave, as I sit back, taking his hard length in my hand, sliding it up and down. His eyes flutter closed. I want him inside me so badly, my stomach drops. Raising myself up, I hold him firm. Lowering myself onto him, I let myself slowly sink, savouring the feel of him around my inner walls.

His eyes open, staring back at me as he fills me completely. I let out a ragged breath.

Nothing has ever felt so damn good. Slowly, I raise myself up, and then sink down again, making small circular motions. His hands tighten over my hips he stares at me with awe and absolute wonder. I continue to move up and down faster. Moving his hands to my upper arms, he slowly slides them down until they reach my hands, entwining them with his. I push him back so I am flat on his chest, our hands above his head. I kiss him, matching the rhythm of us moving together.

"I want to try a different position," I say on a breathless whisper

"Go for it, Baby." He hardens inside me even more.

I adjust myself, bringing my knee up, then swinging my leg slowly over his chest while he's still inside me. I raise myself, but keep the connection as I manoeuvre, my back facing him.

I begin to ride him like this—fucking hell, it's intense.

He leans forward, his chest on my back. His hand grips my hip before trailing his hand in front of me, his fingers stroking my clit.

I come apart around him. As I'm coming down, he leans me forward.

"I want to take you from behind."

I clench again with anticipation.

His hand trails softly down the length of my back. On all fours, I peek over my shoulder.

"Is this okay?" he asks tentatively.

I answer with a nod.

I feel him draw out before he pushes back into me.

"Fuck," I say, the feeling so new to me.

His hands are holding my hips, his pace picking up, in sync with our breathing. He pulls almost all the way out but then slams into me again. I feel a sting from a slap across my butt cheek. It takes me by surprise, sending a spasm right through to my core.

I come so hard I feel tears escape as he loses all inhibitions, slapping into me hard and fast. My orgasm keeps going. His release follows. My elbows give out, and I sink my cheek against the mattress

"That was something else," I say.

"You can say that again. We should go clean up?"

I'm spent; don't think I could muster the strength. Instead, I manage to pull myself up enough so I'm resting on his chest. "Yeah, just need a minute," I mumble. My eyes grow heavy, and I drift off.

I wake to fingers as they tickle a trail along my arm. I smile and open my eyes.

"You crashed out," he says, pouting his lips.

I kiss his nose. "Sorry, how long was I out for?"

"Long enough to miss our reservation, but no apology necessary. I love to watch you sleep, so peaceful and content."

I get lost in his eyes and smile.

If there was such a thing as a person being created for another, I have no doubt in my mind he would have been created for me. I snuggle into him.

"Can we take a rain check on our dinner date?" I ask.

He tickles my side. "I think that's a given, are you hungry?"

"Only for you," I say with a giggle.

"I love you, Flick," he says, placing my palm over his chest. "You feel that right there?"

I nod.

"It beats only for you."

I lean in and kiss him. Taking his hand in mine, I pull his palm to my chest. "And mine belongs to you."

If I could save one memory and frame it, this would be the one.

Epilogue

Eleven Months Later

I don't think I've ever felt this nervous and as sick to my stomach as I do right now. It's like travel sickness, but without the traveling. Charlie has been riding my arse all morning and hasn't eased off, not once.

"Stop it… This is no laughing matter." I cut my eyes in his direction.

"Oh, come on, mate, it is kind of funny."

"Yeah, well, when the roles are reversed, we'll see who's laughing then."

His smile drops. "Why would you say something like that?"

I shake my head. He has feelings for Sophie, and why the hell he's ignorant to the fact is beyond me.

"Good luck, man." He pulls me into a hug. "You have nothing to be nervous about. You got the letter?"

"Yep, it's already in the tree house. Thanks again for helping me out."

He salutes me. "I've always got your back, you know that."

I nod as he makes his way over to his car.

I swear my palms have never felt so sweaty. I wipe them down my thighs, checking my watch every couple of minutes.

It feels like an eternity before Sophie finally pulls up on the drive with my beautiful girlfriend in tow.

I open her door, and she smiles as she gives me the once-over, and a chaste kiss on the lips. She looks stunning—wearing a little summer dress, her wedges bringing her a little closer to my height.

"I just need to grab my bag." She walks round to the boot.

I peer through the open passenger window. "All good?" I ask Sophie.

She nods with a huge smile on her face.

"Yep, and good luck," she says.

I roll my eyes. "Why the fuck does everyone keep saying *good luck*?"

She laughs. "Maybe because you need it, if she's stupid en—*flamingos."*

Flick returns to my side. "What was that, Soph?"

She gives a half shrug. "I was telling Nate about the flamingo tattoo I want."

Hand on her hip, the corner of her mouth turns up. "I didn't know you like flamingos."

"Yeah, love them. Why be a seagull when you can be a flamingo, right?"

Flick chuckles. "I don't think that's the phrase, but whatever floats your boat."

"Ciao," she says, wiggling her fingers.

"Text me when you're home. And thanks again, I had a lovely time."

She blows her a kiss. "Always a pleasure, never a chore," she calls and pulls away.

Her hand in mine, I grab her bag and take it to the kitchen.

"Do you fancy taking a walk with me?" I ask, trying to keep my nervous energy at bay.

"Oh, Nate, you old romantic, you. Let me just pop to the toilet real quick."

I nod as she makes her way out of the kitchen, and pull out my phone.

I bounce on my toes. "Fuck, man, I can't do it… I think I might actually have a heart attack."

Charlie's rumble of laughter echoes down the line. "Shut up, already. You've got this. Pull yourself together and go."

"I'm going to as soon as she's ready, dick wad." I sit down and then stand.

"I'll speak to you later," he says, and I can hear the smile in his voice.

I let out a snort. "I fucking hope not. If I do this right, I'll be too busy."

I hear Charlie guffaw to himself as I end the call.

Flick walks toward me. She looks more radiant than ever, the spa getaway with Sophie most definitely agreed with her. Maybe I should have gone with them. Or at least had a shot or two to calm my nerves.

"Come on," I say, taking her hand in mine. "I want to show you something."

I pull her along. The weather has been perfect for what I've been working on all day.

I feel her gasp on my neck when we get closer. Her eyes float over the tree house, she looks at me, and then back again.

It's covered in fairy lights.

I have to admit, it looks magical. Ever since we were children, she has always had this thing for fairy lights. For a long time, she believed fairies lived in them. I never had the heart to tell her otherwise.

"Nate, did you do all of this?"

I pull her into my arms, sliding my hands over her arse and squeezing. "Yep, and if you think untangling Christmas lights is difficult, you don't even want to know how hard it was with this many."

Her soft, warm lips caress my cheek before she lets out an excited squeal and claps her hands. "It's beautiful! Are they inside too?"

"Yes, come on, up you go." I release her and extend my arm.

I don't need to tell her twice as she grabs hold of the ladder and climbs.

Taking in a deep breath, I follow.

She scans all around her, spinning in a slow circle. Her eyes reflect the glistening of the lights. I lead her to the balcony where I have a blanket laid out, a few nibbles, and a bottle of champagne waiting in an ice bucket.

She smiles from ear to ear, her cheekbones prominent like rosy apples. "Oh, Nate, this is lovely."

I take her hand as she sits, rubbing my thumb over her wrist. I let go to reach for the bottle and get to work popping the cork.

Clearing my throat, I slide my hand on the neck of the bottle. I twist the metal, and after an excruciating battle of wills, I pop the cork and pour.

I pass her a glass and clink it with mine. "To new beginnings."

"New beginnings," she repeats and takes a satisfied sip.

I lower my face toward hers and plant a tender kiss on those luscious lips.

She lets out a contented hum. "Nate, you didn't have to do this."

"Yes, I did. I wanted you to know how much I appreciate you and love you."

She gives me one of her shy smiles—the ones reserved only for me. "I love you too."

I lean behind me, and with a trembling hand, grab the envelope. I turn it over in my hands, my nerves beginning to skyrocket, my chest thumping under my shirt.

I cough. "I've wanted to share this with you, but there just was never a good time…not until now. It's the letter from my Gramps." I hold it out to her.

"Nate, you don't have to. It was private from him to you."

I smile. "It was written to me, yes, but there's something about you in here, too. I want you to read it, please…"

She places her glass down, and takes the envelope from me, slipping the letter free.

I watch her face while she reads, a mixture of emotions playing out across her face: raised eyebrows, her eyes going slightly wide, and then glossy. She covers her mouth with her hand as a few tears fall. She doesn't even attempt to wipe them away.

"Nate, that was beautiful. Thank you for sharing it with me."

I nod. "I wanted you there with me when I first read it. You are a part of me, Flick, and I cannot imagine my life without you in it."

She inhales as the sweat drips down the back of my neck. I consider the possibility of me actually having a heart attack.

"Look inside," I say, nodding towards the envelope in her hand.

She stretches it open with her thumb and forefinger and peeks inside. Her eyes spring back to mine before peering inside again.

"Wow, is that…"

I take it from her and tip the contents onto the palm of my hand. Then I look back to her beautiful face.

I watch as she stares at the ring—the diamonds sparkling, casting a fairy-like dust of rainbow dews across her silhouette.

I move, so I am facing her completely, and take her hand in mine.

"Felicity, will you be my life partner? Today and every day thereafter? Will you say yes to the most important question I'll ever ask? Will you marry me?"

It's always been her. Even when there were other girls, she was the one rooted in my heart. She's the Sharpie that's tattooed her ink into my soul. She's my kryptonite. If I only had one more day, one more hour, one more minute. I'd want to spend it with her.

I reach for her hand. "Flick, I have loved you since the day you said you wanted to marry me for real, right here, in our tree house. And if I've learnt anything this past year, it's that life is too short to hold back. It should be embraced with abandonment."

Her lips part before she bites on her lower lip. Her pulse quickens in her throat, and I see the rise and fall of her chest. All I want to do at this moment is kiss her.

"I know I'm far from perfect, but being with you makes me feel like the best possible version of myself, and I want to be that person and grow old with you." I hold her wedding finger, the ring poised. "I want to see you pregnant. I want to raise our babies here."

She blinks, her eyes wet.

I swallow—it feels like an absolution, waiting for her to answer.

She smiles so big I think my heart will split. "What, for real?" She tilts her head. Her words warm the very depths of my soul.

"Yes, for real, I want to marry you right here under our tree. I want to see you dressed in a white wedding dress when we say our vows, and I want chocolate cake, not that yucky fruitcake."

Her dimple is prominent as she nods her head excessively. "Yes, Nate, of course, I'll marry you. I want all of that and so much more."

I let out a contented sigh, slide the ring onto her finger, and pull her into my lap.

"Thank fuck for that," I say, and kiss her.

Breathless, she pulls back and holds her hand out. "Wow, Nate, it really is beautiful."

"It was always meant for you."

She grabs my face in her hands. "Sometimes I don't think you realise just how perfect you are for me." Leaning in, she kisses me long and hard.

I used to watch my Gramps with my Nan, and I remember thinking how I wanted that someday—to be just like them. They were never afraid to kiss or dance in public, even if there was no music. He lived to make her smile. He could make her eyes sparkle even when she was pissed off with him. He told me once never to go to bed on an argument, said he would pull her close and tell her he loved her. She'd say, "well as much as I don't particularly like you right now, I love you too."

I smile. He said a lifelong partnership meant never giving up, that things worth having never come easy and those are the things worth fighting for. He was right. This girl sitting in my lap is way more than I deserve, and I'll spend the rest of my life proving to her that I'm worthy of her love.

I've never seen her face glow as radiantly as it is in this moment.

"I have one more request," I say, moving the hair from her shoulder and blowing on her neck. "Make love to me."

She looks up. Her eyes are filled with wonder. "I thought you'd never ask."

She reaches up and kisses me.

And we get lost in oblivion.

The End

Letter to Reader

Dear Reader,

Wow, thank you for making it this far. Firstly, thank you for taking a chance on me, and my debut novel.

It's been such a long road. I never thought I would actually make it. After almost six years writing on and off, it has only been the past two years that things came together. And why? I met my tribe. The fact you are reading this means I did it, I made my dreams into a reality. Don't ever let someone tell you it can't be done. If you want it, you can and will do it.

This story really did take on a life of its own. The characters were extras in my first novel, and then they spoke to me. They had their own story to tell. Honestly, if it wasn't for the other two books in the pipeline, this might have turned out completely different. But I believe in the end, this was how their story was meant to be.

I hope my characters resonated with you as much as they did with me. And you are left feeling a little lighter and a lot more hopeful.

What's next you may wonder? Well, I have two more novels on the horizon. Dysfunctional Hearts will follow Charlie and Sophie's story, and Heart of War is the prequel of where it all began. And the best part, each book can be read as a standalone.

There was of course music behind the writing, and if you are interested, you'll find WTHI Spotify playlist here: https://spoti.fi/2CeTqAt

If you enjoyed this book, or you know someone who would, please recommend and leave a short review. Thank you again for taking the time to read this, it truly means the world to me.

Acknowledgements

Mum, I am fortunate and blessed to first call you my mum, but forever my friend. Your strength and determination, but mostly your unconditional love, is what I admire most about you. You are my sunshine. Thank you for being the best housemate anyone could ever ask for. You're all right, you are!

Dad, thank you for being you, and for loving me. Hannah, thank you for blessing us with my little brother and sister, and for all the ink. You get me!

To my siblings I couldn't have asked for a better brother and sister to grow up with, only you understand our kind of crazy.

Carlie, I'm blessed to have a skin 'n' blister as amazing as you. Love you little boo. I'm proud to be an Aunty Lou Lou to your children.

To my pimp, Victoria, I love you bunny. Thank you for always being there for me. Here's to many more years of friendship and shenanigans.

Sam, I've known you since before I can remember. From Boyzone to Motherhood, you are passionate in everything you do. Thank you for introducing me to Mel. Books really do bring people together. Mel, write all the words. You can do anything you put your mind to.

Laura and Andy, thank you for showing me what true love looks like. Laura, I've had some of my most spectacular adventures with you by my side. From New York to Katy Perry's Firework (AD), McFlurry's and B52's… oh, and then there was the one time we all jumped out of a perfectly good aeroplane. Thank you for always making me laugh to the point of hurting. You are doing a wonderful job with the Evie and Zach. Sam and

Libby couldn't be better siblings to the twins. I can't wait for our next adventure!!

To my fam-a-lam, Jon, Tam, Dave, Grace, Alex and Niki, amongst others I don't see you half as much as I should but when I do it's like nothing has changed. You are my people.

To the A-Team, Alison, Andrea and Donna I couldn't be more fortunate to work with a wonderful team of strong, beautiful women. Colleagues I'm now pleased to call friends, you know who you are. Beverlina, you really are a top banana and Michelle love and miss you chick.

My flamingos, Cassie, you are my Yoda, the word whisperer. You've taught me so much, and my words will never be enough to say thank you. Dusti, thank you for always encouraging me, your heart knows no bounds, and your sweet words are forever embedded in my soul. Crystal, you always put a smile on my face and a joy to have in my life. Thank you for being one of my proof readers. Julie, thank you for being so perfectly you. For beta-reading WTHI and giving me the confidence boost when I needed it the most. Steph, I love how you would cross an ocean to fight for me, and the ones you love. One day, girl, we will have afternoon tea together.

Sometimes we meet people and just click, comfortable in our own skin. Like we've known each other a lifetime, we don't have to pretend to be anyone or anything but ourselves. You are my soul sisters, my red threads. The world is complete with you in it. I love you all #TiCs #flamingos

To Kirsten Moore (the Beta Bitch)—you are the bomb, and the book world needs you. Thank you for all your wonderful critique and advice. It was invaluable, even when I know what you read was long, every comment made me smile.

Traci Finlay, girl you know how to blog it like it's hot, and I hope like hell some of it clicked in my writing, please keep it coming!

To the PLN's and the PLN Authors, I wish I could name you all, but I am sure you're all getting bored by now. So, thank you for your unwavering support. Amber, you were one of the first people to accept me when I joined the PLN author group. I can't bloody wait for Gatlinburg.

To Tarryn Fisher, thank you!! Without you, there wouldn't be a we. You have a tribe of women who stand together because you inspired us to fight, to stand tall, and to say *yes we can*. #PLN4life #riseofthewomen

To my most loyal companion, Harley, if ever there was a soul mate in the form of a dog, it's you for me. #girlsbestfriend

About the Author

Leila Pullen is a daughter, sister, aunt and the proud parent of an eleven-year-old Staffordshire Bull Terrier. She spends her week commuting into London for her day job. When she's not working, her passion is reading and writing. She also enjoys art, photography, film, and theatre. In true English fashion, loves Afternoon Tea. Leila is a Ravenclaw.

To keep up to date with her upcoming projects, you can find her on the following links:

Website: http://lspullen.co.uk

IG: https://www.instagram.com/lspauthor

Facebook: https://www.facebook.com/lspullenauthor

Twitter: https://twitter.com/lspauthor

Printed in Great Britain
by Amazon